ON THE EDGE

EDWARD ST AUBYN was born in London in 1960.
His superbly acclaimed Patrick Melrose novels are
Never Mind, Bad News, Some Hope
(published collectively as the *Some Hope* trilogy),
Mother's Milk (shortlisted for the Man Booker Prize
2006) and *At Last*. He is also the author of the novels
A Clue to the Exit, On the Edge and *Lost for Words*.

Also by Edward St Aubyn

The Patrick Melrose novels

NEVER MIND

BAD NEWS

SOME HOPE

MOTHER'S MILK

AT LAST

A CLUE TO THE EXIT

LOST FOR WORDS

EDWARD ST AUBYN

ON THE EDGE

PICADOR

First published in Great Britain 1998 by Chatto & Windus
First published in paperback by Vintage 1999

This edition first published 2008 by Picador
an imprint of Pan Macmillan, a division of Macmillan Publishers Limited
Pan Macmillan, 20 New Wharf Road, London N1 9RR
Basingstoke and Oxford
Associated companies throughout the world
www.panmacmillan.com

ISBN 978-0-330-45397-4

Typeset by SetSystems Ltd, Saffron Walden, Essex
Printed and bound by CPI Group (UK) Ltd, Croydon, CR0 4YY

Visit www.picador.com to read more about all our books
and to buy them. You will also find features, author interviews and
news of any author events, and you can sign up for e-newsletters
so that you're always first to hear about our new releases.

For Eleanor

1

Adam arrived at Brooke's San Francisco mansion wearing the flame-coloured Nehru jacket Yves had brought back for him from Paris. Most people couldn't get away with a Nehru jacket, but Adam, in whose veins the lava of India and the phlegm of England combined with an intoxicating hiss, wore his new clothes with indiscreet self-assurance. Adam was on fire with the truth about the future of the human race and it was not a fire he intended to keep to himself.

'I'm wearing my heart on your sleeve,' he whispered to Yves in the taxi.

'And your soul?' said Yves.

'Always and everywhere,' replied Adam. 'You know I won't settle for less.' His eyes clouded with tears. 'My Shams,' he murmured.

'My Rumi,' answered Yves vaguely.

Adam liked people to have 'a point'. Either they must be brilliant and spiritually evolved like himself, or embarrassingly rich like Brooke. Simple goodness touched him also, at a distance.

Brooke was in fact so rich that no amount of personal

gratification could do more than bail out her sinking ship. The inrush of money was so uncompromising that a few days in bed with a cold would leave her up to her neck in unspent income. The only pump that could save her from drowning was charity, and every morning her secretary brought her a bucket of cheques to sign in the unending effort to keep her afloat.

Brooke treated everyone like a servant, which, given that she had thirty of them already, showed a lack of imagination. Her servants, on the other hand, she treated like family, her own family having thrust her among servants throughout her childhood. Brought up in the reputedly gracious South, her parents were given over entirely to alcohol, horses and other rich people who shared their interests. They had not allowed Brooke's childish cries or lisping enquiries into the meaning of life to mar the elegance of their home. Instead she had been housed with one of the innumerable black families whose unadorned shacks cowered under the fatwood trees, their woodsmoke hanging in the humid air almost as substantially as the membranes of Spanish moss that dangled down to meet it. Brooke had often reflected that she had probably been better off living with Mammy. The riding parties that roamed the plantation in search of the perfect place to have some 'special iced tea', as they jokingly called the gallon of cold bourbon to which a tiny splash of tea, one mint leaf and a slice of lemon were apprehensively added by the cook, never trotted down that particular track which led to Mammy's, its astonishing orange earth making it look more like a river than a road.

When her father died falling off one of his favourite

horses, Brooke had the thrilling experience of being taken to the big house for the funeral party. 'It's how he would have wanted to go,' his friends said, one after another, with a sense of their own gift for the apt phrase, mixed with a certain envy at the spectacle of such a gentlemanly demise. She asked her mother if she could stay in the big house for the night after the funeral.

'I'm surprised at your asking, Brooke,' said her mother with genuine outrage. 'Can you not see that the house is full of your father's relations?'

Returning to Mammy's in the car, Brooke had developed, through a clinging ground mist of misery and incomprehension, a revolutionary fury, a suspicion of rich white people that could have borne cross-examination by Malcolm X, and a determination to find meaning beyond the familial horizon ringed by stallions and empty bottles, without heading too far in the direction offered by Mammy's passion for overeating and fainting in church.

After a psychoanalytic limbo in Manhattan, facing the grey mirror of Dr Bukowski's silence ('At least I'm not a Kleinian,' he had chuckled at their first meeting, but had never lapsed into liveliness again), she headed for the West Coast and its more colourful promises of liberation.

Cured of paying wise men to listen to her, she paid to listen to them instead.

It was then that she met Kenneth Shine, the spiritual teacher, and realized that here at last was the beginning of her real journey.

'You've changed my life,' she told him that first evening.

'What hasn't?' he asked with a kindly gaze, and the question, which she hardly would have noticed under other circumstances, broke her mind open and in that moment she seemed to see the whole impermanence thing, and how we were all changing and the self was an illusion, and everything – he put it so much better than she could, but the sense of it had stayed with her and kept her going over the last five years, working for the good of the world at the level that really mattered, changing people's consciousness.

The 'Human Potential Movement' was rather a grand phrase, perhaps a little pompous, not to be dropped casually into every sentence, but to her ears it had a noble ring.

'You're the Guidobaldo of the Millennium,' Adam had recently declared. She hadn't known what to make of that. Adam could be so bitchy sometimes. Only because he was brilliant, brilliant, brilliant, of course, and he saw human potential so clearly that he got impatient with complacency. At the same time he was complacent about his own impatience, and even his nervous breakdowns and his hysterical tears had something arrogant about them, as if they'd been written by Shakespeare and deserved the closest study.

Anyhow, neither Mammy nor Brooke's teachers at Foxcroft had been too hot on the Renaissance, but Guidobaldo, it turned out, was practically responsible for the whole thing at a financial level. She knew her uses and she was pleased to be useful. 'Everyone has their place and everyone has their pace,' as Kenneth liked to say in his usual memorable way. Adam called him the Bumper

Sticker. There was definitely a rivalry between the two men, but she loved them both.

Kenneth was working on a synthesis of all world religions and philosophies, which he was going to condense into a form that everybody could understand. 'Think global, act local,' was one of his mottoes. He already had a name for his philosophy; the rest would follow. It was called Streamism because of something Heraclitus had said about how you couldn't step into the same stream twice. It was a new stream each time. At this point Brooke got a bit confused. Were you supposed to go with the flow – Kenneth had a whole Tao thing about going with the flow which tied in beautifully with self-acceptance and all those key psychological concepts – or were you supposed to be the rock in the stream, unimpressed by the fleeting manifestations of Time? He was very good on that too. It was part Buddhism, part Marcus Aurelius, he'd told her. She was learning so much, but for a while she remained puzzled, half the time picturing herself as a rock, the other half blithely shooting the little rapids of the stream.

'Of course,' said Kenneth when she had shared her concern. 'You've cut through to the central paradox of Streamism.'

She'd felt quite proud.

'What is God?' he'd suddenly asked with that kindly gaze.

She had blinked nervously.

'The unmoved mover,' Kenneth whispered. 'What must we become?' he thundered.

'God,' she guessed wildly.

'Right!' He gave her a radiant smile, the sort of smile that her father had never given her, and she felt as if she had been airlifted to the mountaintop.

'We go with the flow, but we stay still within ourselves, and by doing that we become gods,' Kenneth claimed, while her head swam with altitude sickness.

'I'm only telling you part of it, of course, you'll have to wait for the book.'

And wait she did. In the meantime she was helping Kenneth out. He didn't want to take an advance from a mainstream publisher. They might cramp his style, and after all his philosophy wasn't called Mainstreamism, he joked.

Kenneth thought unceasingly about Streamism. It was a concept so pregnant with undivulged glamour that he refused to stoop to the pedantry of recording his reflections. If his mind started to wander while he read Lao-tzu, or studied baseball on TV, he couldn't help concluding that a wandering mind was the most uninhibited expression of Streamism, and allowing his thoughts to run dimpling all the way.

In the face of such a comprehensive excitement, he forgave himself for taking Brooke's money and offering her nothing concrete in exchange. (How un-Streamist that would have been, and yet, on the other hand, how Streamist.) He did, however, wince at the memory of his feigned passion for her. It would have been so convenient to find her attractive, but sexual hypocrisy was notoriously difficult for a man to sustain. All the same, he couldn't help feeling a troubling fondness for her. The rich always thought they were being exploited, and here was Brooke challenging that fear with one cheque after another. It was really very plucky.

'I'll be able to pay you back,' he explained while she wrote another cheque for five thousand dollars. 'There'll be the book, and the tapes and a series of pamphlets for people with busy lives, "Streamism and sexuality", "Streamism in the office", "Streamism and your children" . . .'

She was a little worried about Kenneth's pamphlets, but then not everyone could have the privilege of knowing Kenneth personally. She just didn't want Streamism to become vulgar.

'It couldn't be made any more vulgar than it already is,' Adam had snapped.

Honestly, those boys, they were so competitive. She must do something to make them better friends. Maybe they could join a men's group and go to a sweat lodge together. Robert Bly could recommend the best way for them to have a male bonding experience. It was madness for them to fall out, because they really wanted the same thing: to save the world from self-destruction.

Brooke also paid for Adam's apartment in San Francisco. He made sure that this arrangement didn't corrupt him by peppering his flattery with sharp remarks, and occasionally changing his phone number to make sure she didn't imagine she owned him. Hadn't Joyce had his Miss Weaver? And who would remember Miss Weaver without him? Mantegna had had his Sforzas. Their silly intrigues looked very thin now, but his paintings repaid the compliment of their patronage with the far greater compliment of his immortality. And the monks of South-East Asia who survived on the generosity, the *dana*, of the local population, properly understood, bestowed a blessing on those who supported them. No, Adam was completely at ease with the situation, but he wasn't going to allow the fact that Brooke wanted to help him fulfil his God-given purpose to prevent him from gently teasing her now and again.

'I hope I die before you,' he had said that morning after she had bored him with a further list of her good works. 'I want to see heaven before you've improved it.'

'I'll give a party for you when you arrive,' said Brooke, for whom 'networking' had become an uncontrollable habit.

'If *you're* giving cocktail parties, darling, I'll know I *haven't* arrived,' he answered.

'Don't be mean,' she said, as she seemed to say more and more often these days.

'Brooke's getting very full of herself,' Adam had said to Yves after he hung up. 'She'll start thinking she's the Divine Mother next.'

'Ah, *non*,' said Yves sulkily, 'not another one. *Je ne crois pas que je pourrais supporter encore une Mère Divine.*'

Brooke's possible future claims to divinity had been set aside by the time Adam and Yves arrived in her drawing room. Adam's inky unkempt hair flowed down to his flaming jacket which in turn flared over his wide hips and black trousers. Yves, wearing a jacket of the same cut but decorated with swirling sea colours, created a relatively soothing impression. They represented the complementarity of turquoise and orange, the marriage of fire and water, of Yin and Yang, of Rumi and Shams; but only they knew that. To everyone else they looked like a couple of clowns.

Adam, who was deeply suspicious of Kenneth, approached him first. He had recently found out that before his incarnation as a would-be guru, Kenneth had worked for a rock band as 'ambience director', the euphemistic title he gave to his role as pimp and drug courier.

'Hello, Kenneth, what's our lesson for this evening?'

'Humility, Adam, and it's specially for you.'

'Oh,' said Adam, looking around the room as if it were an empty landscape. 'And who's teaching it?'

'Life,' said Kenneth serenely, 'if you're open to it.'

'The Bumper Sticker has spoken,' said Adam in mock awe.

Yves giggled and accepted a glass of champagne from the black butler.

Brooke was still upstairs when Adam and Yves arrrived. Some rumours that had reached her about her mother's behaviour ('Always likes to keep folks waitin',' Mammy used to say) had not been detached by the scrubbing brush of Dr Bukowski's silence, or the laser surgery of Kenneth's teachings.

She was contemplating all the fascinating people she had invited to dinner, 'gurus' as she might have called them five years ago. Now they were just her dearest friends. There were some new faces tonight, new names as well. Her secretary had made a list of them and left it in the bedroom on what Brooke called her 'emergency desk', the one she used when she couldn't get to her study, or office, or library. There was a marvellous environmental campaigner, a fiercely magnetic Irish woman who said we could save the planet by planting bamboo in all the devastated rainforests.

'It's quite important, actually,' she had told Brooke with a patronizing smile. 'We *are* talking about the lungs of the planet.'

The lungs of the planet! We were giving lung cancer to Mother Earth. No doubt the chainsaw operators and timber merchants were heavy smokers. The way we treated ourselves and the way we treated our environment all tied in. Some of her Buddhist friends were particularly good on that theme. Gaia was the Greek goddess of the Earth, and Gaya was the name of the village in northern India where Buddha had achieved enlightenment. How about that? It all tied in. Brooke hurtled on in an associative frenzy.

She also had a marine biologist coming tonight who had discovered that whales were suffering from AIDS. New plagues were springing up in a world out of balance. Marburg, Ebola, Sin Nombre – her secretary had written them down; it was the marine biologist's first time and she had him on her left at dinner – bursting on to the scene from the untamed expansion of human populations. It was like that old Chinese curse, 'May you live in interesting times.'

Realizing she was late, but unable to move from her dressing table, Brooke ran through the gallery of what had by now become apocalyptic platitudes, almost soothing in their familiarity.

'Always likes to keep folks waitin',' she heard Mammy's voice say again.

'Oh God, I'm turning into my mother,' she screamed with sudden savagery, throwing down her lipstick and then hastily picking it up again. Her face was almost as wrinkled now as her mother's had been when her father died. Adam had called her a 'menopausal mystic' during their most violent squabble. That had almost finished them off, but after a long conversation with Kenneth about the meaning of forgiveness she had given a special dinner for Adam.

'That man's like a nuclear winter,' said Kenneth when he learned who she was forgiving. 'All he can do is fall out with people. That makes it, eh, even more of a privilege,' he added soothingly, 'to have helped reconcile you.'

Brooke unglued herself from the dressing table and, with a last toss of her head, as if the mirror had insulted her in some way that was beneath her attention, headed out of her bedroom grabbing the list of new names. She was worried about the late arrival of her house guest Crystal Bukowski. Yes, she was the daughter of old Dr Bukowski, now dead it turned out, and they had met three weeks ago in New York at a fascinating gathering given by some people *very* close to the Dalai Lama.

What a coincidence, she would have said in the old days, but now she only used the S words, serendipity and synchronicity. Crystal's mother, her hostess had told her, had been one of her father's patients who had become accidentally pregnant and then, realizing that he wasn't going to leave his family but was prepared to pay her not to ruin his practice, she had joined a series of weird cults, taking little Crystal with her.

Crystal was just emerging from a very difficult romance with a Frenchman and Brooke already felt protective towards her, although there was going to be an ugly gap on Adam's right if she didn't turn up soon. Still, Crystal had a kind of honorary familial status due to being Dr Bukowski's daughter. If not a black servant, he was at least a Jewish employee, most of whose family had been wiped out in concentration camps, and on whom she had showered vast sums of money during seven years of analysis.

They'd had to look long and hard at the pleasure she got from paying for missed sessions. It had enabled her to spend money in two places at the same time; it all tied in with having two homes. Really, he had helped her a lot, but in those days she had been so self-obsessed; now she was working for the world. She didn't regret the years with Dr Bukowski. 'You have to have your feet on the ground to touch the sky,' as Kenneth said.

Crystal Bukowski was in fact on board a delayed flight from New York and had no chance of making it to Brooke's dinner. Not that she was going to California to hang out with Brooke, but to attend the Dzogchen meditation retreat at the Esalen Institute.

She knew she was headed for the right place when she started fantasizing about sliding a chainsaw through the thick trunk of her neighbour's neck. With a face of unfathomable stupidity which could only have emerged from the most deeply inbred valleys of Kentucky, perfected by generations of blood feuds and wood alcohol, with a haircut that had just come out of a Marine shearing shop, and a pair of jeans so tight they offered every hope that he would be the last of his line, this hillbilly from hell had writhed in his seat, scratched his balls and tugged at his trousers from the moment the plane left New York. At other times she might have taken refuge in a pair of headphones and a cool chanting tape, but he nudged her with his elbow each time he had a scratch, and now she was obsessed.

What was her anger telling her? That she was feeling hostile towards men right now? That she wanted to scratch her own genitals? That she was feeling dumb about the way things had turned out with Jean-Paul? That she was guilty about being so restless, about burning up her father's surprise legacy to continue her mother's soul-searching migrations? Yes, yes, yes, yes. So her mind was projecting again – left to its own devices that was pretty much all it ever did – but she was so bored with catching herself out, she just wanted to go with the aggression today, give in to the hatred she felt for the Caliban beside her.

Crystal closed her eyes and breathed deeply, concentrating her attention on her hara, her navel chakra.

She tried to quiet the part of her mind that kept flashing little analytic mirrors. It had been bad enough having an absent father who had been an analyst without falling for a French philosopher who was training to become one.

Last month she had persuaded Jean-Paul to take psychedelics with her in the wilderness, figuring he needed a rocket launch to lift him into the dimensions beyond his busy intellect. Psychedelics cut through the analytic tic which was currently wasting her time, and took her into the zone where meaning was immanent, tangible and numinous. Unfortunately the mescalin and the magic mushrooms seemed to have the opposite effect on Jean-Paul.

The worst part was what had happened afterwards. Somewhere below the plane Jean-Paul was galloping across the wastes of a North Dakota reservation pretending to be a Lakoda brave, something even the Lakoda had trouble doing. He was living in one of those Third World rubbish dumps which the Federal government had offered the Native Americans, like a mugger tossing a subway token at his bleeding victim. He had even written to the passport authorities in France to say that he wanted to change his name to Little Elk. They had not complied.

It was no use blaming their guide, Robert, he was just a suburban kid from Sausalito who thought he was the reincarnation of a Hopi elder. In any case he said that the Hopis came 'originally' from Tibet, so he had all the options covered.

In the end she blamed herself for giving Jean-Paul the psychedelics. He had been enthusiastic, of course, as an anthropologist. He had read Huxley and Leary and so forth; he'd done a lot of reading in his life, he just hadn't done much else.

Jean-Paul had even started lecturing her on the value and function of psychedelics in primitive and developed societies, on their way from Moab to Canyonlands in their Cherokee four-wheel drive – no doubt Robert would have hired a Hopi four-wheel drive had there been one, although he had said that he 'honoured the Cherokee Nation' when she had made a mild joke to that effect.

With her eyes still closed and her arms pressed to her sides, out of range of Caliban, Crystal reluctantly replayed the movie of her trip with Jean-Paul. She had gone over it before, but like a tongue nagging at a fragment of trapped food, her memory returned again and again to those events in the hope of dislodging the truth of what had happened.

Almost immediately Crystal's thoughts were interrupted by another violent nudge from her neighbour. Caliban had just had a particularly vigorous tug at his jeans. She opened her eyes angrily and scowled at his apparently unconcerned profile. Part of her was relieved to be interrupted. Perhaps she had made him nudge her.

'I'm sorry to be so moving in my seat,' said her neighbour in broken English.

He wasn't a hillbilly at all, he was a Swede or a German.

'I have, um, problem with the skin. I come to California for doctors.'

'Oh, God, I'm sorry,' said Crystal, as much in apology as sympathy. 'I hope you get the help you need.'

'Thank you,' he smiled. Really, he had very nice eyes, and she seemed to see in them a glint of pained intelligence, showing that he'd picked up what she'd been thinking about him.

What a teaching, thought Crystal, as the plane landed at San Francisco airport. 'What a teaching,' she murmured in the baggage-claim area. What an incredible teaching, she mused contentedly in the taxi, nodding her head in gratitude, incredulity and embarrassment.

Brooke had relaxed a little about her dinner party. Moses was taking the herb tea around, and everyone was evidently having a marvellous time. They were mostly a little drunk or high and agreeing with each other about things they already knew they agreed about, and planning fresh opportunities to discuss saving the world at each other's seminars, conferences, workshops and performances. Brooke was talking to Dave, the marine biologist. She had just delivered her list of plagues bursting from their 'natural reservoirs' – she was very proud of that phrase – on to the human scene. Unfortunately, with so many new names to remember, she had included the Irish environmentalist.

'Isn't it dreadful about Ebola, Marburg and O'Hara?' she had said, shaking her head sadly.

Dave didn't seem to notice the mistake.

'There's a symmetry there,' he said, looking at her from within the parentheses of his sunbleached blond hair. 'We have a viral relationship with our habitat and we become the habitat of the viral.'

'But isn't that like saying that AIDS is divine retribution?' said Brooke, who knew it wasn't but felt like beating up some fundamentalist white trash.

'Not really,' said Dave politely. 'It's just like saying that what goes around comes around. Karma is not retribution, it's just the way things are. At another level, the reality we inhabit is a function of the paradigms we use to describe it. Most of those paradigms are way too reductionist.'

'But isn't there something real underneath it all?' said Brooke, fascinated.

'Sure, there's the energy which takes the form of matter, light and everything else.'

'But I don't want to think of this table as an energy field,' said Brooke, removing her elbows in mock alarm.

'Why not?' said Dave. 'It's cool.'

Why not? thought Brooke. She smiled at Dave. Dave smiled at her. She was learning so much.

Adam rose to his feet, tears streaming down his cheeks. Everyone fell silent.

'The whales have AIDS,' he sobbed. He had only learned this from Dave half an hour before, speaking across the gap of Crystal's absence, but he had already appropriated it as his own tragedy. 'What are we doing to this beautiful planet?'

He paused and made a visible effort to remain calm.

'The people in this room, gathered here by . . .' Part of him wanted to say 'the Madame Verdurin of the New Age' but the wine and the fire won over and he said, 'our Eleanor of Aquitaine . . .'

Brooke, who had been expecting Guidobaldo, was lost for a moment, but could tell from the smiles that the comparison was flattering. She must get a research assistant to deal with Adam's conversation, her poor secretary had enough to do already.

'The people in this room,' Adam shrieked, 'are the only people who can save the world from utter destruction. This is the most important gathering that could take place at this moment in history. We are witnessing a new mystical

Renaissance that is struggling to be born against terrible odds in the rubble of our dying civilization, and it's up to us, scholars, poets, scientists, public figures, dharma teachers, to go out there and *wake people up*.'

And then he started to sing, pushing his thick hair back with the fingertips of one hand, and touching his heart with the palm of the other.

'O just one word from Shams and I would gladly give my life,' Adam warbled.

> 'His life is before me, and through his
>   love my heart has become pure, my breast has
>   imbibed every virtue.
> One smell of his perfume and I walk light-headed
>   on this path.'

Adam suddenly thrust his hand aside with a gesture of contempt.

> 'O cupbearer, enough of your wine, I am drunk
>   on the wine from his cup.'

Moses stood by, unsure whether to offer Adam some herb tea. He'd heard plenty of singing in his day and he felt that Mr Frazer needed lessons, as well as new material.

'I hope I'm in good voice tonight,' said Adam, audible over the small patter of applause.

'Rumi is the supreme guide to our age,' he continued with a new pedagogic calm. 'He has a literary genius equal to Shakespeare's, and a spiritual genius as powerful as Christ's. He brings us eternal news of perfect being, and of the fire of transfiguring love. And,' he concluded with a disconcerting rush of colloquialism, 'he reminds us to get off our fat arses and sing.

> "I'm tired of cowards, I want to live with lions,
>   With Moses, not whining teary people.
>   I want the ranting of drunkards,
>   I want to sing like the birds sing,
>   Not worrying who hears or what they think." '

Moses, whose loyalty to Miss Brooke was unfathomable, nevertheless drew the line at being propositioned in public, and left the dining room with subdued indignation.

Adam sat down and smiled modestly, but soon resumed the luxury of his new torment.

'The whales,' he said to Kathleen O'Hara, like a child whose adored puppy has just been run over and is offering his inconsolable torment to his mother.

'There,' said Kathleen, instinctively maternal. What a lovely sensitive man, she thought, so in touch with his feminine side.

'It's terrible what we're doing to the oceans,' she said. 'They're our natural filter systems, the kidneys of the planet.'

Everyone was embarrassed by Adam's speech. The idea of being the most important gathering in the world, and the excessive responsibility it brought with it, made them anxious to return home. Crystal's arrival could only act as a small counter-current to the tide of departures. When Moses showed her into the dining room, Adam was talking excitedly to Yves, Brooke and Kathleen about the vividness of his spiritual life. He was feeling charming, as he often did once he had discharged the anguish and hysteria which haunted his nature.

'Crystal, darling, we missed you over dinner,' said Brooke.

'And *you* missed a wonderful dinner,' said Adam, getting up.

'I'm sorry,' said Crystal to Brooke. 'By the time I knew the plane was delayed, your number was in the hold with my baggage.'

Brooke introduced her to the other guests.

'You must have been the empty space on my right,' said Adam.

'Form is emptiness and emptiness is form,' said Crystal in her Indian guru voice. Adam Frazer was a minor celebrity on the alternative scene and she wanted him to think she was interesting. There she was again, she reproached herself, still looking for approval from a powerful man. 'The two are really one,' she warbled.

Adam laughed. 'Not being *completely* enlightened, I prefer this delightful illusion to the more austere one I had over dinner.'

'You are tossed on the restless sea of samsara,' said Crystal, shaking her head sadly. 'Just turn your mind back to the source,' she urged him, quoting the great Poonjaji.

'Adam,' said Yves, who thought that Adam might be having fun with somebody else, 'it's getting late.'

'Oh, my love, are you tired?' asked Adam. 'We'll go home this instant.'

'Brooke, it's been a wonderful evening,' said Kathleen.

'Here's that thing we talked about,' said Brooke, half-discreetly, giving Kathleen an envelope. 'For the Foundation.'

'For the lungs of the planet,' said Kathleen compulsively.

When the others had left, Brooke took Crystal up to a guest room. It was so much cosier than sending her up with Moses. She sat on the small sofa at the foot of the bed and told her how welcome she was and to treat the house as her home while she was in San Francisco.

Crystal was touched and a little saddened at the same time, because the places where she had lived had been her homes for such fleeting periods, often under the precarious conditions of hospitality. Of course she had long inhabited the paradox of feeling at home with no home, and she tried to think of the glutinous satisfactions of property as a bribe it was noble to refuse. Instead of a memory oppressed by the tropical air of nostalgia, her memory had a swifter quality, as fugitive as the shadows of starlings flitting across the ground, but capable of delivering high notes; whole cities, whole atmospheres, whole passages of thought and feeling, as vast and suddenly present as the smell of the sea.

Brooke's own wounded sense of home made her almost excessive in her hospitality, but the two women ended up both feeling moved by the rituals of welcome.

'As you know, I'm going to Esalen on Sunday,' said Crystal. 'So I'm only really here tomorrow.'

'Oh, I should have told Adam,' said Brooke. 'He's teaching Rumi there next week. He's teaching Rumi everywhere every week,' she laughed. 'Make *sure* you contact him now that you've met. I don't think I could bear to have two friends in the same place who weren't in touch.'

2

Crystal couldn't sleep. Interrupted on the plane, and by her arrival at Brooke's, her thoughts returned compulsively to Utah and to the events which seemed to have tipped Jean-Paul into madness. They had talked in almost hallucinatory detail about that trip.

He had told her afterwards that he had found the landscape of Canyonlands overwhelmingly strange even before they had taken the psychedelics. Everything had been all right at first, driving through a semi-arid landscape of rolling hills and Ponderoso pines familiar to Jean-Paul from the countless Western movies he had devoured as a child.

It was only when he got out of the Cherokee and walked to the edge of the canyons that he was thrown by the complete strangeness of his surroundings. His first reaction was incomprehension and nervous laughter. From that height the wind seemed to have caressed the pink and yellow sandstone into sinuous and elliptical shapes, flying saucers and waves and mushroom caps. More than the vast scale and the exotic colour, he was overwhelmed by the fact that he had never seen or imagined such a landscape before. Without the consolations of history or analogy he was unable to make anything of it and so he resisted letting it make anything of him.

He realized that he had come in a predatory frame of mind. Like the trappers and the miners after whom the West was so often named, he had come to pillage. He was looking for echoes of the American codes he had already deciphered, fresh troops of imagery to enforce his arguments and observations, and 'typical' American experiences, such as the cult of the wilderness, which he could deconstruct, exhume and subvert with his tireless intellectual audacity. Ideally, he would have written the book in Paris, as Fredric Prokosch had written *Asiatics* in Chicago, but Crystal had persuaded him to get a pair of hiking boots.

Every millimetre of Europe had been drained, ploughed, terraced, built on, fought on, named, hedged or written about, but this American 'wilderness' was the site of irony and scandal. To begin with, it was inaccessibly expensive. By the time planes had been caught, a Cherokee, tents and sleeping bags hired, permits acquired, new clothes bought, three hotel rooms taken at the Ramada Inn on the way in and the way out, and a guide engaged at three hundred dollars a day, he worked out that they could have stayed in the Plaza Hotel in New York for the same number of nights. Instead of sleeping in stinking clothes under a swirl of snow in the company of Robert, the would-be extinct Native American white boy, they could have been channel-surfing in matching dressing gowns, searching for the Westerns whose Oedipal substructure he had written about in some of his most magisterially impertinent paragraphs.

Jets and smaller planes flew over constantly. The 'wilderness', he reflected, had no vertical extension, it was only a thin layer of the biosphere, a symbol of freedom subject to more prohibitions and regulations than Parisian traffic. The most ordinary acts – cooking, drinking, excreting – were subject to detailed methodologies enforced by a special bureaucracy of rangers. Walking around freely was fiercely discouraged. A trail scarred the canyon and along it they must trudge.

When they had gone to collect their permits, the rangers at the station, immigration officers for this land of harrowing novelty, had warned them not to walk on the 'kryptobiotic soil', a living soil which took eighty years to grow and could be destroyed by the brush of a boot. The true lover of the wilderness would avoid visiting it altogether. Once wilderness turned into 'The Wilderness' it became the most officious and fragile aspect of nature. Even Robert referred to his business as the 'wilderness industry'.

On the third day of camping in this controversial landscape, they'd left Robert behind and taken the psychedelics.

About an hour later, Jean-Paul's legs started to shake uncontrollably and he collapsed on the ground. The light, he told Crystal, was flashing swiftly over the tops of the sagebushes, like helicopter blades catching the sun. Realizing that he'd fallen through a trapdoor into a realm in which anything could happen, he sank lower on the ground, retreating from the menace of the steely sun.

When he turned to Crystal again and tried to speak he could only manage a solitary gasp.

'Strong.'

She nodded, speechless too.

He pictured antechambers of unease starting to honeycomb the universe, each crowded with petitioners pushing one another aside to secure his attention.

He was dying of cancer. He was going mad. He had never known and would never know the real meaning of love. The rotten floorboards of his pride gave way one after another and he fell through clouds of dust into a bottomless basement. Small hypocrisies cut into him like axe blows, and unacknowledged vanities rose up in all their monstrous plumage.

Just as a man releases millions of sperm to fertilize one egg, Nature spawned millions of human beings for the glory of one breakthrough in consciousness, one watershed in the history of sensibility, one invention like the alphabet, that made a real difference, one song that might be remembered, one book that might be read in a hundred years. What was he but one of those doomed sperm, part of the numerical pressure of evolution, unable to step personally into history, unable to define the nature of its emergence, let alone to shape it? Knowing he could leave no vivid trace of his passage, and shocked by the absurdity and strength of his desire to do so, he writhed as he watched the part of him that had not accepted his own historical impotence accept it now.

He spun as he sensed his own death encoded in the spirals of his DNA. It was his own cells and organs that would kill him, his own heart that would break him in the end.

He longed for Nature to rise up and, with the cool precision of a lizard's flickering tongue, eliminate an arrogant and parasitical human race, but at the same time he could not bear the thought of the smallest thorn scratching the thickest skin of the dullest person on earth.

All these thoughts assaulted him instantly, and intensely, with the same aggressive rapidity as the blades of light that strobed across the landscape. He realized with white panic that each second contained a lifetime of horror, that the most intimate sadness could become universal and the most universal proposition intolerably personal, that the many winding paths between the mind and body had been blasted into thundering motorways. He did not relish watching his mind and body locked into each other's decline, like a pair of pitbull terriers biting furiously into each other's bleeding mouth as they spiralled down over the edge of a precipice.

'*Oh, la vache*,' he gasped.

He had to take a break, the images were too strong. He closed his eyes and breathed deeply. Fluorescent dodeca-hedrons whistled past him in a thick meteor shower which was clearly about to smash apart the spaceship of his identity. Even geometry was out to get him, even Euclid could not cool the fever of his unhappiness. He opened his eyes again and burst into flame.

Oh, fuck.

Should he tell Crystal that he'd burst into flame? What was the etiquette of insanity? How could he ask her to save him when he had no idea who she was? He knew something about her back there in the other world, but now that he was on Pluto having his teeth examined by Dr Mengele, while the laws of physics were being redefined several times a second, whatever he had thought he knew meant absolutely nothing.

'Where are we?' asked Crystal with a breathtaking mastery of language. 'It all looks the same.'

'Whuh,' he managed, dragging the water bottle out of his backpack. Being on fire was thirsty work.

Why had she said that? Why had she introduced the further disturbance of pointing out that they were lost? Everything *did* look like everything else. They were in a fractal landscape: the smallest cracked pebble contained canyons that lay on the ground of canyons that branched off wider and wider canyons in a land of wide canyons. And those cracks led to gulleys that ran into streams that flowed into tributaries that disgorged into the churning ochre drain of the Colorado. Seen from above, he knew that this vascular system, contained within the echoing canyons, created another layer of resemblances to various anatomical, botanical, crystalline and zoological formations.

There were star-shaped flowers and, no doubt, flower-shaped stars, but these multiplying resemblances which might at other times have spoken to him of an intricate design, or at least of an intelligible vocabulary, now crushed him by annihilating the space between what had become purely mental objects.

A more primitive and chaotic collapse of space took

place when he tried to make out where they were sitting. The pink and yellow rock shimmered and shifted like an exasperating piece of optical art, but instead of being able to step out of the pretentious gallery in which it hung and into the visual liberation of the street, he was installed in the centre of this little conceptual joke, caught like a loose hair from the paintbrush in the pigment that surrounded him on every side.

Surrounded and invaded: his own flesh was also a pink and yellow landscape which he could not help imagining flayed in a butcher's window, a few sprigs of sagebrush arranged at the base.

These thoughts, which would have taken so long to formulate, took no longer to think than a wasp's sting to sting.

As if this weren't enough, he seemed to be in a landscape crowded with debris from an era of reptilian giants. Its petrified iguanas, tortoises, lizards and dragons were swapping positions at high speed, receding and rushing forwards like the garish chariots of a funfair ride.

'I see what you mean,' he said.

Each gasped word, particularly 'I', 'see', 'you' and 'mean', seemed to lead down hazardous mineshafts of communication designed by narrow conventions, held up by rotting props and filled with dead canaries. 'What' preserved a comparative innocence.

He knew that the only way to gauge real time was to move through real space, that the only way he could stop the poisonous vine of malaise from strangling him completely was to pit his most fundamental resources against it. This was not an experience to relax into but an enemy to defeat at any cost.

A low bank of earth rose nearby. If he could get to the top of it he might see something that would lead them back to base camp, to water, to food, to someone whose mind was not ravaged by psychedelic drugs, although he secretly believed that the disappointment of these consolations would tip him into permanant madness.

Crystal hoped the trip wouldn't get any stronger. The beauty of the psychedelic realm was eluding her right now. She felt she was being taken further away from her centre, not deeper into it. The truth was she had wanted something for Jean-Paul.

When she had introduced him to Lama Surya Das at the New York Open Center he had said how many interesting questions he had about the nature of meditation. Surya Das silently made the gesture of unscrewing Jean-Paul's head and throwing it away.

'Ah, so you understand that I think too much,' Jean-Paul said with satisfaction.

'A lama understands everything,' Surya Das replied with a self-mockery as gentle as everything else about him, except his passionate desire for full realization.

She'd thought that Jean-Paul might get 'out of his head' in a constructive way but now she wasn't sure, watching him sway on all fours like an infant on its first crawl.

Jean-Paul clutched at the ground as if it was the last bush on the lip of a precipice, his fingernails filling with dirt. When he reached the top of the little mound he turned around and sat down heavily on the ground. The busy landscape, dancing with strobe lights, was as indecipherable as before, apart from the distant green haze of the first leaves breaking out on some cottonwood trees. He could remember seeing cottonwoods in the creek that ran parallel to the trail. He raised his arm and pointed in their direction.

'There,' he said.

Ostensive definition, was that all he could manage? He, whose student essay on Hegel had been the talk of the philosophy faculty of the Sorbonne for one heady week, was now reduced to pointing. He whose commentaries on Lacan were considered seminal by the analytic community in Paris was unable to form a sentence. Drugs had reduced him to an imbecile.

Crystal turned slowly and smiled at him. Maybe being a real man and finding the way home would help. There she was again, more focused on the other person than on herself. With this hint of self-reproach she felt the eruption of old feelings about her father. He had loved her even when he wasn't there, he had never stopped loving her. Therapy had taught her to name and map her abandonment, but Poonjaji had shown her that he had loved her even when he wasn't there, that he had never stopped loving her. For years she had been angry and filled with mistrust, but after seeing Poonjaji last year in Lucknow, she had gone down to Goa and spent a week lying on the beach alone feeling wave after wave of liberation. Every suffering turned into a teaching, and when she pulled at the oldest and heaviest chains of her soul, they tore like paper decorations in a child's hands.

Turn the mind back to the source, that's what Poonjaji always said. Yes, it was there, that humming, that deeper reality. It was there all the time, all she had to do was turn her mind back to the source. She felt the turning like a muscular contraction at the centre of her brain, and her attention vaulted over the thoughts that sensation pro-voked, over the thinking that enabled those individual thoughts to exist, and plunged itself into a limitless field of light. And then she knew, without needing to argue or to formulate it, that thinking was a degradation, a falling away, a clamorous and vain insistence on distinctions which had their conceptual charm, but no ultimate reality. The ruling force was not argument, or logic, or personality, or the individual manifestations of life, but life itself, the organising principle that germinated seeds, exploded novas, and deserted the body at death without leaving it any lighter. This mysterious, weightless and invisible force pointed to a genealogy more fundamental than the history of the things that had happened to her. She experienced it as not only transcendently grand but touchingly personal. Her whole body was taut but completely relaxed, as if she were locked into and held gently at the first stages of an unstoppable orgasm.

'There,' Jean-Paul reiterated hoarsely.

He was pointing to something.

'Is that the way home?' she asked.

He nodded. Crystal, while overflowing with loving kindness towards Jean-Paul, couldn't help taking a mis-chievous pleasure in his speechlessness. When she had tried to tell him what happened when her sense of self was wedded to a sense of life that didn't require her to think in the normal sense, he had scolded her, 'But this pure Being is a linguistic scandal! There can be no thought without language and no language without culture. Even being asleep is a cultural act! We bring to it our expectations of the language of dreams, we bring to it quotations from a thousand books. When we say we are in a state of Being we place ourselves at the centre of a complex cultural argument, not beyond that argument.'

God, the French were crazy. All she'd been able to say was, 'It doesn't feel like a cultural argument. It feels great.'

'But culture is great, culture is fantastic,' he'd said. 'Also, it's all we have.'

Jean-Paul half rolled and half crawled back down to Crystal's side, and with the awful defiance of a dying king heaving himself from his bed to sign the orders for a last batch of executions, staggered to his feet. The price he paid for this effort was to burst again into clear yellow flame. His skin prickled with pinpricks of sweat and he stumbled forward, supported by unreliable knees, his arms outstretched to catch a fall. He imagined his blackened flesh peeling like curled butter and falling softly to the ground. He felt everything false and shallow and cunning falling away with that burning flesh, and wondered nervously what was left.

Crystal resigned herself to following Jean-Paul's wavering return. He obviously needed to be going home in some sense, even if home was a tent where he'd only spent one night. Guilty about the pleasure she'd taken in his speechlessness, Crystal started chanting to the female Buddha,

OM TARE TUTARE TURIE SOHA, and immediately felt a downpour of reassurance, falling like a pelting rain of honey into the starving mouths of humanity. OM TARE, she imagined it falling onto Jean-Paul, TUTARE, she imagined it falling onto her, TURIE SOHA, their blood turned to liquid gold.

Jean-Paul's flesh burnt away again and again. What was left? What was essential? He longed for a diamond body, an incorruptible and incombustible diamond body, but he could see only a charred corpse, a black-and-white war photograph as banal as it was hideous. In the burning ghats of Benares, beside the Ganges, the only other time he'd travelled exotically, he'd seen the bandaged corpses sit up as they burnt, sit up and burst from their bandages, resurrected by the medium that consumed them, but that was just a moment when fact and symbol made an amusing marriage. It meant nothing, nothing.

Sinking deeper into scepticism he started to contemplate with fresh anxiety the substructure of language, hidden like the submerged section of an oil rig under the opaque and frothing sea that separated the conscious from the unconscious mind. The garrulous and busy platform was language itself, the site of visible industry, but underpinning it was Chomsky's deep grammar, the web of relations that made the acquisition of language possible. In the beginning was not the word but the grammar, a skeleton waiting for semantic flesh and giving it order. If the eye socket was not waiting for the eye, the eye might turn up on a kneecap or in an armpit. He'd too often glibly equated thought and language by expanding the term 'language' to include all patterns of imagery, but there could certainly be no thought without grammar. It was the hard wiring of the subject–object relation, and the thinker was always a subject even if, or perhaps especially when, he was the object of his own thoughts.

The reason Jean-Paul found these otherwise familiar reflections disturbing was not only that he experienced his own analogies with complete conviction, feeling his eyeball sliding down to his kneecap, or squinting out of the steamy and hirsute darkness of his armpit, but also because he felt his own deep structure being exposed to the danger of alteration. If his grammatical core was being corroded, if some fundamental girder was being removed or replaced, then a sense of self that went far beyond education, nationality, personal history or sexuality could be disrupted and he would lose not just himself but his opportunity to regain himself by reading the world in a way that made sense.

He had taken a drug, his body would metabolize it and everything would be all right. He had taken a drug, his body would metabolize it and everything would be all right.

Crystal felt engulfed in the golden cascade of her first mantra and, just as an espresso can be welcome after a rich meal, for those who still eat rich meals and haven't given up caffeine, she chose to switch to the Dzogchen mantra, the ultimately laconic 'Ah'. She immediately felt the change of energy. Clarifying, all-accepting, Ah, immersed fully in the moment, Ah, all the rocks vibrating with the same frequency, Ah, expression of wondrous surprise and deep simplicity, Ah, all sounds, all mantras, all colours converging in that one syllable, Ah, her chakras flowering in time-lapse bursts, like the purple convolvulus untwisting in the morning sun, Ahhhhhhhh.

Jean-Paul's paranoia was relentless, but he staggered on. If he was left only with madness, it would be his own madness. The thing he could call his own in an inferno of alienation was the alienation itself! Hadn't Nietzsche said that the measure of a person was his ability to embrace contradictions and hold tensions in place? He forced himself to look up from the dusty tips of his hiking boots and try to admire the landscape.

Crystal was exquisitely aware of every footstep she took as she wove her way mindfully among the patches of kryptobiotic soil and bare rock and fruitless sand. She felt the Earth calling to her and to millions of others, to rise to this level of kryptobiotic mindfulness. With one careless footstep she could disrupt the habitat of the tiny creatures that made up this living soil. She was deep into the interconnectedness of everything, tendrils of desire springing from her feet and webbing with the roots of all the plants of the Earth.

The silence now was as deep as a cathedral bell. The colours, the blue sky washing over the yellow stone and running into the pale-green sagebrush, spoke of a subtle harmony. She felt herself joining the landscape, not in some vaporous interfusion but with a groan of surrender.

They had just hit a patch of brilliant grass, each porcelain blade streaming with light.

'Look,' she said.

'What?'

'A Colorado bluebird.'

And yet we are in Utah, thought Jean-Paul, and still it persists in its scandalous blueness. This bird is a disrupter of nomenclature, a categorical dismemberment, a crosser of borders, an inhabitant of the margins.

Crystal sat down on the grass and watched the bluebird. Perched in a thornbush, it looked to her as vivid and brilliant as a painted tile from Isfahan, a songbird in the jewelled tree of a Persian paradise. She willed it to come closer and the bluebird dipped towards them and came to rest on a nearby bush. She imagined its darting perspective and felt she had entered the mystery of its consciousness, seeing the world reflected in the dark beads of its eyes. The bird flew closer still and turned at the last moment, revealing the darker blue plumage of its back, its radiant feathers dyed with a concentrated solution of the sky against which it moved.

The flight of this complex bird moving from bush to bush, thought Jean-Paul, traces the line of a telephone wire dipping and rising outside the window of a train. But what message does it bring along the wire? For two days he had been trying to impose comparisons and extract metaphors from this landscape. When the rocks, with their usual disturbing plasticity, had conjured up a city of minarets, pyramids and camels, he had pondered both the coincidence of this constellation of imagery – had one image triggered another? – and the inescapable fact that the Anasazi, the now extinct 'original inhabitants' of these canyons, could not have seen any camels or minarets or pyramids, unless of course they were Egyptians, as Robert no doubt believed. How had these unmistakable signs appeared to the Anasazi? Did they see things which resembled those objects in their own culture, or did they read the elements of the picture with a radically different gaze?

Just as the vapour trails of jets criss-crossed overhead in the lost wilderness of the sky, the traffic of analogy moved from one object to another, plundering every language, every culture, every landscape, and creating an ever more opaque web of connections, a mirror increasingly scratched. But out of this apparent reduction of resources, hybrids would arise, increasingly complex combinations of increasingly exhausted elements. Would these images constitute novelty or merely decadence?

Crystal watched the low white clouds beginning to flow into the canyons. Although the weather had been extreme and unseasonal, scorching for an hour and then snowing heavily, these clouds had a decorative innocence. Near the camp there was a large round cactus that reminded her of a geodesic dome made of tightly packed segments. She had seen it the morning before, beads of dew clinging to its steely spikes, and in the seams between its segments, the buds of red flowers gleaming like drops of blood. Two of the flowers were open and blazed with astonishing intensity against the grey-green of the cactus's skin. When she returned from her hike these blood-red cups were filled with crystals of snow. It was so beautiful.

God, she could feel the mushrooms starting to come on. The urgent luminosity of the mescalin was giving way to the more sumptuous eruptions, the hesitating fountain of the psilocybin. An iridescent sheen played over the mother-of-pearl surface of a cloud. She watched it shifting lazily from a baby's sleeping face – it was her own face, how peaceful she looked – to a team of heavily maned white horses kicking up a cloud of mauve dust with their galloping hooves. Oh, yes, it was like a slow fuck, this erotic divulgence of Proteus to her fervent imagination. The unfurling leaves of the cottonwood trees were now a few yards to the right, the slender branches pulsing with spring, leaves like unclenching fists surrendering to the warmth and generosity of life.

Another jet flew overhead and she remembered Thich Nhat Hanh saying how you could use the ring of the telephone like a meditation bell to cut through to mindfulness, and so she imagined the passage of the jet through the sky like a blade cutting through the canvas of a tent and opening outwards on to the sparkling darkness.

Yes, that sound was her mantra. The mushrooms contained such extraordinary teaching. She was deep into the sacred nature of psychedelics which revealed the sacred nature of everything else. They were one of the gateways into the luminous field.

'The mushrooms are coming on,' she called quietly to Jean-Paul.

'Mushrooms!' said Jean-Paul. The word alone was enough to infuse his bloodstream with the spoors of a deeper paranoia. 'This trip will get stronger?'

'Different,' said Crystal. 'Sexier.'

'Sexier? You mean the first part was sexy for you? For me it's not so sexy to have an angry man with a blowtorch trying to dismantle the structure of my identity! Even le Marquis de Sade, with an unusual but imperative continence, would have resisted the concept of sexual excitement on this occasion.'

'Don't use so many words,' smiled Crystal, 'just look at stuff.'

'But when I look at stuff I see "stuff".'

Crystal walked over to him and kissed him on the mouth. '*Calme-toi*,' she whispered.

Jean-Paul smiled back. He was far too anxious to think of making love to her. Besides, rangers were no doubt on the ridge with their government binoculars, ready to shoot them for rolling around in the kryptobiotic soil. He pretended to be persuaded by her kiss and resumed his homeward march.

Where was the eternally derailed train of his thought? Oh, yes, this landscape, this obligation to be in awe. If he fell to his knees, what would he be worshipping? Wind erosion? Sandstone? The weather? The relative scale of human and inhuman phenomena? No, he would be worshipping the spirit which Rousseau had marketed so cunningly for the Western mind, the spirit of egotistical sublimity. But surely the essence of this landscape was its inhumanity, its harshness, the way in which it stood just out of range of the eager reach of pathetic fallacy. The civilized landscapes of Europe, the Alps, Provence, Tuscany and so forth, were the nymphomaniacs of the sublime, constantly accommodating the sensitivities and reflections of every visitor, lying down and gasping as one after another they brought their intimations of immortality, their sighs of appreciation, or their easy conviction that, as Rosanov had said, happiness consists of picking one's nose while watching the sunset.

Canyonlands, on the contrary, was the coldest of virgins who could only be approached on her own terms, through a grille in the convent wall. She was not interested in one's longings, only in one's worship, and in the end she was not interested in that either. She simply embodied something so strange and extravagant that the road of Rousseauesque communion with Nature forked towards incomprehension on the one hand and self-annihilation on the other.

How would one 'surrender', what mental act was involved in that 'awful daring'? Was it something to do with humility, a subject on which he was no expert, or was it, on the contrary, a sense of special destiny which filled one with universal awe?

He tried to force himself again to look at his surroundings rather than read them, and then to feel them rather than look at them. He only had to make these decisions for them to be fulfilled, but he found himself feeling something other than universal awe. He and it, subject and object, inside and outside, seemed to be superimposed on each other, as if he were looking at a glazed painting through a shop window on a sunny day, but instead of the vitreous ghosts being effects which he witnessed from a known centre, he felt that there was no part of the ghostly scene that was not animated by his presence. By the same token this dispersal of himself into the shimmering fabric left him utterly lost, as if the echoed flash of sunlight caught on the bumper of a passing car and reflected in the window could steal his soul, so dangerously thinned by being interfused with everything.

Was the problem that he needed to describe what was happening and the description contained the very terms, like 'subject' and 'object', that were abolished by the experience he was attempting to describe? He must know the answer now!

'It's called "Don't know mind",' said Crystal, pausing on the trail. 'Sometimes you have to stay with the position of not knowing. I don't know why I said that . . . I guess I have to stay with the position of not knowing. God, it's one of those loops.'

'But it's incredible,' said Jean-Paul. 'I was thinking how I *must* know what things mean when they are happening.'

'I guess I picked that up.'

'What does it mean to "pick that up"? We are having telepathic communication?'

'Don't know,' Crystal had said, hearing the scepticism and alarm in his voice.

Contemplating the changes that had swept over Jean-Paul after that day, Crystal had often wondered if it was the idea of telepathic communication and the permeability of his own mind which had disoriented him beyond recovery.

She sat up in bed. It was three in the morning in San Francisco, and she had to see a bunch of people the next day. She crossed her legs and breathed out deeply, trying to dispel a feeling of guilt and abandonment. Eventually she relaxed into meditation, and from there into exhausted sleep.

3

'Is there any chance of your going back to Kleinwort's?' sighed Mrs Thorpe.

'I don't know,' said Peter, to whom it seemed rather less likely than an invasion from Sirius. Kleinwort's was utterly remote to him at the moment. Over the last few days the rest of the world had receded like clouds melting in the heat of an atomic blast. He didn't dare tell his mother that he'd forgotten her telephone number.

'You must be running out of money,' she said hopefully.

'Not yet.'

'You can't just say you don't know,' said Mrs Thorpe.

'Even if it's the truth?'

'But I don't think it is true, not deep down.'

'You mean the deepest thing about me is my potential re-employment by a merchant bank?'

'You sound so different,' said his mother. 'You used to plan for the future.'

'Well, just now I'm trying to live in the present.'

'That's what animals do, darling, *we've* got minds.'

'And what are they for? Buying life insurance?'

'I can't make out whether they've turned you into a socialist or a Moonie,' said Mrs Thorpe.

Peter looked out of the telephone booth. The Pacific, sparkling among the dark branches of a cedar tree, made him pause long enough to disarm.

'You're probably right in a way. I don't really know what I'm up to,' he said. 'We're all so fragmented, perhaps we can never know ourselves as a whole.'

'Are you all right?' said Mrs Thorpe, her opposition replaced for a moment by maternal concern. 'You're not cracking up, are you?'

'No, I mean, I had this strange feeling the other day. Maybe I felt whole then, or maybe it was just a new bit of me emerging.'

'You *are* cracking up,' said Mrs Thorpe, no longer in any doubt.

They fell silent for a moment and then Mrs Thorpe bravely resumed.

'Fiona rang. I had to admit that I had no idea how to get hold of you. I don't think she believed me, which is absolutely maddening because as you know I think she's perfect for you. She blames that Findhorn Foundation. What I can't understand is why you went there in the first place.'

'To get away from Fiona for one thing,' said Peter.

'Well, you didn't have to go to a Moonie place, you could have gone on one of my Serenissima Tours. They're such fun. We're going to look at castles on the banks of the Danube next month.'

'If you really want to know, I was also pursuing another woman.'

'*Cherchez la femme!*' said Mrs Thorpe.

'That's exactly what I was trying to do. We only spent three days together but I've never been so happy in my life. Then she just disappeared saying nobody owned anybody else.' Peter watched Brad lolloping past the phone booth in a faded pink T-shirt.

'Hey, Peter,' said Brad.

Peter waved at Brad. 'I had no desire to own her,' he went on explaining to his mother. 'I just wanted to hang with her.'

'Hang?' said Mrs Thorpe, vaguely remembering a disgusting article about American adolescents who hanged themselves in the shower for sexual titillation.

'Oh, it's just an expression they use here, an abbreviation for hanging out – you know, spending time with someone.'

'Well, it should be abolished,' said Mrs Thorpe. 'How long do you propose to go sleuthing after this inveigling woman? Sex isn't everything, you know. I learned that from your father. If you went back to Kleinwort's you could get a private detective to find her. When he succeeds you'll be able to pop out and join her. Frankly, she doesn't sound that keen anyway.'

'She was very keen at the time, that's the puzzle. Anyhow I haven't got a photograph of her and I don't know her last name, so the detective would have to be a psychic.'

'I'm sure there's no shortage of those in the circles you move in these days,' said Mrs Thorpe, pronouncing the word 'circles' with cool irony. 'Do you make a habit of going to bed with women whose last names you don't know? As you know I'm not easily shocked . . .'

'But you're easily shocked . . .'

'No, no, I realize that standards change, I just wish they sometimes changed for the better.'

'Listen, I'm running out of money,' said Peter, ignoring the heaps of change scattered on the wooden ledge under the phone.

'Are you going to tell me where you are?'

'At Esalen.'

'What's that?'

'A personal growth centre. I know . . .'

'It sounds like something a doctor should have a look at,' giggled Mrs Thorpe.

'Ah, there goes my last coin,' said Peter. 'I'll call you soon.'

He was not surprised that his mother found it hard to understand the changes he'd been through in the last four months; he found it even harder, despite the advantage of having lived through them himself. She at least rested in the certainty of her disapproval, whereas he was at once disapproving and overwhelmingly grateful, flooded with a new sincerity and convinced, sometimes by the same sincerity, that he must be deceived.

His life had been a forced march through the Cotswolds of English respectability, interspersed with periods of equally brutal idleness among the same irreproachable hills. Now everything was in doubt. His pursuit of Sabine seemed to have translated him to a Himalayan landscape where the sublime and the ridiculous alternated with horrifying suddenness. His feet could freeze while his face burnt. He sometimes found himself gasping beyond the tree line of everything reassuring and familiar, but the view from those rocky slopes made him reluctant to accept the bribes of homecoming, those dripping oaks and bleating sheep, the gusts of warm stale air in the underground on his way to work, the reiterated sense of belonging. Without knowing what it would mean to look on the world nakedly, he knew that he had never done so. The cataracts of habit and conditioning clouded his eyes; the world he looked on seemed to have been wrapped by a demented florist in swirl after swirl of noisy and distorting cellophane.

He had always been too busy to daydream, except about unexpected sex and unexpected promotion. Everyone had time for that. Peter heaved himself up, stepped out of the phone booth and ambled down to the Pacific with his hands in his trouser pockets.

When he'd met Sabine on a banking trip to Germany, and actually had some unexpected sex, he'd made the mistake of telling Gavin about it, in Gavin's terminology.

'Met a really stunning German girl, physically, apart from anything else, really stunning.'

'Jammy bastard,' said Gavin.

Gavin was an acquaintance of his from school who had been so struck by twice belonging to the same institution as Peter that he'd prophesied they would become 'bloody good mates' at the bank. Although Gavin's dinner parties in Parson's Green, with their smoked-trout mousses, and the weekends playing Monopoly for real money left Peter cold, he had fallen in for a while with Gavin's fantasy of friendship, through the same combination of resignation and vague reluctance to cause offence which had determined most of his social life.

'She said the oddest thing,' Peter had told Gavin, quoting Sabine in a funny German accent. ' "We meet, we come together. Don't grasp me. If we meet again we let the universe decide." '

'Sounds like Loony Tunes to me,' said Gavin. 'All I can say is I hope the universe, whoever he is when he's at home, has a bloody good address book. What on earth did you say?'

'I said the universe was very wise, not without a pinch of sodium chloride,' Peter added, hoping to fall in with Gavin's oppressively fluent facetiousness.

'More like a bloody shovelful I should think,' said Gavin. 'Trouble with these stunning women, they completely blow your gasket in that department.' He pointed to his trousers with an expression of alarmed bliss. 'Plus of course the mysterious depths of the female psyche,' he conceded, 'and then you find out they're completely and utterly barking. One day you're having a nice weekend of off-piste skiing, if you know what I mean, and the next you're on the blower to Directory Enquiries, "Excuse me, do you have the number for the Priory?" By the way, old boy, you may find that three weeks in the bin for some loony Kraut isn't included in your medical insurance,' Gavin guffawed.

After this speech Peter had stopped confiding in Gavin, or anybody else. The truth was that Peter had always been more sensitive and intelligent than he'd let on, and now the extremity of his obsession with Sabine had no place in the world in which he moved.

He ached for her limbs and her lips. He thought he saw her disappearing round corners, or rumbling past in buses, broke into an incredulous run, and then realized he was going mad. She was the only star in the utter darkness of other people. He thought about her so much that she became more intimate to him than he was to himself.

The memory of her physical presence would shimmer towards him, like a swimmer breaking the surface of a pool. He would stop everything, in case he missed her warm breath against his cheek. Sometimes he howled out loud, thinking of her perfect body, white as the moon, buckled on the corner of the bed, and the way she had said, 'Does it please you?' with a worried frown.

At first he'd returned to Frankfurt, to the cafe where he'd met Sabine, and the streets he could remember walking with her. He felt increasingly distraught, remaining silent while lover's speeches raged in his head. The obsession grew stronger with time, and his secrecy created an increasingly eerie gap between him and the rest of the world. He loathed himself for telling Gavin about her and crushed speculation when it occurred.

'This German sex machine hardly sounds like wife material,' Gavin hazarded one day, sensing that he was being deprived of news.

'Oh, that's all over,' said Peter, furiously preoccupied with his computer screen.

'Can't marry a girl just because she blows your socks off,' said Gavin.

When Peter managed, with great difficulty, to get three months off work, Gavin was incredulous.

'Jammy bastard, going walkabout, eh? Wouldn't have anything to do with a certain Fräulein Leg-Over?'

Despairing of Germany, Peter had decided to visit the places he could remember Sabine mentioning: the Findhorn Foundation; a bookshop in Los Angeles called the Bhodi Tree; and the Esalen Institute, where he now stood on the brilliant lawn, looking at the sea.

He had arrived a couple of days earlier, and taken room and board until Sunday when he was going to attend the 'Moving on and Letting go' workshop which he had chosen rather haphazardly from the catalogue. Not entirely haphazardly of course, since he really did have to return to England the following weekend if he was going to go on working at the bank. Maybe he had to move on and let go of Sabine, or maybe he had to let go of the bank. That was the trouble: he wasn't sure what to let go of even if he found out how to do it.

In a way Fiona was right, the Findhorn Foundation had started him on what she would no doubt have called 'the slippery slope'. He had been nervous enough himself when the taxi driver from Inverness airport, at first sycophantically mistaking him for some kind of sportsman, spat him out disgustedly at the doors of the rambling former hotel which housed the educational aspect of the Foundation. On the way in, he briefly overheard the conversation of two men with grey ponytails.

'What are you doing here?'

'Inner Child.'

'That's with me!'

'Oh, I didn't realize it was with you!'

They rubbed each other's backs appreciatively.

Inside, after ignoring some notices from the Housekeeping Department, signed with hearts, he found himself in the hall with three groups of people. In front of him stood a couple in a long, charged hug. Over on the stairs an earth mother massaged the shoulders of a ragged-haired girl with a nose-ring. And in the corner an earnest trio consoled a crying woman.

He soon realized that the notices he'd ignored had been about removing muddy shoes before entering the house. During the months he subsequently spent in the winding souk of spiritual growth, nothing turned out to be so certain as the obligation to remove and replace his shoes dozens of times a day. Laces were as helpful as handcuffs to a juggler.

Sweaters, on the other hand, played a part analagous to armour in the lives of those medieval French knights who drowned in the mud of Agincourt, so weighed down by the armigerous language of swans and shields and falcons that they could no longer move without crane or horse. Peter felt bald in his dark-blue knitwear, when the sweaters of the initiated were bristling with rainbows, twinkling with stars, threaded with silver and gold, pulsing with hearts, populated with endangered species, embossed with purple burial mounds, and swirling with nameless mandalas. Homemade, these sweaters were also expressive of a love of creativity that scorned the judgement of the world. Everywhere, he found an art measured by its sincerity, not its results. Art itself seemed to take on a blurred but pretentious existence on the borders of therapy and craft, where it was deliriously liberated from difficulty as well as talent.

For his first few days, Peter endured the fulfilment of his prejudices in the hope of getting an address for Sabine. The New Age seemed to be a bomb shelter for people burdened with unusual names. Even those with ordinary names made subtle changes, putting a K in Eric or dropping an N from Anne. If all else failed, they simply changed their names to Shiva or Krishna, defying their birth certificates for the higher truth of their longing for deification.

He also encountered the first hints of a new vocabulary in which rules were called 'suggestions'. This was one of the promises of the Aquarian Age, a coercion not exercised from above, but enforced from every side by the asphyxiating pressure of collective beliefs. The net would replace the pyramid as the model of human relations, but consensus could be as oppressive as authority, and the cult of group activities, while it seemed to point forward to a democratic future, also led backwards to the mentality of the schoolyard, where popularity and the ability to exploit a special slang were the currency of power. The shadow of the pyramid in any case prevailed, crumbling, compromised, questioned, but still present. He found at Findhorn, and again elsewhere, a slave population of long-term students who paid reduced rates to work for nothing, a priesthood of teachers who passed on the open secrets of the New Age, an aristocracy of administrators, and a merchant class of consumers like himself, paying for the teachings of the priests.

Peter was at first annoyed by the 'focalizers' – a clumsy term used to sidestep the hierarchical implications that 'leaders' or 'teachers' would have conveyed. Everyone in his group would learn from everyone else, but they 'held the focus' by the simple device of deciding what everyone would do for the 'Experience Week'. Krishna and Lolita suggested that Peter move out of the local hotel he had mistakenly thought he was allowed to stay in, but Peter, who had come to pursue an amorous obsession, not to return to the primitive conditions of a hostel dormitory, suggested that he would rather leave the group than the hotel. Krishna and Lolita climbed down, but only after Peter had assured them that his separate accommodation would not prevent him from 'fully participating' in the Experience Week.

He had hardly tasted the thrill of out-suggesting the focalizers than he found himself in a strange crisis, wondering if he was addicted to telephones and hotel rooms, and feeling guilty about the conflict between his promise of full participation and his undisclosed reasons for coming to the Foundation. Somehow, the atmosphere of self-enquiry had already encroached on his private schemes.

On the first evening there was an 'attunement', a preliminary to all activities in which the help of 'unseen presences' and the 'Angel of Findhorn' was invoked, and the members of the group, sitting in a circle around a candle and some scattered leaves, 'shared' their feelings.

'Oh, we are nine!' exclaimed Oriane, a nervous and melancholy French woman whose face seemed to have been polished by too many tears. 'It's a sacred number.'

Peter found that few numbers escaped this accusation at one time or another. The number ten clung to a certain steely practicality, gleaming like a Swiss army knife among the smoky relics of numerology, although there was no doubt some 'system' in which it too bowed down before the tyranny of the esoteric. As a banker, his relationship with numbers was at once corrupt, since numbers were always figures, standing for a sum of money, and at the same time serene because, even in the debased form of a bottom line or a grand total, they spoke of a separate reality, infused with a meaning less slippery than language and less ephemeral than emotion. To see this Platonic realm press-ganged into the tricky service of symbolism was strangely disturbing to him. He felt a similar flicker of indignation at the thought of astrology. Why should the other planets, which spun out their lives beyond the reach of palpitating human concerns, be dragged into that unfortunate melee?

As the sharing went round, Peter became anxious about giving an account of his motives for coming to Findhorn. His heartbeat quickened and his mouth grew dry. He was far too preoccupied to notice what the others said, except that each one seemed to be 'going through a transition' and won appreciative nods from Krishna, Lolita and the others for using this phrase.

'I'm going through a transition too,' said Peter defensively. 'It's difficult to talk about because, well, I'm sort of right in the middle of it at the moment. I work in a bank and the thing is it suddenly seemed *completely pointless* and I had a bit of a nervous breakdown . . . that's all I can say just now.'

He blushed at the thought that he might be believed as much as at the thought that he might not be. What disturbed him even more was that he started to believe what he had 'shared'. On his way through the dark woods that led down to the village of Forres and his hotel, he began to feel that he really was having a bit of a nervous breakdown, that banking did seem completely pointless, and that he was in fact going through a period of transition.

Back in the hotel, he was told there was a function in the Sunderland Room, but that residents were of course welcome to avail themselves of the bar facilities. He drank whisky in the bar and wondered what kind of mirror the group was setting up. Why should he start to worry about the things he said in front of the group? Why did it seem to act on him like some magnified and collective conscience? Why could he not wear some adequate disguise, and when the office opened the day after next ask if they could remember a German woman called Sabine, and when he had an address for her, leave Findhorn and its silly rituals? That's what he would do, that was definitely what he would do.

The next morning on his way to breakfast, Peter saw the man with the grey ponytail he had overheard on the first day. He was again in earnest conversation.

'He was saying that when you bring things together

with love, either pieces of yourself or people in a group, that the sum is greater than the parts, and that in that context one and one equals three . . .'

Here, perhaps, was the sacred arithmetic that explained the strange power of the group to impress him more than its constituent members.

The fact that the first thing he heard in the morning seemed to address the very question he had been asking himself in the bar the night before was one of those funny little coincidences of which the people around him made such a cult.

'Here at Findhorn,' said Krishna before that morning's attunement, 'we suggest you make "I" statements. Out there – ' he thrust his chin towards the uncomprehending world that lay beyond the window – 'you often say "you" when you really mean "I", but here we like to own our feelings.'

Jill, a crushingly shy nineteen-year-old from Glaston-bury, wanted to leave the group. Lolita was with her now, Krishna explained, trying to persuade her to stick it out at least for the sacred dancing they were going to do after the attunement. Krishna asked everyone to hold hands by crossing their arms over each other as if they were weaving them into a rope.

'Feel the energy going round the circle,' he said. 'Receive it, take what you need and pass it on.'

Peter felt the flow come through one hand and pass out through the other. Was his neighbour sending the flow the same way? Did it matter?

'Let's focus on Jill and hope that through our love we

can persuade her to remain part of this circle of new friends.'

Peter, who despite himself was enjoying being roped to his neighbours, was jolted into rebellion by this promiscuous use of the word 'friends' to describe the bunch of nervous strangers who had met for the first time the evening before.

The sacred dance was focalized by Ulrike, a German woman who had been 'heavily into the lesbian and biking scene in Berlin' before she got into sacred dance; now it was her life.

They stood shoeless in the former ballroom of the hotel, no doubt the site of many functions in its day, a painting of a unicorn, as pleased as Punch beside a woodland stream, now defacing its principal wall. Outside, ribs of dark grey cloud were packed tightly overhead. Peter looked longingly at the cars parked at the back of the building. He hated dancing. They were trying to brainwash him into some collective trance in which community, communism and communion formed a noose around the beautiful neck of capitalist individualism, the sole route to cultural achievement and personal happiness. He was going to scream.

The circle was the sun, Ulrike explained, and each person was a sunbeam. 'We will dance the sun meditation and maybe the sun will come out,' she smiled.

Fat chance, thought Peter.

Ulrike asked everyone to look at each other while they danced.

The music from the *St Matthew Passion* swelled from

a ghetto-blaster in the corner. They started to move in a simple step, looking by turns into each other's eyes, trying to move harmoniously round the room.

Peter looked at Lolita and she seemed to be serious and kind. Krishna, too, had a serious expression in his eyes. He looked around the room and saw candour, yearning and woundedness. Only Jill looked resolutely at her feet. She was young, excruciated, lost. Her skin was bad and her clothes defiantly ugly, but instead of dismissing her as he would have in the predatory streets of London, Peter found himself longing to reassure her and put her at her ease. They moved around, ceremonious and slow. If only she would look up, he would rain kindness into her eyes.

There were further dances, including a vegetarian allegory in which a hunter, startled by the beauty of his prey, spared its life. Peter continued to note the ideological pressure he was under, but it no longer bothered him as much. He was more intrigued by the strange sense of goodwill that was welling up in him. Why not approach people with trust instead of suspicion? Why not be helpful instead of opportunistic? Why not be heartfelt instead of calculating?

The clouds had thinned, melted and fragmented, and the sun poured down on to the lawn and through the tall windows onto the blond floorboards of the ballroom. What was going on?

'You see, we've brought out the sun!' Ulrike laughed.

Over the next few days, he kept rediscovering this sense of goodwill, even when the experiences it accompanied seemed to take place on moonless nights of rhetoric and credulity. His concern for the rest of the group gradually rose to a pitch at which his happiness seemed inseparable from the happiness of the others. Everyone developed a sense of each other's vulnerability by telling their 'stories'. Instead of having to lower the portcullis of a false self in order to avoid being hurt, they pre-empted the pain by showing that they were all hurt already. There was a great liberation in feeling that the worst had already happened. This mutual concern was how family life should be, but of course never was, and that was its seductiveness.

There was a hint of a primordial scene as everybody told their stories, if not around a campfire, at least around the fat candle that always burnt at the centre of the circle.

Peter had not devoted much time to what Gavin called 'navel-gazing', although Gavin himself once admitted to a 'bout of the blow-your-brains-out' on an otherwise meticulously rowdy skiing holiday in Klosters. Peter had no very clear idea of what he felt about the big issues, except a general sense that God was bad taste in some forms, boring in others and mad in the rest. Nevertheless, he started to reflect that even if we were just dying animals, burdened with self-consciouness and the certainty of death, telling ourselves stories about the world in order to pass the time and relieve our troubled minds, then they might as well be good stories and they might as well be true. And so he told the group his real reasons for being there and about Sabine and how he'd been happy for the three days they'd spent together, happier than he'd ever been.

Everyone was touched by what he'd said and nobody seemed to worry that he'd not said it before.

'Oh, it's so romantic,' said Oriane, 'it make me want to cry.' And cry she did.

'I want you to think of room ten as your room, Peter,' said Evan, a buck-toothed and awkward Australian, aching to do good for the world in ways it was hard for him to put his finger on. Room ten had been assigned to Peter before it became known that he was staying in a hotel.

'It's actually rather a special room, because it was Eileen and Peter Caddy's family room,' Evan went on, unaware that this would not represent an additional temptation to Peter, who found the mythology of Findhorn and the lives of its founders, often recounted with the portentous detail of a biblical parable, one of the most tiresome aspects of his Experience Week.

'When you were telling your story, I was thinking what a pain in the ass God is,' guffawed Xana, an American woman who became friends with Peter, despite her initially disconcerting habit of bringing God into every sentence. She helped to persuade someone in the the office to look for traces of Sabine, and miraculously, as they all agreed, one of the names that emerged was indeed 'Peter's Sabine', as he could tell from the address in Frankfurt she had unfortunately been leaving at the time he met her. At least he was now fortified with her second name, Wald.

A morning's work was part of the Experience Week and both Peter and Xana ended up working in the kitchen.

'I'm Gawain, I'll be focalizing the soups today,' said the friendly man who greeted them in the kitchen. 'And this is Bettina, who'll be focalizing the salads.'

'Hi,' said Bettina.

There was an attunement and everyone shared what was 'going on' for them that morning. The sharing went around in what Peter was coming to think of as the usual way, until it reached Lisa, a young Argentinian woman who was part of the established kitchen team. Lisa's English was immediately exhausted by the enormity of her mood.

'I feel,' she began, and then broke into gesture, wriggling her palms towards each other on different planes, like tadpoles hurrying towards a doomed rendezvous. 'I have to be careful, because I may not really be here . . .'

You what? thought Peter.

'When I was a healer in Brazil,' continued Lisa, 'I couldn't work at night, because I would leave my body and go off on the astral plane. Sometimes it was very hard to come back and I think maybe last night,' her right hand shot up into the air, 'I spoke to my angel, and I have to share one thing: my angel tell me no work this morning.'

This was what Gavin would have called 'skiving off work without a chit from Matron'. You didn't need a chit from Matron here, just a chat with an angel.

Gawain, whose name sounded so like Gavin's but whose tone was so different, asked the Angel of Findhorn to help them work as a team, to open their hearts and to clear their minds. He invited everyone to be conscious of the noises in the kitchen and of the spirit helpers, as if this enjambement of whirring blenders and fluttering wings were the most natural thing in the world.

The strange thing was that they *did* work as a team,

the atmosphere was wonderfully collaborative and charming, people glided round the kitchen, anticipating their fellow workers' needs, sliding saucepans and knives to each other, handle first, with a silent smile, moving out of the way without stopping work, preparing food for hundreds without apparent effort, and enjoying themselves as well. What had happened? Again, there seemed to be something precious hidden among the rustling tissue of ritual and rhetoric. Gawain's prayers had been answered, and even if prayers were just the setting up of a fervent expectation, they had worked.

Elated over lunch, Peter and Xana discussed what had happened while eating the food they had helped to prepare, which tasted to them supremely good. Perhaps the attunements were not just an amiable waste of time. Peter had always assumed it was best to bully his way through his feelings. When he set off for the bank feeling sad, or hungover, or bored, or desperate, or in some other way unfit for work, he found that these moods usually evaporated as they hit the hotplate of action. There was of course a price to pay, a vague general depression, the lost habit of reflection, sudden bursts of frustration that seemed inexplicable because the trail that led to them had been obscured by a thousand urgencies, and by the trick of calling unhappiness 'a lousy day', and by the agreement of everyone around him that nothing surpassed the thrill of selling expensive loans and securing cheap ones, in order to enter a nirvana of ownership and hobbies.

At that evening's group attunement, Peter shared that he liked the group much better than he'd expected.

'Are we supposed to be flattered?' asked Xana, breaking the rule of respectful silence.

Stung by this mild mockery, Peter felt that sense of intense betrayal that sends children running from rooms. This raw sensitivity had of course to be 'processed', and led to further opportunities for bonding and trust. Xana and Peter climbed on to the roof and Peter, who had always been the one who said 'Oh, I missed it' when someone pointed out a shooting star, saw four that evening.

'You know they're no bigger than a swimming pool,' said Xana, 'burning up as they hit our atmosphere.'

That night Peter, who never remembered his dreams, dreamt vividly. Gawain and Gavin were engaged in an elaborate medieval jousting match. From behind the stockade where he stood among the rude serfs, Peter could see Sabine seated next to the King. Peter was crushed when he found that the jousting match was a computer game he was playing at work, and that with this shift in perspective Sabine was reduced to a few dots of light on a liquid-crystal screen. Caught playing games instead of investing, Peter was furiously berated by his boss, but he couldn't concentrate on his chastisement because he was too pre-occupied with the pair of dirty pigeon's wings which grew out of his boss's shoulder blades. In the next scene he was swimming with Sabine among the stars, in mildly electrified water that made them both unbearably excited. Their swimming pool suddenly tilted out of orbit, hurtled through space, and flared on the edge of the Earth's atmosphere.

'Awesome,' said Terry, a black American woman who

had given up her job in order to do past life regression work, dream work, and body work. 'You were definitely on the astral plane.'

'Was I?' said Peter, looking up from his porridge.

'Definitely.'

'Maybe I can skive off work,' said Peter.

'What?' said Terry.

'Oh, nothing.'

'The King's your higher Self,' shouted Terry, as he set off to the kitchen.

He didn't skive off work, although he soon wished he had. Gawain, who had focalized the kitchen so beautifully the day before, had been replaced by a tall bearded American called Warren. Perhaps Gawain had lost his jousting match, thought Peter, who found himself shuttling increasingly fluently between waking and dreaming.

'Have you been the butt of a lot of small-people jokes?' Warren asked Xana as she came into the kitchen.

'What?' said Xana, amazed.

'That's just me,' said Warren. 'I like to push people's buttons. I've got to be myself, right?'

Despite this warning, Peter, lulled into needless candour by the touching group attunements, mentioned his real reasons for being in Findhorn.

For the rest of the morning, Warren shouted, 'Is this the one?' whenever a woman passed the kitchen window. He danced with special glee when the ancient overweight postmistress came to deliver the mail.

'Hey, Peter, this is definitely the woman of your dreams. It was her dress sense that got to you, right?'

Whenever he was near Peter he sang the old Crosby, Stills, Nash and Young song 'If you can't be with the one you love, love the one you're with'.

Under Warren's guidance the food gradually declined.

'This is my grandmother's secret receipt,' he said, emptying a bottle of vinegar into a saucepan full of cabbage leaves. 'She smuggled it out of the Ukraine in the lining of her overcoat.'

'We want to go to the sanctuary to meditate,' said Xana at noon, when there was a theoretical right to do this.

'Tough shit,' said Warren.

'We're going anyway,' said Xana, undoing her apron.

'Great,' said Warren. 'That's called stating your needs.'

'You know, Warren,' said Xana with clipped patience, 'when you asked me about the small-people jokes, I happened to be with my god.'

'Did you get back to him?' said Warren, suddenly leaning closer.

'No, I wasn't able to do that,' said Xana. 'I think we've all come to Findhorn to develop our personal concept of the Divine. It so happens I *have* been the butt of lots of small-people jokes, and I'm all right with it, but you didn't know that. You just planted a bomb and walked away.'

'I could see you were all right with that issue,' said Warren, as if he'd been in control of the situation all along. 'I make people confront their issues, it's kind of a twisted gift I have,' he said. 'Think about it: what's your god worth if he can't survive a small-people joke?'

'That's what I'm going to the sanctuary to find out,' said Xana, hanging up her apron.

Peter started to follow her.

'Have *you* got an issue with me?' asked Warren, fixing Peter in the eye.

'Not really,' said Peter, for whom the word 'issue' had, until recently, always been preceded by the word 'bond'. 'I mean, it was a lot more fun working yesterday,' he recovered feebly.

'I don't give a shit,' said Warren, striding back to the cauldron of sour soup he was preparing for the community. 'I say that,' he shouted over his shoulder, 'but really I care profoundly.'

Outside Xana and Peter burst out laughing.

'I wasn't with my god when he asked about small-people jokes,' Xana confessed.

'Weren't you?' said Peter, slightly shocked.

'I just thought I'd throw *him* for a change.'

'Rather naughty of you,' said Peter admiringly.

Instead of going to the sanctuary, they went for a walk and talked about how horrible Warren was.

Apart from anything else, Warren had managed to destroy the alternative way of working which Peter had glimpsed the day before. A more familiar pattern had taken over; everyone retreated into their private thoughts and watched the clock, workers intimidated by an unpleasant authority. When Peter stopped chopping beetroot for a moment to stretch his back, Warren, who spent most of his time bouncing around the kitchen making flippant remarks, instantly caught him out.

'Got a backache, huh? Try working through the pain,' he suggested. 'You see, I'm not just good-looking, I'm psychic.'

Peter realized with some bewilderment that he felt protective towards the fragile revelations he'd had over the last few days, and that the great anxiety about whether to stay, which seemed to be the principal preoccupation of the entire population of Findhorn, might not just be born of a reluctance to leave a warm bath of licensed self-obsession, removed from the economic pressures of 'the wider community', but also spring from the loyalty he could feel stirring quietly inside himself, if only in opposition to Warren's malign influence.

Perhaps Warren had performed a valuable service after all. No, no, he couldn't start thinking like that; that's how they thought.

On the free afternoon that came just before the end of his Experience Week, Peter went to see David Campbell, a local laird who had been a friend of his father's. He had planned this escape while he was still in London, thinking it would offer a harbour of sanity in a lunatic week. Shivering his way among the silver dunes, with the North Sea licking icily at the beach and a few purplish clouds shrinking towards the horizon, he wished he'd stayed at the Foundation, and talked about his feelings with someone in his group.

Campbell lived in one of those high-rise cottages which are called castles in Scotland. Except for the inevitable rumour that Bonny Prince Charlie had passed through, dressed as a baker's wife, nothing had happened on this unprofitable stretch of frigid coastline until it became the landing site for a New Age settlement.

Campbell sat in the corner with yellow-white hair, coughing and smoking in a paisley dressing gown covered in ash and coffee stains.

'I call them the Gestapo,' he said. 'The women tend to wear long dresses and flowing robes and carry their babies on their backs instead of having prams and pushcarts like everyone else.'

How different history might have been, thought Peter, had the Gestapo worn long flowing robes and carried babies on their backs.

'Item number one,' said Campbell, 'they're selfish. They're not interested in the people around them. They pretend to be but they're not, because they think they're more important. Mrs Brown, who looks after me, was collecting for the local oldies, and I told her to jolly well go and rattle her box at the Foundation. She didn't want to go because it's another world to her.' Campbell paused, taking the opportunity to clasp a glass of warm vodka with his arthritic hands. 'Not a penny,' he said, sucking from his smudged tumbler. 'They said they hadn't got any money, although according to her they were all tucking into huge plates of delicious-looking food.'

'It's easy not to have any money because you don't have to pay for anything,' said Peter.

'Item number two,' said Campbell, 'a lot of them drop out of the Foundation and buy houses nearby, but they don't make themselves very popular because they keep themselves to themselves. We're at the end of the road here, there's nothing between us and Greenland.' He waved his cigarette towards the draughty and peeling window.

Realizing that Peter wasn't going to participate in satirizing the Gestapo, item number three turned out to be that 'they do no real harm'. As Peter left, his host went further and said, 'I suppose some of the things they say about trees and so forth make a hell of a lot of sense, but it's not my sort of cup of tea.'

By the last evening, Peter was in a fever of reciprocated and complex concern about the other members of his group. He not only knew what Evan thought of Xana and what Xana thought of Evan, but what Xana thought about what Evan thought of her. The web of connections was so intense that it promised to be permanent, as if the solution created by dissolving all these individuals together had formed a crystalline structure of its own during the course of the week.

As they shared for the last time, a young German woman called Lara told about the death of her three-week-old child. Hardly able to speak, let alone in a foreign language, she made exasperated gestures, as if she were tearing up vast sheets of paper, then she joined her knuckles together and pressed them hard, rocking her upper body.

'That morning I was so happy, yes? When I looked at my child ... her face was so peace, yes? Umm, I am very happy. Then I see she is not breathing, and I think, no, this is not possible. How can this happen when I love her so much? How can she stop breathing?'

Oriane burst out of the deadly silence that followed.

'It make me so angry. How can you believe in God when this happen?'

Later, Oriane was upset by her outburst and Peter was upset that she was upset, and they were both upset that Lara was so unhappy, and Xana was upset by it all too. After having a long speechless hug with Lara, Peter took a cup of tea to Oriane's room, and then he brought Lara to Oriane's room, and Lara said it was all right because anything anyone said was hopeless but she knew that Oriane felt the sadness in her heart, and Oriane burst into tears and so did Lara, and then Peter and Xana couldn't help bursting into tears as well.

On the last day they all spoke about their week. Lara said she felt as if she were dissolving in an ocean of love. Krishna said the love was so palpable you could cut it like a slice of cake. Peter said he knew something important had happened but he didn't yet know what.

'I hesitate to share,' said Oriane with a sigh. 'I always hesitate in my life and now I hesitate to share because I don't want to sound negative. This morning when I hoover the carpet I cry because I am so happy to be a slave, no, not a slave, a servant, but I am so happy not to make decisions. It's incredible what this group has shown me. I have a therapist for many years but he never show me how much I hate myself. This week I have seen how much I hate myself and I am very shock.'

Xana said she wished she'd had a mother who was as heartfelt and enthusiastic as Oriane, and Oriane burst into tears.

Krishna explained that they would end with a dance, as

they had begun. He taught them the steps of another simple dance and Lolita, after putting Pachelbel's *Canon* on the sound system, ran from behind the controls to join the others.

The group started to step slowly round in a circle, holding hands, each person in his place and then each person in everyone else's place. The sun was setting through the bay windows of the room they had met in all week. It seemed to sink under the weight of the baroque melancholy wrung from the speakers. No longer inhibited, Peter circled around effortlessly. Tears fell from Oriane's eyes and from all the other eyes as well. There was nothing to hold them back.

Peter knew all about their failed marriages, and their sick children, and their heartless mothers and their high ambitions, and they knew that he was a romantic and demented figure under his banker's garb. He would probably never see any of them again, but they were webbed together for ever by the emotional pressure of the week, and their connections would be preserved in some other dimension like the veins of a petrified leaf.

It was not that they had made friends, like holiday-makers bonding by a poolside, but that strangers had found a way of cutting directly through to intimacy, without the meanderings of social life or the precarious exclusivities of sex. Flowing through the room, along with the music and the tears, was the conviction that this was how people were meant to live, with nothing left to hide. The idea that all human beings could be loved had always struck Peter as either an unappetizing journey to a subbasement of species loyalty, or a rumour started by a Sunday school. Now it seemed to him to be the ground of all relations. Everything had been complicated and wrong; now it was simple and right.

Peter tried to restrain this delinquent effusion of goodwill, but it was no use. He was shining with conviction and, besides, the self which might have made sceptical judgements and qualifications was changing so fast that there was no position from which to make them. At the same time he kept meeting people who presented combinations of qualities which the outside world had lazily encouraged him to think of as mutually exclusive, people who were inarticulate and interesting, vulnerable and strong, unsuccessful and contented.

When it was time to leave, Peter threw his air ticket away and decided to return to London by night train so he could have a final drink in the pub with the group. Although after the closing ceremony there was a strangely awkward and anticlimactic quality to this meeting, Peter promised himself that this was just the sort of flexible behaviour that would characterize his life from now on.

In any case, he started to remember the excitement he felt as a child on the two occasions he had travelled by night train with his parents. He could suddenly picture how exhilarated he was by the crowded panel of light switches and air vents, by the concealed basin, and the clanging chains wrapped around the wheels for the Channel crossing, the blind that lowered on darkened countryside and sprang up again on startlingly new landscapes, with mountain torrents thin as threads of smoke, or umbrella pines that arched over a sea rippling with the reflection of an orange cliff, like blue silk set on fire.

When he booked his ticket he was told that the dining car wouldn't be attached until Edinburgh, but there would be a trolley service available at the front of the train. Instead of feeling disillusioned, Pachelbel's music still circled solemnly in his memory, keeping him on the cusp of an elated poignancy. He hadn't found Sabine Wald, but he was no longer suspicious of the world she moved in, and he decided to continue his search for her, only stopping briefly in London. Fiona wouldn't be pleased, but she would preserve that air of martyrdom which seemed to design her for disappointment.

Still feeling spontaneous, Peter decided that before he left the hotel he would call Gavin, who had played such a strangely insistent role in his thoughts during the week.

He got through to Gavin's extension, but Gavin didn't answer.

'I'm afraid Gavin's not here,' said Tony Henderson.

'When's he back?' asked Peter.

'Look, you obviously haven't heard, so I'd better tell you straight out,' said Tony. 'Gavin's topped himself.'

'Oh, my God.'

'Apparently it was a chemical imbalance. He had too much lithium, or too little lithium, or something.'

'Of all people.'

'I know.'

'How did he do it?'

'Bloody unpleasant, actually,' said Tony. 'He stabbed

himself in the heart. Not how I'd choose to go,' he added discriminatingly.

'Christ,' said Peter.

'The trouble was he didn't do it very well,' said Tony. 'There were a couple of stubbed-out cigarettes in the pool of blood next to him. Passing the time while he waited to bleed to death. Poor old Gavin, he always said he'd rather die than give up smoking,' added Tony, for whom this remark was already established as an office joke.

Peter could say nothing to match its levity.

'We looked into his computer,' Tony went on. 'There was a bit of a scare that he might have been doing something silly with other people's funds, but all we found was that he'd printed out page after page covered in zeros. Very symbolic, really.'

'Yes.'

Peter sat on the edge of his hotel bed for several minutes, staring at the carpet. Was it Gavin's suicide that had made him think about him so often during the week? Had Gavin been haunting him? It was a far-fetched but irresistible idea. Would Oriane, he wondered with a sudden spasm of bitterness, have claimed that a hundred pages of zeros made a sacred number? No, he knew Oriane now, what was he thinking? Was he angry with Gavin for reminding him of buried moments during his adolescence when he'd longed to kill himself? Why hadn't he? Was it because it was even more difficult than not doing so? Something had happened and he, like almost everyone else, had got used to the habit of life. Perhaps that was all life was: a habit that resisted the adventure of death. Perhaps Gavin, behind the camouflage of his ridiculous slang, had never acquired that vital habit, had never stopped being excruciated.

Realizing he must tell Fiona that he would only be passing through London briefly, Peter called her from the train. He swayed from side to side in the carpeted cubicle, watching the credit hurtle down on his phonecard.

'Awful about Gavin committing sui,' said Fiona.

'Doing what?' said Peter.

'Committing suicide.'

'Did you say "committing sui"?'

'Yes, I suppose I did,' said Fiona uneasily.

Peter was silent. Somehow the full horror of Gavin's life being cut short was unveiled by Fiona's cosy abbreviation.

'He didn't seem the type,' Fiona soldiered on.

'The type?' said Peter. 'What type? We could all do it any time.'

'I *suppose* so,' said Fiona with a reluctance that was at once exaggerated and frivolous, as if she had been asked to play croquet on a particularly wet lawn. 'Isn't it usually intellectual types who do it, or real proper loonies?'

'The intellectuals probably buy another black polo neck instead,' said Peter, realizing he wouldn't have said anything so silly except to Fiona.

'Shall I stick my head in the oven or buy another polo neck?' she guffawed.

'Listen, I'm not going to be spending much time in

London. In fact I'm going to be flying out before the weekend.'

'But we're going to Daddy's.'

'I know. I'll just have to cancel.'

'It's a bit late to chuck.'

'I'm sorry.'

'You're not giving me the old heave-ho, are you?' said Fiona, with a sudden burst of vulnerability as grating as a missed gear.

'God, no,' said Peter, 'I'm just . . .' he searched for the right phrase, and then he remembered Gavin's formula, 'just going walkabout.'

'Men!' said Fiona, and he could hear her eyeballs rolling skywards.

That night Peter could not sleep in his airless berth. He didn't bother to lower the blind as the train screeched its way into the crowded south. The bunk, which had been so perfect for an eight-year-old, no longer suited him, and he couldn't abandon himself to playing with the light switches any more.

The rhythm of the train cajoled him into a mysteriously pensive insomnia. Had Gavin's suicide been a momentary madness, or a long-postponed rebuttal of an unbearable suffering? Was suicide the most courageous and authentic thing he had ever done? Why had Peter learned about Gavin's suicide just when he was so elated and open to life?

Peter was unable to answer any of these questions, but as the night wore on, his imagination tracked Gavin's fate, crossing to that realm of bored and plaintive ghosts, to see if he could find Gavin still smoking idly beside a pool of his own blood. Gavin's suffering gradually merged in Peter's tired mind with Lara's unspeakable loss, and for one astonishing moment, as the train shot through an empty station, its deserted platforms still uselessly lit, Peter suddenly lost himself in this pool of other people's tears, re-emerging as the windows darkened again, shaken but somehow washed.

Yes, Fiona was right, Findhorn was responsible for the start of some change in him which he could never stop for long enough to assess. After leaving London he hadn't contacted her again until he got to California, and then he'd just written an evasive letter filled with vague neutral phrases about 'needing space'.

And now he was at Esalen, still looking for Sabine, but less sure of his pursuit. Esalen was the last of the questing stations he could remember Sabine talking about. She had been especially nostalgic about its sulphurous hot tubs where the traumas unearthed by its workshops were transformed into a voluptuous catharsis.

Peter turned away from the wooden railing where he had been standing beside the lazy diamond ripple of the Pacific, and went back to his room to collect the dirty laundry he had accumulated in Los Angeles.

4

Peter watched his tumbling laundry, daydreaming to the faint clicking of his shirt buttons against the metal drum. What would he do if Sabine walked in right now? He still thought about her continually, but he thought about her more as a preoccupation than a person. He could no longer browse through the much-thumbed anthology of their three days together and expect to find any detail he didn't know off by heart. What fascinated him now was the perseverance and the recklessness of his fascination. His latest and most exotic frustration had taken place only a few days before he arrived at Esalen, when he was looking for Sabine in Los Angeles.

One day the whole world was going to look like Los Angeles, he decided, not a city, nor the absence of a city, just ruined countryside, with houses squeezed between highways which never tired of whispering the lie that it was more interesting to go somewhere than to be here. The entire westward drive of American history seemed to have piled up on the beach, and the descendants of wagon-crazed pioneers, refusing to accept completely the restraint of the world's widest ocean, frantically patrolled the edge of the West, like lemmings in therapy.

The breathless obesity of the city was mirrored by the way in which work and play spilled into each other and formed a perpetual suburb of hedonistic commerce. Every deal had to be closed with a game of golf, every party was the occasion to flex the muscles of a feeble career instead of going to the trouble of making conversation. These confusions spread to all the details of life. Menus couldn't decide whether to advertise dieting or eating. Often the contents of salads and sandwiches hung around shyly among the real stars: the ingredients that had been left out, and the pointless variety of methods by which the sodium-free, unbleached, sugarless, decaffeinated, coffee-free coffee could be vaporized, sun-dried, skimmed, scorched, and served in sixteen different sizes of cup.

Already running low on money, Peter had slept on the sofa of an ex-girlfriend who had the good fortune to play the English wife of the maverick Lootenant McMurphy in the evergreen television series *Cop Story*. She really wanted to play something serious, Caroline never tired of explaining, but *Cop Story* paid the rent.

The night before Caroline threw him out because she said that his passionate search for Sabine was undermining her sexual self-esteem, she had taken him to a party given in the offices of a lawyer specializing in the entertainment industry. She abandoned him at the door in order to network with a producer, and Peter fell prey to Jerome, a man with electric blue eyes and chaotic grey-brown hair who plunged into speech without any introduction.

'I feel everything is coming together tonight,' he said hoarsely. 'I'm getting a lot of vibrational energy from the Moon.'

'Is that nice?' said Peter.

'It's great.'

'Oh, good.'

'I've written a sequel to *Easy Rider*, and I've just met a man with a direct line,' Jerome karate-ed his hand emphatically, 'to Jack Nicholson.'

'But don't all the principal characters get killed in the original movie?' asked Peter.

'We've got round that.'

'Aha.'

'I'm only doing the film project to make money. My real passion is for the spiritual autobiography I'm writing. It's called "You invented the Ego because you forgot you were God".'

'Catchy title.'

'Yeah, but I'm thinking of calling it "Too Deep to Dig".'

'It's hard to choose,' said Peter.

'The central idea is love, love, love. Forget your suffering and your petty squabbles, just love, love, love. Forget your drinking and your smoking, because when you understand love, you'll love yourself too much to do that stuff. That's pretty much a quotation from the book,' said Jerome, to excuse the eloquence of these remarks. 'Why doesn't God alleviate our suffering?'

'I've often wondered,' said Peter.

'Because he doesn't see it as suffering.'

'Clearly he's less bright than one imagined.'

'The thing you notice that you haven't noticed that you don't have is the thing that really matters,' said Jerome, beaming vibrational energy at Peter. 'Think about it.'

They stood beside a wagon-wheel with candle-flame light bulbs, hanging low over a conference table that groaned with bright orange triangular chips and a tub of oil-free herbal dip. Peter was desperate to ditch Jerome, but Jerome, having got Peter abreast of his business projects, was ready to feign an interest in his career.

'So, what are you doing here in California?' he asked.

'Well, I know it sounds ridiculous, but I'm looking for a woman I'm in love with. I don't suppose you know her,' said Peter wearily. 'A German girl called Sabine?'

'Sure I know her,' said Jerome. 'Tall, brown hair, very cute . . .'

'Christ,' said Peter, leaning on the table. 'Yes, that's her. From Frankfurt?'

'But originally from Hanover,' said Jerome, in a perfect impersonation of Sabine.

'I don't believe this,' gasped Peter. 'Where is she?'

'She's here in LA.'

I knew it, thought Peter, I knew there was some point to my being in this ghastly place. Perseverance *is* rewarded, serendipity *does* work, life *is* beautiful.

'We could see her later tonight, if you want,' suggested Jerome.

'If I want, if I want . . . I've given up my job, I've spent three months looking for her, I've almost run out of money . . .'

He reflected that in the movie version of this moment he would probably break down in tears.

'Your search is over,' said Jerome, rubbing Peter's back soothingly. 'Let's go see her.'

Caroline wanted to come along too.

'I wouldn't miss this reunion for all the world,' she sighed.

Jerome was also bringing a friend, a thickset and pock-marked lawyer called Julio, who had just joined the entertainment lawyer's firm.

It was raining heavily outside and Jool's car moved slowly through the steamy darkness and the sudden torrents of increasingly narrow roads.

'Where exactly are we going?' asked Caroline.

'Place in the valley,' said Jerome.

'Do you have any legal representation here in the States?' said Julio, straining backwards with a grunt.

'No,' said Peter, 'but I don't do any business here.'

'No, no,' said Julio. 'You're putting the carriage before the horse. You gotta have legal representation, then you get the deal.'

'Do you specialize in entertainment?' asked Peter politely.

'No, I'm in personal injury,' said Julio.

'Is that legal?' asked Peter.

'Sure it's legal, it's a branch of the law.'

'I was just joking . . .' mumbled Peter.

'Julio is working on the patent of my water-purifying invention,' Jerome explained. 'It changes the molecular structure of the water and makes it lighter, so it doesn't produce such tight-rooted vegetables.'

In the shadows of the back seat, Caroline crossed her eyes and stuck her tongue out to indicate her opinion of this scheme.

'It doesn't use any chemicals,' said Jerome. 'I met a healer in Tijuana said cancer was caused by chemicals that are everywhere around us. They change the molecules, parasites move in and they explode into cancer cells.'

'God, how terrifying,' said Caroline in a bored voice. 'Look, I don't want to be a party-pooper, but how far is it exactly to this place? I've got an acupuncture appointment early tomorrow morning.'

'Acupuncture,' said Julio. 'Guy sued the other day, 'cause he said it didn't make no difference. Had to get the AMA to adjudicate. They said nothing had happened, no improvement.'

'Don't believe anything you read in the newspapers,' said Jerome. 'Everything you read in American news-papers is not the truth, it's a story they're putting out. Of course acupuncture works. The body is an electrical system.'

'Look,' said Caroline, 'could you answer the question? How far are we?'

'Not far,' said Julio, scratching his neck. 'Rain slowed us down, look at this rain . . .'

'Repent,' said Jerome, 'that's a beautiful word. It's *repentare*: to think again. It's so beautiful. Later on it became associated with guilt. They invented guilt.'

'You realize we're going to be murdered, don't you?' Caroline whispered to Peter reproachfully.

Peter frowned at her to show that he felt she was exaggerating.

'What about the Fall?' he said to Jerome.

'The Fall,' laughed Jerome, as if this was a great joke. 'Knowledge of good and evil. Before the Fall, when we lived in Atlantis and Lemuria, we had these incredible powers, and we're going to get them back,' he said, slapping the steering wheel. 'We're going to get them back, but we've had like ten thousand years of guilt and good and evil, and distinctions and ego, but we're going to get back those powers we had in Lemuria.'

'What's the source of that?' asked Julio.

'I gave you that book,' said Jerome.

'Oh, yeah, yeah. It's because it's in the DNA, right?'

'No,' said Jerome angrily. 'Let's get cause and effect right. It's because it's like that that it's in the DNA, not the DNA that caused it.'

'Yeah, right, right,' said Julio, conceding the justice of this point.

The conversation petered out in these fathomless philosophical waters. Caroline crossed her arms and stared tragically out of the window, as if to burden Peter not just with her own death but with the death of all the Ophelias she would now never play.

'We're here,' said Jerome.

They got out of the car in front of a black wall with a black door in it, and a pink neon sign saying '222'.

'What is this?' asked Caroline.

'It's a place Sabine loves to hang out,' said Jerome.

'You always had strange taste in girlfriends,' said Caroline ironically.

The dimness of the interior failed to hide large areas of baldness in the red carpet. A number of unusually tall women in sequined evening dresses hung around the bar. One of them sat on a gashed banquette with a hollow-cheeked man in a leather coat.

Jerome went over to the bar and whispered to one of the girls.

'You realize what this is, don't you?' asked Caroline.

'A low dive,' said Peter.

'They're trannies.'

'What?'

'Transsexuals. I'm going to call a cab – we may still be able to get out of here alive.'

'I want to introduce you to a friend of Sabine's,' said Jerome.

'Look here . . .' said Peter.

'Sabine's coming here later to meet up with her.'

'I'm not sure I believe you,' said Peter.

'Are you saying that my friend is lying?' asked Julio.

'No, I'm—'

'Because if you were saying that,' said Julio, 'that would be a very serious accusation.'

'I forgive you, Peter,' said Jerome, putting his hand soothingly on Peter's back. 'Come and meet Shalene.'

'Shalene, this is my very good friend Peter.'

'Hello, Peter,' croaked Shalene, almost as hoarsely as Jerome.

'Hello,' said Peter. 'You're a friend of Sabine's, are you?'

'That's right, honey,' said Shalene, taking a cigarette out of her velvet evening bag, and leaning over to Peter for a light. Her jaw was square but clean-shaven, her make-up thick and white.

'So, eh, when do you think . . .' Peter began, but Shalene leant over coquettishly and interrupted him.

'Do you want me to suck your cock?' she asked.

'No, thank you,' said Peter, fumbling with a book of matches on the counter. 'It's awfully kind of you but—'

'Do you want to suck mine?' said Shalene immediately, as if to save embarrassment.

'Yours?' said Peter. 'No, I'm afraid I don't.'

Clearly, Shalene was still saving up for the full operation.

'So what are you doing here?' asked Shalene, suddenly dropping her exaggerated femininity for a male aggression which was equally exaggerated, if only by the backdrop of false lashes and paste bracelets.

'I've told you . . .'

'Who the hell is Sabine? She's making me jealous,' said Shalene, pouting. 'You gotta tell me your fantasy. That man told me to say I knew Sabine, that's all I got to work with . . .'

'Where is Jerome?' asked Peter anxiously.

'He left. Was Sabine another girl like me who was a special friend of yours?' persisted Shalene.

'No,' snapped Peter, realizing the implications of Jerome's departure.

Caroline drifted over to the bar casually.

'They're on their way,' she said through gritted teeth.

Shalene's manner had changed to open hostility.

'If you don't wanna have sex, what the fuck are you doing here?'

'Look,' said Peter, feeling Shalene's indolent and well-built girlfriends closing in on them with sympathetic hostility. 'Normally I would, of course, I mean you're frightfully attractive and all of that, but I'm with Caroline this evening and I think she might be shocked.'

'Maybe she'd like to watch,' said Shalene, narrowing her eyes and twitching her lips seductively.

Christ, she has an answer for everything, thought Peter.

'I don't think so,' he said firmly.

'Ask her,' said Shalene, with a stiletto in her voice.

'Caroline,' gulped Peter, turning round slowly, 'Shalene wants to know whether you'd like to watch while she sucks my cock.'

'Humm,' said Caroline, and to his horror Peter could see that she was thinking of taking her revenge. 'I . . . I don't think so,' she said, smiling at Shalene. 'Thanks anyway.'

'Aren't you in *Cop Story*?' asked Shalene.

'Yes,' said Caroline reluctantly.

'Oh, my God, you're Lootenent McMurphy's English wife.'

'Yes,' said Caroline.

'I love your work,' cooed Shalene, clasping her breast

and rolling her eyes to heaven. 'We've got a star at the bar!' she called out.

The other girls swooped down hungrily.

'Mrs McMurphy from *Cop Story*,' said Shalene with a flourish.

Everyone was thrilled.

A black girl, six foot four tall, with blonde hair and a diaphanous bodystocking revealing the glories of a full operation, came mincing out of the corner with a silver hairbrush.

'Can I brush your hair?' she asked.

'Why not?' said Caroline, rather pleased to be the centre of attention.

Peter slipped towards the door to check for the cab.

'I'm sorry to break this up,' he said triumphantly, 'but our cab's arrived.'

'Ohhh,' groaned the girls. 'Can't you stay a little longer? Don't you like us?'

'It's been *such* a lovely evening,' said Caroline, autographing Shalene's cigarette packet, 'but I'm on set at *dawn* tomorrow.'

'We understand,' said the girls.

Caroline and Peter left together, surrounded by appreciative comments.

'She's such a lady,' said the hairbrusher, with a crack in her voice as deep as the San Andreas fault.

'I discovered her,' said Shalene proudly.

For a while in the back of the cab, Caroline couldn't disguise her relief, but she soon worked up a rage at the fear she had experienced earlier in the evening.

'You must be fucking crazy chasing this German girl you hardly know . . .'

The cab screeched to a halt.

'What's going on?' asked Peter.

'I'm going to have to ask you to get out of the cab,' drawled the spotty young driver.

'What?'

'I can't have any abusive language in my cab.'

'I promise we won't say another word,' said Peter.

'Abusive language is the belching of Satan,' said the driver. 'I'm going to have to ask you to leave.'

'Oh, for . . . for our sake, please make an exception. It's raining and we're both very tired. Show a little charity, please. Look, here's an extra fifty dollars.'

'Please leave the cab,' said the driver, turning round with a can of mace in his hand.

'Do you have Christ in your heart?' said Caroline.

'I certainly do, ma'am,' said the driver, 'but I believe that you have Satan in your heart.'

'But you know,' said Caroline, breathing hard, 'being with you I feel this tremendous pressure in my chest, and I think it's Christ trying to enter my heart. Are you going to let Satan win my soul, or are you going to win a soul for Christ?'

'Well,' said the driver, confused. 'Are you ready to be baptized?'

'Oh, yes,' sobbed Caroline.

'Will you swear,' said the driver, putting away his can of mace and taking out a copy of the Bible from the glove compartment, 'that you will accept Christ into your heart?'

'Let's walk,' said Peter.

'You walk,' said Caroline. 'I swear.'

'Oh, I suppose I swear as well,' said Peter.

It was four in the morning when they were dropped home.

'Fucking wanker,' said Peter as he closed the door.

'Arsehole,' added Caroline, kicking the cab door.

'This is my kind of town,' said Peter. 'I'm seriously thinking of coming to live here.'

'Well, you'd better look for another address as from tomorrow morning. "Let's walk", you idiot!'

The tumble-drier groaned to a halt and Peter collected his warm shirts from inside the drum.

5

Barny approached the overflowing park bin with an air of half-defeated curiosity. Scattered on the downtrodden mud of Clapham Common, polystyrene fast-food cartons trembled in the chill breeze.

'Barny!'

Jason tried to sound angry but he was cut short by the faint wagging of Barny's tail as he sniffed at the nostalgic odour of something like meat.

Poor Barny, did he dream of butchers' shops? Was he kept awake counting uneaten sheep? Did he dangle all night from the meathooks of memory? Some memories had to be searched for, thought Jason; others find you wherever you are.

Haley had said that they were responsible for Barny's 'spiritual welfare'. After a long debate about what a dog's spiritual welfare might be, she had triumphed as usual, and Barny had been put on the Veginugget Vegan dog-food diet. A once happy hound who used to bark excitedly in the hall, his nails scratching the Victorian tiles and his black Labrador's tail beating loudly against the door frames, Barny now moped about, his forehead ridged with fleshy furrows of self-pity and bewilderment.

'He looks fucking miserable,' said Jason. He realized he'd grown used to being consoled by Barny's foolish eagerness when he returned empty-handed from another record company.

'That's because he's getting the toxins out of his system,' said Haley. 'You can't imagine what they put in the average can of dog food.'

'Toxins?'

'Yes, horrid toxins for a nice doggy. Poor Barny's addicted to toxins, aren't you, you silly doggy?' Haley grasped Barny by the ears and shook his head. 'If we put him on Vegginuggets he'll probably come back as a human being in his next lifetime.'

'Now you're really making me feel guilty.'

'Don't be so cynical, he might be the next Gandhi. Yes! Who's a clever Gandhi-doggy?'

'But Gandhi's dead already,' Jason protested.

'Poor Gandhi-doggy, living with such a boring old pedant,' said Haley irritably.

Barny drifted away from the park bin and Jason's thoughts returned irresistibly to the frustrations of his career. In his twenties, driven on by the belief that bad news was infectious and optimism self-fulfilling, he'd been in the habit of saying things like, 'all the signs are good . . . the record company is really interested . . . we should close the deal before Christmas'. The discovery that he was known as 'all-the-signs-are-good Jason' put an end to his assumed cheerfulness. A period of tight-lipped silence was soon followed by his present policy of talking very generally and bleakly about 'economic conditions'.

At thirty-two he was getting too old for a big break in rock music; perhaps he'd been too old for a long time. It was his birthday soon. As an Aries he was supposed to be explosive, ambitious, driven and shallow. Haley said that even Jung thought there was something in astrology. Jung thought there was something in everything. He even talked encouragingly to his kitchen equipment, just to be on the safe side. Haley also said that thirty-three was a really crucial age, when Christ had been crucified and Buddha enlightened, but Jason didn't want to start a world religion, he just wanted to make a record – and then start a world religion.

He frowned sensitively and sang into an imaginary microphone. Like phosphorescence in a churning sea, bulbs flashed from the adulatory crowd beyond the edge of the stage. His face caked in make-up, his eyes blinded by the sting of sweat and the glare of spotlights, he no longer shifted about restlessly in his diffident and troubled skin but blazed with the certainty that he had become a turbine for momentarily transforming the frustrations and desires of a million raw souls. He closed his eyes and inhaled the exhilarating liberation of fame, and his new identity, a mirage of falsehood and calculated carelessness, stood up and walked away like a confident ghost from the corpse of his old uneasy self.

Yes, yes, he wanted it so badly. He kept his eyes closed to sustain the vision a little longer. To become completely phoney and to be worshipped for it, and then to be thought 'real' because he gave in to his wildest vices. He threw back his shoulders and felt himself grow taller. Bliss, it would be bliss.

Barny, who could not be expected to know that his master had transformed himself into a global icon, one of those truly famous people who are recognized everywhere, in Vanuatu and Kathmandu as well as the King's Road and Fifth Avenue, barked feebly by his side.

Jason, realizing that he was on Clapham Common rather than the stage of the Hollywood Bowl – he thought fondly of Johnny Rotten saying, 'Do you ever get the feeling you've been ripped off?' when the Sex Pistols left after playing only two songs – started running homewards clapping his hands and shouting, 'Come on Barny!' to his exhausted pet.

Tomorrow, he and Haley would be flying over the Hollywood Bowl, not in order to gulp down the nectar of his stupendous popularity, but on their way to a workshop to repair their ailing relationship. As soon as Haley had suggested the workshop, Jason had started to feel that things were really about to happen for him musically, but he was in no position to refuse. She might throw him out of her house.

She had recently declared that their relationship was 'totally sick' after going to a Co-dependency Group on three successive Wednesdays, and returning home with a grisly new friend, Panita, who believed that 'self-satisfaction', as she called it, was the aim of life and that it could only be achieved by violently breaking off relations with every-body she had ever known, including 'old selves'.

'She should break with her new self while she's at it,' he had commented sourly.

'I think that's a really abusive comment,' Haley said.

'Oh, piss off,' said Jason.

'No, Jason, it's typical: I make a new friend and so you have to put me down. Is it because you find it threatening? Jason losing control of Haley, is that what you dread?'

'Oh, go abuse yourself,' he'd shouted, slamming the door.

'King Baby!' she screamed. 'You're the archetypal King Baby.'

The terrible truth was that he did find it threatening, knowing that the price of admission to the inner circle of self-empowerment and ill temper was the freshly dripping head of an 'abusive' lover or parent or employer.

Nowadays, when he reached for his Nirvana *Unplugged* tape in the car, so he could sing along in sweetly tortured emulation of Kurt Cobain, his hand had to push aside a clattering heap of Pia Melody tapes, about chucking your boyfriend on to the street, as he paranoiacally imagined, not having heard any of them, but just *knowing* that they were muscle-building exercises for Haley's determination to boot him out.

He would willingly have donated his dole cheque to a minicab in order not to be driven to the airport by Panita. She was arriving in a couple of hours and that morning he'd been unable to resist complaining to Haley.

'Don't you think it's "totally sick" of her to want to drive us to the airport when you've known her for less than a month?'

'No, Jason, I actually think it's typical of the sort of kindness you can expect from a person who's really trying to get their life together, not that you'd know much about that . . .'

And so another argument had started, and he'd had to take Barny out of the house for another walk.

'Your partner doesn't seem to understand what you're going through at the moment . . .' Haley read the words with mixed satisfaction. The trouble with finding her private thoughts figured in the dance of the planets, as reported in *Aromatherapist*, the magazine for professionals like herself, was that Jason had the same Sun sign as her. It was so true, he didn't understand her, but if the horoscope was true, she didn't understand him either. Anyway, Sun signs weren't real astrology. Mars and Venus, morbid Pluto and dissolute Neptune, Uranus, Saturn, Jupiter and the Moon all told their vast symbolic stories. The Moon was enthroned beside the Sun, Mercury was their chamberlain and Mars their chief of staff. So many influences, cardinal, fixed and mutable, evolving through their progressions, blocked and amplified by their aspects, acting through different signs in different houses, could describe the potential and the waste, the weakness and the strength, the obsessions and the ignorance of any shade of personality. When a fiery sign could be in a watery house, or an earthy house filled with planets in an airy sign, anything was possible. Her own chart afforded moments of solemn reflection. Her Saturn was conjunct her Sun. Either she would crumble completely or develop a strong identity through overcoming Saturnian challenges and frustrations. Saturn was also conjunct her Mercury, which might mean that she was very stupid or – like Einstein, whose Saturn was conjunct his Mercury – that she would prove to be a deep thinker. Haley tended to favour the second interpretation.

They were both Aries, but Jason had Libra rising, that mask of facile charm hiding the thoughtless and immature energies of spring. If only she could persuade him that he needed a radical change to get his career going, an internal change, a – yes, she was going to use the word – spiritual change.

She knew it was humiliating for Jason to be living in the house that her father had bought her and off the income she made from her aromatherapy business, but it was annoying for her as well. It was certainly a confusing time to be a woman. Of course she was into challenging stereotypical gender roles, but it would be nice to be taken out to dinner for a change. In any case, challenging gender roles seemed to have become a stereotype of its own.

They argued about everything, without either of them knowing what could be gained by arguing; they just couldn't stop. That's why she was taking them to Esalen for the 'Letting go and Moving on' workshop. She was blowing most of the five thousand pounds her father had given her for her thirtieth birthday. The packaging business had been good to him, as he never tired of pointing out. What Jason didn't know was that *his* birthday present was a further weekend in a Tantric sex workshop. Haley had secretly decided that this was a make or break week. Either they were going to have a really deep transformational experience, or she would flood the stage with arguments about their relationship being totally sick. It wasn't as if arguments would be hard to find, and she knew she had the support of her friends in CoCo: the Co-dependent Co-operative.

Jason slouched home apprehensively. He didn't want to argue all the way to California; on the other hand he resented being terrorized by Haley's new habit of exhuming incidents from the graveyard of their past, and carrying them off with bitter triumph to the pathology lab of her meetings. She used to show the same amnesiac brio which characterized his own approach to life, but now he felt that there were thousands of labelled jars in which these diseased moments were murkily preserved.

'We're on the way out,' he said to Barny, and Barny whined as if he understood the pity of their situation.

Panita arrived half an hour early. 'In case you have plane fever,' she explained.

'If we had plane fever, we would have asked you to come half an hour early,' said Jason sarcastically.

Orphaned, single, friendless and unemployed, Panita was an almost discarnate co-dependant, not weighed down by the actuality of a relationship, but perfectly englobed within her self-diagnosed anxiety. She was the concentrated essence of what Jason hated, floating free of the compromises made by ordinary co-dependants with other states of being, and existing in a pure state of passionate psychological handicap.

'Weird route,' he commented on the way to the airport.

'I'm just going the way I know,' said Panita.

'Back-seat driver,' said Haley, sensing trouble.

But Jason couldn't be stopped, and after the briefest pause he leant forward and asked in a voice of mock concern, 'Is there anybody you're co-dependent on at the moment, Panita?'

'I hope not,' said Panita.

'Haley, for instance?' asked Jason.

'I think I'd know the signs by now,' said Panita with grim expertise.

'What are the signs?'

'My eating, for a start.'

'Oh, have you got an eating problem?' asked Jason with undisguised delight.

'Not at the moment, my recovery's very solid.'

'You had a healthy breakfast, did you?' said Jason.

'Oh, give it a rest,' said Haley.

'I'm worried about our new friend,' said Jason. 'I couldn't bear it if you girls turned out to have a totally sick relationship.'

'Calling us "girls" is really patronizing,' said Haley.

'Yeah, really patronizing,' said Panita.

'What would you like me to call you? Old hags?'

Panita drew over to the side of the road.

'Get out of the car,' she said.

'What?' said Jason.

'You heard me,' said Panita, suddenly empowered. 'I'm not having any inappropriate behaviour in my car.'

'Oh, gimme a break.'

'Get out!' screamed Panita. 'I'm sorry, Haley, but I

don't have to take inappropriate behaviour in my own space.'

'Yeah,' said Haley, disconcerted, 'but we've got to get to the airport.'

'He can take the Underground, I'll take you and the luggage.'

'Can't you just apologize?' said Haley.

'It's gone beyond apology,' said Panita. 'I've been abused.'

'But isn't that what you secretly want?' said Jason. 'So you have something to talk about at your meetings.'

'Jason!' screamed Haley.

'Get out of my car, or I'll call the police.'

'Officer!' screeched Jason hysterically. 'This man said I was co-dependent, I've been inappropriately abused.' He clambered out of the car, laughing at his own joke. 'Right, son!' he went on in his PC Plod voice, leaning back through the open door. 'I'm apprehending you and taking you down to the station to listen to some inappropriate tapes.'

'I'll drive *you* to the airport if you like,' said Panita to Haley.

'Oh, God, I'd better go with him or he may not turn up,' said Haley.

'You do think I did the right thing, don't you?' said Panita. 'I really need your support on this.'

'I suppose so,' said Haley, 'but it's a real pain in the arse.'

'I don't want to make judgements,' said Panita, 'but I think you two have a really sick relationship.'

'Well, at least we're in a relationship,' said Haley

slamming the door. 'You stupid wanker,' she said to Jason, 'you can carry my fucking case.'

'I'm being abused!' cried Jason facetiously.

'You think you're really clever, don't you?' said Haley. 'You get us stranded in the middle of Hammersmith Broadway and all you can do is make stupid jokes.'

They struggled to the Underground station together, Haley's indignant voice battling like a furious swimmer against the roar of the traffic.

6

Stan and Karen Klotwitz had made the move to Santa Fe because they wanted the dry climate of the south-west without the geriatric belligerence of a retirement community in Arizona. Neither of them was interested in joining the Grey Panthers and they both loved having young people in their lives. Stan had been in the insurance business in New York and Karen had been 'just an average American housewife', as she said with true modesty, but also in the hope that folks would find it hard to believe when they saw what an Awakened Being she'd become. They'd settled in their new home seven years ago and they thanked God every day that they had chosen Santa Fe because they had such an incredibly rich life there, and had made so many incredibly special friends.

Stan said that life began at seventy and that you were only as old as you felt; Karen, who was more mystically inclined, said she was not attached to her 'earth suit'. Stan wasn't particularly attached to it either and that was why he and Karen were going on a Tantric sex workshop at a unique resource centre in California.

'Get some of the old fire back,' said Stan with a wink,

as he barbecued a couple of steaks in the patio area. Somewhere along the line, Stan had got the idea that mental health consisted of talking about his sex life to complete strangers.

'Spring will return to the mountain,' said Walking Eagle, who had only met Stan and Karen the night before at the Omega Center. He had led an incredibly unique, ancient, secret ceremony which he claimed the elders of his tribe had said he could share with other nations because the Dark Times were approaching.

Ever since he contracted arthritis, Stan had refused to wear anything but sportswear. Many of his friends also dressed as if they were about to take part in the Olympics, although they often had trouble getting out of a soft armchair. Walking Eagle was decked in silver and turquoise jewellery which set off his thick silver hair and his faded jean shirt in a way that Karen really appreciated. Karen herself was a pastel swirl, as if a watercolour study of candyfloss had been left out in the rain.

Stan and Karen's home was very unique. All their friends had unique homes as well, but theirs was perhaps especially unique. The ceiling of the living room rose thirty-five feet in a 'cathedral effect', and if you included the patio area, there was a sixty-five-foot sweep of open space from the front door to the back wall of the garden. Somewhere further along the line Stan had gotten the idea that hospitality consisted of behaving as if you were trying to sell your house to a prospective buyer. After softening up his guests with some statistics, it was time to move on to his mental health.

'I'll be honest with you, Walking Eagle, I've been impotent for the last eight years,' said Stan, flipping a steak expertly with a giant fork.

'My people have a ceremony to help with that,' said Walking Eagle gravely, over the sizzling sound made by the scorched meat.

'They do?'

'It's a secret ceremony, but for a friend . . .'

'Well, God, that would be a really unique privilege. We're going to go with this Tantric thing first, but when we get back we'll get right on to you about that.'

'You're such a caring person,' said Karen, who couldn't help thinking that Walking Eagle didn't look as if he had any problems with impotence.

'How long will you be away?' said Walking Eagle, taking out his diary.

'Well, we're going to sort of a Gestalt thing first to get us mentally prepared,' said Stan.

'Mind, body and spirit,' said Karen, 'you can't separate them.'

'There are ways,' hinted Walking Eagle.

Ding-dong went the doorbell. Walking Eagle offered to go, seeing how Karen had broken her ankle, and Stan was preoccupied with the steaks.

Karen had broken her ankle in one of the most unique car accidents – she preferred to call it a car destiny – that anybody could possibly imagine.

She had been on the corner of Hacienda and Aztec completely lost in the magic of Deepak Chopra's *Quantum Healing* tape. Anything with healing in the title captured

Karen's curiosity, and who could resist 'quantum', surely one of the most mystically mysterious words in the English language? Wasn't it Einstein who had said that God wouldn't play dice with the universe? Even if God had wanted to play dice, Karen suddenly reflected, who would he have played with? She couldn't bear the thought of anybody being lonely, but it was the uniquely sad thought of God's utter loneliness which had paralysed Karen's reflexes as she drifted into the side of a Jeep Cherokee.

Then an even more incredible thing happened. The young man in the Jeep got out and apologized. It turned out that he had been listening to a tape of Scott Peck's unbelievable *Further Along the Road Less Travelled* (which happened to be one of Karen's most unique tapes) and he felt responsible for the accident.

And that was the story of how she had met Robert, who was now walking through the exquisite pastel shades of her living room, with his arm in a sling.

'Karen!' he greeted her.

'Robert! My meant-to-be-accident,' said Karen, shaking her head at the wonder of the universe. 'I guess you met Walking Eagle.'

'*Hey waka jo hada*,' said Robert.

'Hey what?' said Stan.

'*Hey waka jo hada*,' said Robert. 'It means "May you walk in beauty" in the language of the Cherokee nation.'

'*Hey waka jo hada*,' said Walking Eagle.

'Isn't that . . .' Words failed Karen. 'I love the way you two have just – excuse my language – cut through the crap and gotten right to the heart of things. "May you walk in beauty", oh, that's, oh.' She put her hand on her heart and caught her breath. 'I can't tell you what that does for me. I feel all tingly in my fingers . . . Can you write that down for me? You guys are just so amazing . . . Can you believe that, Stan?'

Stan put his hands on his hips and shook his head as if he'd completed a long run and was too breathless to speak.

Gradually Stan and Karen's patio area filled up with as many unique people as anyone could reasonably hope to fit in one place at one time.

'He's not just some New Age Indian,' said Stan in a loud whisper, indicating Walking Eagle with his giant fork, 'he's the real thing.'

Walking Eagle looked a little nervous, cornered by Robert who seemed to know a disturbing amount about Native American language and mythology.

'A lot of the nations are worried about having their culture co-opted by white people,' said Robert. 'What d'ya think of that?'

'I think that the white people need our wisdom,' said Walking Eagle. 'To walk in beauty means to give from the heart.'

'That's true,' said Robert, 'but the power mustn't fall into the wrong hands.'

'I try not to be political,' said Walking Eagle. 'So what kinda business are you in, Robert?'

'Oh, I'm in the wilderness industry.'

'Man's an omnivore, right?' said Stan, dangling a steak at Walking Eagle. 'I like to tease the vegetarians. Many of our friends are vegetarian but I'm too old to change.'

'We must accept the animal's sacrifice,' said Walking Eagle, holding out his plate.

'That's a nice attitude,' said Stan.

'It's the animal that has to accept his own sacrifice,' said Robert.

Stan moved over to another part of the patio where Karen was discussing Princess Dux, a local celebrity, with Gary, one of the most spiritual hairdressers in Santa Fe.

'Whether she's an ambassador from the court of Lemuria or not,' Gary was saying, 'she's one powerful lady.'

'I think she's a phoney,' said Stan. 'I don't believe she's three hundred years old.'

'Stan is still learning,' said Karen, apologizing for her husband's backwardness. 'I believe that Princess Dux is here to show us the future of the human body.'

'Obesity?' asked Stan.

'What is it that Chris Griscom says?' Karen went on, slapping Stan on the forearm for being flippant. 'Until you can bilocate, until you can levitate, until you can astral travel, don't talk to me about the limitations of the human body?'

'I'd be satisfied with a reliable erection,' said Stan candidly.

Gary looked at him astonished, but Karen persevered.

'I think that Princess Dux is here to prepare us for the Great Change. Evidently, we're soon going to be capable of ten thousand simultaneous telepathic communications.

I read a book which said that people who weren't prepared were going to think they were going insane.'

'I think I'm going insane already,' said Stan. 'Sometimes the old insurance broker comes out in me and I think, what kind of rating am I going to give a three-hundred-pound, three-hundred-year-old princess from an underground civilisation that most people think has been extinct for thousands of years?'

Stan still had one or two knots in his otherwise flawless learning curve.

'I'm married to a conservative,' Karen wailed affectionately. 'Wasn't it William Shakespeare who said that there are more things under heaven and earth than are dreamt of by philosophers? *He* believed in Lemuria.'

'Is that right?' said Stan, prepared to bow to a greater authority. 'My wife's a great reader,' he added proudly.

'With my schedule I haven't got the time,' complained Gary.

'They're mostly audio books,' admitted Karen.

Karen's literary tendencies were plainly displayed for anybody who cared to use the bathroom.

On the wall was a list called 'A hundred things I'll try to remember every day'. It ranged from the practical, 'Drink peppermint tea to cleanse my auric field', through the ethical, 'Try to achieve psychic calmness in my sendings and remember that every being, whoever he or she may appear to be, has his or her unique part to play in the great mystery we call life', and upwards to the metaphysical, 'Aside from the rarest exceptions, humanity came to our planet from the Moon.'

Beside the lavatory itself was something simply entitled 'Poem'.

> I walk with Great Spirit through the dew
> He makes me feel so shiny and new
> I am happy as a child
> In his embrace so firm yet mild.

Everyone agreed that, as usual, Stan and Karen's barbecue was a unique success. Karen asked Walking Eagle if he would help them close with a blessing. Walking Eagle, who felt constrained by Robert's presence, made the closing ceremony almost indecently abrupt.

'Mother Earth, Father Sky,' he called out, raising his palms to the stubborn blue patch above the patio. 'We ask your blessing as Stan and Karen go on their Tantric workshop. May spring return to the mountain.'

'I appreciate that,' said Stan, raising his glass and giving Karen a squeeze.

A murmur of approval rose from the guests and dissipated in the dazzling light of the afternoon.

7

During Saturday lunch Brooke had again urged Crystal to get in touch with Adam Frazer when she arrived at Esalen. Kenneth allowed his forbidding composure to be punctuated by sarcasm when Adam came up in conversation.

'Like all very brilliant people he can be difficult sometimes,' Brooke admitted to Crystal.

'Like all very difficult people he's difficult the whole time,' Kenneth corrected her.

'I've noticed dumb people being difficult too,' Crystal pointed out, in the hope that they could all find some common ground.

Now that she was driving down Route One, only a couple of hours from Esalen, Crystal started to wonder what she should do about Brooke's suggestion.

There was no doubt that Adam was clever and charismatic, with rows of mystical medals shining on his chest, but he had publicly turned his back on Mother Meera, one of the gurus he had earlier publicized with unbridled eagerness. Once trapped in the supreme truth of his latest enthusiasm, he was forced to tear up yesterday's manifesto with a screech of renunciation, or face the unpleasant prospect of keeping his mouth shut. Apart from uncomfortably recalling her mother's pendulum of devotion and disappointment, Crystal was uneasy because of her own more hesitant but respectful relationship with the avatar of Thalheim.

The most consistent thread in all Adam's work was the conviction that whatever happened to him was of global significance. Had he operated in the 1930s, he might well have written a book called 'Why I'm a Communist', followed, hotfoot, by a book called 'Why I'm not a Communist'. Now, in the portentous shadow of the millennium, he pursued the same tango on the mystical plane. He experienced the Divine as a series of compliments paid to his sensitivity, and if he ever lapsed into humility it was the most extraordinary humility the world had ever seen and was immediately turned into a book or a film. Crystal had seen a film about his conversion to Mother Meera in which he often seemed to be on the verge of tears at the thought of what he'd been through in order to become so special. Even his laughter was lachrymose, like the giggling of a child who has been tickled for too long.

Whoever he was announcing or denouncing, taking up or dropping, Oedipus and Narcissus were two figures who commanded his unquestioning loyalty. Exiled from his magical Indian childhood by the treachery of his adored mother, he was installed in frigid England where he developed that prancing, bucking intellect with which he hoped one day to kick down the stable door.

At heart he remained unconsoled, even by his own brilliance, and when he met an Indian woman calling herself Mother Meera he was powerless to resist the rumour of her omnipotence and resumed his magical communion with the subcontinent. She was bound, by the same somnambulant logic, to betray him, as his own mother had done. This she did, or so Crystal had heard, by failing to share Adam's excitement about his forthcoming marriage to Yves.

Again he retreated from devotion to scholarship, but Rumi, despite his intoxicating emphasis on the wine and fire of Divine love, could not last for ever. A friend of his had told Crystal that Adam's attention was being drawn towards the Virgin Mary, the mother of all mothers, who had the advantage of already being elaborately mythologized and, thanks to being dead, was less likely than her predecessors to let him down or tell him how to run his life.

Or was she?

The race was on. Would Adam at last find in the Mother of God a parent adequate to his special needs, or would he end up staring into the glamorous pool of his own personality with an ever more candid admiration?

Crystal liked people to be fascinating, but she didn't want them to be charismatic – charismatic meant that they expected other people to find them fascinating. Adam, having led the charge towards Mother Meera, was no less charismatic in retreat. Some of his plodding followers might be forgiven their sprained ankles and their spinning heads.

As usual his personal experience contained a message it would be mad for the world to ignore. He'd squabbled with Mother Meera, and so the age of the guru was over. With Yves's approval and support, he was prepared to strike a posture of total independence from any mediated experience of the Divine. Gurus were fallible human beings like the rest of us, and it was dangerous to attribute magical powers to them. Of course it was, thought Crystal, but they still might know something worth finding out.

Adam had become the anti-guru guru, teaching his listeners to turn their backs on all their teachers (except himself) and strut about in garrulous self-sufficiency. This desire to abandon the people who'd helped him, driven by the deep conviction that in the Dodge City of maternal betrayal you have to shoot first, was not to everyone's taste. It was all very well to kick away the ladder once he was on the roof, but what about those who had not yet run through most of the star rimpoches and avatars currently crowding the planet?

No doubt the transition from external authority to inner conviction was an important passage in spiritual life, but of all revolutions it must be the most bloodless; nothing could falsify it more conspicuously than the need to stab. Any real awakening embraced a past which appeared to have led with newly unveiled precision to a higher perspective. Whereas ordinary well-being always dragged along its gloomy companions, 'How long can this possibly last?' and 'If only I'd known this earlier', awakening divulged the secret of ripeness, redeeming time as well as understanding, promising that every drop of suffering had been purposeful and that things would never be the same again.

If only it happened more often.

The past contained implacable enemies of liberation, from the most general unnegotiable conditions, like the structure of the human brain, or the karmic chain of cause and effect which seemed to enslave every incident to a deep and eventually unknowable set of causes, down through the genetic codes inherited by each individual, and finally in the distracting drama of personal history. It was only by appreciating the asphyxiatingly conditioned nature of each thought and action that Crystal had developed that passion for freedom which might enable her to punch her way through the icecap of conditioning. She was well aware that this passion and the moments of spaciousness which it sometimes gave her might also be determined. Until these tricky questions were settled more precisely by science and philosophy, every choice might be contained in the invisible prison of another category of determinism.

However irrational it might seem, she felt instead that there was collaborative impulse at work, as if her passionate refusal to inhabit this frozen domain was being answered by a pitying Nature, which stooped down and lifted her from the ice with the same impersonal tenderness with which she sometimes lifted a struggling insect from a swimming pool. And then an idea like ripeness would descend on her with utter conviction and, like the insect opening its wings again in the sun, everything was perfect just as it was.

Crystal's relationship with gurus and spiritual authority was far from simple, and she recognized in her reading of Adam's predicament the shadow of some of her own doubts and difficulties. Adam was a kind of authority himself, not only in his own eyes, but also in the part of her that was still impressed by his cleverness and notoriety. Why else would she be wondering whether to approach a man whose behaviour she found silly and corrupt? Was she expecting to acquire mystical prowess by association? And if she was, how different was that from his ruptured faith that, bathed in Mother Meera's omnipotence, he could realize an omnipotence of his own?

Crystal, too, had longed for paraplegics to rise from their beds as she passed, longed for emotional knots to unravel in the clear light of her presence, and longed to crown these powers with the touching modesty of disclaiming them. Perhaps the only difference between her and Adam was that when she had these longings she realized that, under present conditions, she was wasting her time.

In order to see Mother Meera, Crystal had been forced to overcome reservations about going to Germany at all. Most of her father's family had died in the Holocaust, and her sense of her father's absence from her childhood was exacerbated by the ancestral void that lay behind him. Germany was the Fatherland of her fatherlessness, a personal wound that took the preposterous form of a nation state, it had bequeathed her not only a family which she didn't know but one she could not know. Her loathing of its Nazi past cut across all her ideals of forgiveness and compassion. She went there to challenge her hatred and indignation, and found her desire to give them up challenged instead.

Thalheim lay in what might have been called the heart

of Germany until, arriving there, it seemed wiser just to call it the middle. The ugliness of the surrounding villages would have been dazzling enough without the hostility of the population to reinforce it, but the stony-faced family who ran Crystal's boarding house in Dornburg chose to underline the atmosphere of dutiful depression with a particular grimness of their own. Frau Varden treated her clients as an insufferable imposition, as if they had been billeted on her by an invading army, while her two lumpish sons had perfectly decanted their sibling rivalry into a competition for the role of village idiot, knowing that the loser would always be welcome in some humble capacity at the local abattoir.

Walking around Dornburg, Crystal's thoughts grew wilder and wilder. She longed to haemorrhage against the walls to add a little colour to the scene. All the buildings were white, the gardens trim, the designs utilitarian. Post-war Germany seemed to be punishing itself for the extravagances of its past. If its internally shuttered houses and tight-lipped inhabitants were also trying to renounce world domination, the discipline carried with it a hygienic ferocity reminiscent of the drives it was designed to extinguish. No wonder the Germans had spent their history invading other countries. Who could blame them for wanting a holiday from their own *Kultur*? When she reached the edge of the village on her first walk, shivering in the December snow, she found a cute sign, decorated with a cow and a few buttercups, saying, AUF WIEDERSEHEN DORNBURG! It reminded her that on the flip side of every bully was a sentimentalist, like those smiling pigs painted on a butcher's window, wearing a lop-sided trilby and a willing expression.

The devotees in her boarding house added to her isolation by drowning all the fine distinctions which had crowded her mind since she had first heard rumours of Mother Meera's divinity. For them the focus of controversy was not her status, but their own status, as measured by where they sat during *darshan*, the silent encounter with Mother Meera which was the climax of their pilgrimage.

Crystal discovered this preoccupation at her first breakfast, and learned the nicknames of some of the Meera entourage, jokingly called the '*darshan* Police'.

'I didn't want to be in Kansas in the fucking kitchen,' complained one American woman.

'I was in the bookshop,' her friend groaned, 'and every time anyone wanted to get past me, they tapped me on the shoulder. Moustache Boy gave me a really nasty shove. You know, that was abusive. The only way I can figure it is that I had to learn something about my body.'

Boris, a ponderous Russian living in North Carolina, controlled the little group through the power of his mind.

'Please!' he said, as if he were asking someone to remove their car from his driveway and couldn't be expected to keep his temper for much longer. 'Read Jung!'

Everyone, it turned out, had read some Jung already and so Boris badgered them from another angle.

'Jung only wrote one book for the public, that is *Man and His Symbols*, the other books are too esoteric for the public'

'Oh, I kinda liked *Memories, Dreams, Reflections*,' said Robin, the woman who had been abused by Moustache Boy.

Boris gave her a furiously soulful and patronizing glance with which he conveyed that she had not understood its inner meaning. When he heard that Crystal was living in California, he became bitter.

'Ha! California,' he said, 'the capital of spiritual materialism.'

It was too cold for Crystal to refuse a lift that evening, but she paid the price of overhearing Boris's dream interpretation.

That afternoon Robin had dreamt that she was driving a six-wheeled truck. Before she could say anything more, Boris explained that 'Six is the number of the higher intelligence.'

'Why?' asked Robin.

'Because it is the sixth chakra, the brow chakra, which is the chakra of the higher intelligence.'

'Well, there are so many systems . . .' Robin began, but she was soon silenced by the Rasputin-like power of Boris's self-belief.

'It is very clear: you are being driven by a higher intelligence,' said Boris, turning into the municipal car park.

Crystal, who was going to *darshan* for the first time, was able to break away and go to the head of the crowd, a privilege reserved for newcomers.

A lecture on *darshan* manners, delivered on the edge of the dark and foggy car park by a skeletal and lamp-eyed man with a monkish haircut who looked as if he'd been interrupted illuminating a twelfth-century manuscript, advised Crystal not to look at the other devotees but to turn her attention inwards and meditate during the three hours she would sit in Mother Meera's presence.

While she stood there waiting to leave, Crystal overheard a snatch of conversation between two American men.

'What did you say this guy's name was?'

'Poonjaji. He can really shift your perspective,' said a man in a blue bonnet.

Crystal felt a burst of affection for Poonjaji. She remembered her private interviews with him and the way he always went straight to the point.

'Are you and I the same?' he would ask in the warbling Indian accent she loved to imitate. 'Is there any difference between you and my guru?'

Nothing about the content of these questions could in itself explain why she had felt all the walls come down at once, and the undulation of a universal rhythm flow through her unresisted, not with the loud bliss of psychedelics but with perfect naturalness. The trouble with Poonjaji's teaching was that there was no supporting practice, and it only took a long plane flight, a bout of flu and an unreliable man to turn this openness into a sense of agoraphobic naivety, quickly followed by closure. Having thought she was beyond meditation, she resumed with grim discipline. She couldn't fly to Lucknow every morning for half an hour but she could sit on a cushion.

What would be the Mother Meera effect? What would it show her, if anything?

When the group of newcomers finally set off, the man who had spoken about Poonjaji was at the front of the pack.

Someone came abreast of him. 'First night, huh?' he asked sarcastically.

'Oh, yeah, well, like I figured I deserved a place in the big room,' said the man in the blue bonnet.

He's lying, thought Crystal. He's on his way to see someone who he thinks is either God or a fully realized human being and he's lying in order to get a better seat. What's the deal here? Hasn't it occurred to him he might be blowing it?

And here she was on her way to see the same person and getting annoyed by the behaviour of a stranger.

The group advanced swiftly and quietly through the streets, approaching a house with a large room on the ground floor and a dimly lit window upstairs. Ah, thought Crystal, uplifting her thoughts, that's her home, that's where we gather downstairs, and from her bedroom Mother Meera engages in her lonely work, sending the Paramatman light into the world.

It was not the house. They moved on to a stubbornly ordinary village house and stood in line, having their names checked by a man with a clipboard and a mustard-coloured tie.

Inside, Crystal sat down in a room crowded with rows of white plastic chairs; its wallpaper was silky and white, the floor tiles white marble, and against the wall stood a large armchair draped in pale floral silk. On the ceiling the light bulbs were contained by opaque glass lotuses, not with a thousand petals but with six, each petal patterned with sinuous tendrils of clear glass.

Crystal sat down and closed her eyes.

She was astonished by the speed and directness with which she was javelined into concentration. It was a ferocious state of mind, piercing her with a sense of urgency. Why was she holding back from the final generosity, the final embrace of life? How could she bear to run along the gleaming tracks of a determined and yet fugitive experience?

All the touching deathbed scenes she had ever imagined flashed over her at once. Smiling serenely at her inconsolable friends, she would be wise and kind, a reconciliation in one hand and a legacy in the other, courageous in the face of pain, witty at the end.

Why wait? Why wait until she had a hospice for an address? Why wait until she was twiddling the dial on a morphine drip?

Why not do it now? If not now, when?

She opened her eyes and looked around her, ostensibly to check whether she was participating in a mass psychosis, but also wanting to steady herself with the reassuring metallic flavour of irritation with which Germany and Boris had provided her so conscientiously over the last twenty-four hours. Who were these devotees she had fallen among? What context did they provide for her prickling sense of urgency?

Not surprisingly, visiting someone called 'The Mother', there were various connoisseurs of the maternal: earth mothers, lost boys with pursed lips, thin unsuckled daughters. She looked around, relieved by the triumphant return of her critical mind.

The honey-blond crew who discussed the enneagram over coffee in their lovely homes. Gold jewellery. Very long fingernails. They hold the saucer under their chins as they sip from the cup. They brush the crumbs from the corner of their mouths with pinched napkins. No minds to speak of, but a kind of gooey generalized lurv. Easter bunnies melting next to a fake log fire.

And the hippies who'd done India and done acid and done communal living. Hair still long, but grey now. Experts on altered states who thought that Mother Meera might give them a hit that would take them back beyond the detoxifying diets, beyond the ashrams, back to the *early* trips.

And old people who would hardly be able to get on their knees to rest their heads in Mother Meera's consoling hands. They wanted to be less scared of death, of all the things they'd done and hadn't done. Who could blame them? Who could blame any of them?

'The Mother' came into the room and they all rose, eagerly, coolly, arthritically. She's a small Indian woman with a moustache and a fancy sari, thought Crystal, but she felt a visceral recognition during the avatar's swishing passage through the room, and sensed a masterpiece of concentration housed in that fragile body.

Crystal closed her eyes again and shifted instantly into

an intense reverie. She saw an image of pale-yellow roses beaded with rain, and felt that this vivid picture was somehow accompanied by an elaborate anecdotal atmosphere.

She was seeing these roses in the early morning, after talking all night in a curtained room with someone who was not yet her lover but would be soon. And then she'd gone outside. Wet grass, almost as laborious as sand to walk through, and the melancholy excitement of a new day without sleep, the smell of rained-on earth and, round the corner of the house, the roses, against a stone wall, their heads stooped with water, but also stooped from having to mean so much, like a newborn child who inherits a famous name, not just wet flowers but old roses.

Behind her closed eyes she closed her eyes again, and the smell hit her in the middle of the brow like a picture nail. The inner sensation of beauty disarmed her predatory mind which, a few moments earlier, had been watching for something to condemn, like a cat beside a mousehole. Now, she had merged with an imaginary rose and was nodding carelessly on the edge of a symbolic realm, pregnant with the atmosphere of amorous adventure.

Far out.

If only I could sustain this awareness for ever, thought Crystal, immediately losing it, recognizing the inevitability of the loss, and finding a new centre. The operation was over in a second. Some things were lost, some remained. The thing was to see what was there, instead of moping about what was lost and hoping it might return. The enigma of how things became available to consciousness was some consolation for their apparent loss, as well as a promise of further loss. She had spent so much of her life chasing after half-concealed thoughts, like a diver hurrying towards a glint in the seaweed, only to find when she got there at last the lid of a tin rocking limply in the current.

The roses were gone but she had cut through their loss with a bracing sense of present reality.

This Mother Meera was quite something; or the collective expectation that she was quite something was quite something. What did it matter? In her presence Crystal was able to hover on the thermals of impermanence without needing to beat a wing. And if those warm currents, caused by appreciating the insubstantiality of her own thoughts, were removed, and she hovered in pure emptiness, beyond even acknowledging the emptiness, would she have to flap a wing?

She experimented, relaxing completely into the knowledge of her own death, taking groundlessness as her ground, and free fall as her playing field. Instead of spiralling downwards, she found a still more essential poise. Her eyelids parted slowly, her lips parted slowly, and her slowly exhaling breath seemed to last from the beginning of time to the present moment, so solid was her sense of connection between those two non-events, passing like a rod through the centre of her body.

Quite something, the little Indian woman was quite something.

Curious to watch the process of *darshan* more closely, Crystal beamed in on the devotee who was kneeling in front of Mother Meera, his head in her hands. After a few moments he gazed up into Mother Meera's eyes. Crystal was trying to discern the exact quality of the transmission when she was distracted by the sound of muffled crying.

Only a few seats away from the avatar's armchair sat the source of the noise. Her face was crumpled, halfway between the tear pump of a devouring Picasso hysteric and the glycerine leakage of the sickliest devotional postcard. Tears streamed down her cheeks with such hydraulic prowess, it was hard to believe that she was not connected to the mains water supply. As one fluid ounce followed another into a chain of soggy handkerchiefs, Crystal started to imagine the slates of a mountain lodge glittering in the spring thaw; Venetian floods submerging the chequered piazzas, and eventually, in pure awe, Noah's ark bobbing under a dehydrated sky.

The reason she couldn't find her way to compassion was the repulsiveness of the display. It seemed to be divorced from direct suffering and to spring on the one hand from a simple rage that Mother Meera was getting so much attention, and on the other from a veil of piety suggesting that only she, Wasserworks, understood the exact nature of the sacrifice the Divine Mother had made by descending into the charnel house of human incarnation.

Crystal tried to persuade herself that this was the core of suffering, the suffering of self-centredness, and that it too required compassion, but she only grew more exasperated. Wasserworks's strategy of draining attention towards herself was bad enough, but the dissonance of her calamitous expression as she looked at *darshan* was like going to a concert with someone who stoutly whistles another tune during the performance. Crystal tried all the usual self-accusations to discover why she was so annoyed by this woman, but finally had to give up and be annoyed by somebody else.

Immediately behind Wasserworks, and in comic contrast, was Mrs Ecstasy, who had her hands folded over her heart and her head cocked to one side and a grin from ear to ear. She looked like a clown on a circus poster.

Crystal tried to stop but she simply had to accept that she was doomed to shuttle between passages of exquisite insight and blasts of annoyance and disrespect.

Ah, there was the liar, without his blue bonnet, looking shifty as hell. The Macbeth of *darshan*, whose victorious proximity to Mother Meera was utterly compromised by his means of winning it, was sweating on his throne. Whatever self-righteous pleasure Crystal might have taken in his punishment collapsed at the thought that she must soon present herself to Mother Meera. Who was she to condemn Blue Bonnet, or anyone else? What was so pure, after all, about her own state of mind?

She realized she was asking these questions in order to be able to look without malice into the eyes of what might be God, whoever she was, or an agent of the Paramatman light, whatever that was. The calculated nature of this correction made her feel even more phoney. She realized that any pretence would give way like so much sodden paper, and that this too was an effect of the context she was in. She exhaled and let it happen, finally coming to rest in the knowledge that she had come to Talheim, however misguidedly, because somehow she wanted to be a force for good in the world. That was true. She could rest there.

She started wishing that they had been given numbers so that the timing of her own *darshan* could have been taken out of her hands. Instead, she found herself waiting apprehensively, half relieved and half frustrated by the constantly renewed line of kneeling devotees waiting in the aisle. Eventually deciding to treat the queue as a reassuring interval in which she could reverse her decision, she knelt in the aisle herself.

What could she bring to Mother Meera? The outcry of a lost child? The humble devotion of a pilgrim? The highest notes of her own consciousness? What were those anyway? In a blur of panic and indecision she staggered up to the waiting chair and watched the last *darshan* before her own.

Kneeling in front of Mother Meera, almost fainting with nervousness, she bowed her head until it was parallel with the avatar's knees. Mother Meera pressed her thumbs gently either side of the central line of her skull and Crystal felt, or imagined she felt, two rods of light being slotted into her head. They would dissolve over time, she decided, keeping her bathed in a state of illumination.

These thoughts gave way to a sense of flotation in infinite space, without images, and without speculation about the state itself. Mother Meera removed her thumbs and Crystal looked up, no longer wondering which gaze to use. Her awareness had briefly flipped from a point in space to being space, the pure category without the limitation of a viewer. She offered this transformation, not without scholarly enthusiasm, to Mother Meera, who instantaneously met her at that level, but met her with eyes that hinted, without reproach, that she could take it further.

Crystal left *darshan* with an unprecedented sense of devotional simplicity. It did not last.

Boris had picked up a pink-cheeked Englishman whom he was also driving back to Dornburg.

'God,' said Robin, 'did you see that man who went up twice? He snuck up at the end and had a second bite . . . Can you believe that?'

'The sari she wore tonight was really special,' said Robin's friend.

'So,' asked Boris witheringly, 'did anyone achieve full realization?'

'The way I see it,' said the Englishman with an engaging smile, 'is that we're all realized already, we just don't realize we're realized.'

'But isn't realizing we're realized realization?' asked Crystal.

'That's what Mother Meera does.'

'But she can only make you realize how much you realize at any particular moment.'

'I think she can make it all happen at once.'

'Maybe,' said Crystal, 'but you still can't project it backwards . . .' Why was she arguing? She could see that the leaves and twigs of logic were not going to dam up the flash flood of his conviction.

'Apparently Adam Frazer used to have his own special slippers during *darshan*,' said Robin. 'And when someone asked him to take them off, he said, "They're not shoes, they're slippers, and anyway, *I'm* allowed." '

The memory of this exotic detail recalled Crystal to the present and her doubts about associating with Adam. She had left Thalheim dismissing fraud, but uncertain whether Mother Meera was wise to call herself 'a divine personality', a phrase which never entirely escaped the atmosphere of a Long Island cocktail party. Perhaps she was someone who had never forgotten the unity of the realm from which she had descended into incarnation, or a yogic master, or a good person with exceptional powers of transmission who had fallen in with the mythologies of her culture and the longings of her entourage. 'Avatar' was just a word from the treasury of hyperbolic spiritual claims. She chose not to get too hung up about whether to believe it or not, and to concentrate on the way Mother Meera had amplified her highest meditative state. There seemed to Crystal to be no enslavement inherent to the process, it was just what Mother Meera did. If that's what you wanted, you could get it there, like gas at a gas station.

8

Sunday afternoon was Peter's last chance to have a hot tub before his workshop began. After several visits, the sulphurous stench of the baths had gradually become delicious. Associated with unknotting muscles, heavy eyelids and blameless drowsiness, the atmosphere of rotting eggs now assailed him with an invitation to pleasure. The nudity no longer disconcerted him either; he even enjoyed watching the subsiding thermometer of his self-consciousness.

As he soaked in the tub, purgative sweat started breaking out on his forehead and trickling down his cheeks. He sank lower in the water, allowing it to cover his shoulders, and rested his back against the gritty wall of the bath, sighing with relief. Slipping his head under the water, his heart pumping hard and his cheeks swollen, he felt his hair sway, like seaweed in a current, in the current of his paddling hands.

As he broke the surface and gasped for air, he saw her stepping into the bath. Politely refusing to linger on her slender legs or try to make out the colour of her pubic hair in the murky light, he shifted into the corner.

She smiled at him. He knew it was not seduction but

ease that made her smile, ease that was more seductive than anything. Holding her nose, she arched backwards into the water, her belly gleaming for a moment like the back of a diving whale. He noticed the ring in her navel and wanted to reach out and touch it, touch it with the tip of his curving tongue.

Where was his loyalty to Sabine? Maybe she had been the pretext for launching him on a quite different adventure, Peter reflected. He might be better off with this sexy girl opposite him in the tub.

Mad thoughts, fainting heat, sulphurous fumes. Peter clambered out of the bath and steadied himself for a while. He wanted to go over to one of the massage tables and cool off.

Sitting down naked in front of the Pacific, cross-legged on a padded white table, he watched the sea foam violently below. As it broke over the black and orange rocks, it yielded flashes of purple, like liquid sparks. He looked further out and saw waves unfurling southwards along the curve of the bay. Under an inky sky, silver streaking the horizon, an opening in the clouds conjured up a flood-lit stadium far out to sea. He half expected Prospero or the Grateful Dead to come splashing onto this aquatic stage. The air was already electric with the promise of a storm.

The stage faded again and he closed his eyes, feeling dizzy as his body cooled off in the breeze. He let loose a deep staggered sigh, as if he'd exhumed himself from a long burial, and suddenly his chest seemed to burst open like a torpedoed ship and flood him with nameless emotion.

From behind the double darkness of lids and clouds, his eyes swivelled searchingly like the restless upturned eyes of the blind, and his mind disappeared by flashing too brightly, like a sword catching the sun. Between his pounding heart and the pounding waves, between his hissing blood and the electric air, between the spinning galaxies of his molecular structure and the spinning galaxy which his molecular structure inhabited, the membrane of his skin grew translucent and all distinctions dissolved in the light of their resemblance.

What was happening to him?

He felt a moment of pure bliss, and then as he clutched at it, trying to repeat the mental process that seemed to have led there, he watched it recede. He was almost grateful for the disappointment, feeling that the filament of his sense of self was not designed to carry such a current.

What had happened to him? Words and explanations rushed towards the emergency of an incomprehensible experience, their sirens wailing. It was the change of temperature; he had been 'enlightened'; he shouldn't be eating so many salads; his mother was right, he was cracking up; he had suddenly been liberated from a false model of himself he'd been carrying round for years . . . but none of these paramedics could perform the vital operation of describing what had happened. Changes of temperature usually gave him a cold, and 'enlightenment' raised more questions than it answered. The experience preserved an exciting mystery, it was a flash of something other which he must protect from the glare of analysis. Shivering now from the cold, he hurried back to the hot tub.

'Are you all right?' asked the girl with the navel ring. 'You look kinda stunned.'

Oh God, not conversation, not after that. Like a man hurrying out of a curfewed city with a hungry infant under his cloak, he was not inclined to chat with strangers. Still, he'd never been good at lying, despite countless attempts, and he'd fallen into the habit of answering questions honestly.

'Well, I was sitting on the table and I felt very, um . . . open.'

Open? Open? A door could be open, a shop could be open, a public lavatory could be open. How could he force what had just happened to share a descriptive label with these achingly trite situations?

She smiled at him encouragingly as if she knew exactly what had happened, despite the thinness of his adjective. She was pretty too, and maybe she knew where he could find Sabine. Maybe she could replace Sabine after all this time. He cancelled the thought hastily, but it drifted guiltlessly back into his mind.

'Are you here in a workshop?' she asked.

'Ya, I'm in the Martha Goldenstein workshop tonight.'

'Oh, too bad we're not in the same group. I'm doing Dzogchen meditation, "A Week of Noble Silence".'

'That sounds perfect,' he said. 'I wish I was facing a week of noble silence instead of what will no doubt turn out to be a week of ignoble chatter. Ever since I can remember I've been trying to avoid making a fool of myself in front of groups of strangers; now it's become a way of life.'

She laughed. She was really adorable, he decided.

'How come you booked for a week of ignoble chatter?' she asked.

'Well, to be honest, I didn't really look very carefully at the catalogue. I just wanted to stay on here for another week. It's a long story . . .' He paused.

He felt excited and confessional but the strategic part of his mind threw up a few flimsy barriers to a full disclosure. What sort of buffoon would she think he was if he told her that he'd given up his job in order to spend three months pursuing a woman he'd only known for three days?

'I'm looking for a friend of mine I've lost touch with,' he said. 'She used to mention this place and I thought I might find some traces of her here.'

'Is this someone you're totally in love with?'

'I suppose so,' he said cautiously, and then decided to play the role of the wry Englishman with which he had had some success during his travels. 'I mean I was in a fairly gloomy state about the whole love business. I thought, "I won't bother with romance or marriage any more, just find a woman who hates me and buy her a house."'

'Sure,' she laughed, 'but you still have to find the right woman.'

'What's your name?' he asked.

'Crystal'

'With a C or a K?'

'A C.'

'Well, I'm Peter with a P,' he said. 'The thing about

Sabine,' he added, 'is that I saw her so briefly, and haven't seen her for so long that perhaps I'm no longer pursuing her so much as the hope she gave me.'

He'd never said this before, but didn't want to give this charming woman the impression that he was completely unavailable.

Some new people started to climb into the tub.

'Hi,' said a white-haired man with glaring blue eyes that seemed determined to defy insincerity even in the gathering darkness.

'Hi,' said Crystal.

Stepping into the tub behind Blue-Eyes was a woman whose blonde hair, tortured into the tightest curls, seemed to be a homage to Africa, and a whimsical gesture of regret at not being black herself. Peter was shocked to find himself irritated by Crystal's friendliness towards the new-comers. Although these people had as much right as he had to be in the communal tub, they were interrupting his conversation with her.

'I did a past lifetime thing,' said the African Queen. 'I didn't really know what to make of it, but it made a lot of sense. I'd been a slave at one point and suffered *a lot*.'

Peter instantly hated her. She was paying huge hair-dressing bills to create a cosmetic continuity with a former lifetime of abject suffering in the hope of justifying the overflow of her self-pity.

Whatever had happened on the massage table, it had done nothing to make him more tolerant.

'What I don't understand about Chinese and African cultures,' said Blue-Eyes, 'is that if reincarnation is true then we're our own ancestors, and really we're worship-ping ourselves.'

'Maybe it's like you've got to worship yourself before you can worship anything else,' she suggested.

'Sounds good,' he admitted. 'One of the coolest things I ever heard,' he added, turning the full glow of his innocent and sketchy features towards the African Queen, 'was that religion is for those who want to avoid hell, and spirituality is for those who've already been there.'

A real little fount of wisdom, thought Peter.

'Cool,' she affirmed.

'I think Deepak Chopra is going too far when he says that the water you drink is also the water Christ bathed in, and so the whole body of water is sacred.'

'It's a lovely idea though,' she said, as if she were looking at the brochure for a Caribbean holiday.

I think I'm going to be sick, thought Peter, sinking quietly into the steaming water. When he emerged again, Blue-Eyes was still pumping out the wisdom.

'North or South, they both lead you to the same place. I didn't say that, Suzuki did.'

He's unstoppable, thought Peter, I'll have to leave. He looked over at Crystal. She answered his look and, although there was complicity in the way she smiled, there was somehow no condescension towards the others. Peter was troubled by the contrast between the delicacy of this position and his own fermenting irritation.

'Martha Goldenstein says that every moment is a gift,' said the African Queen, 'and that's why it's called "the present".'

Peter surged noisily out of the water and grabbed the standard-issue pink towel that was just too small to wrap around a human waist.

'See you later,' he said to Crystal.

'I hope so,' she said.

Peter didn't have to wait long to see Crystal again. He found her a couple of hours after they had met in the tubs, queuing up for dinner in the lodge. Her short T-shirt left her belly exposed and he saw the navel ring again, the skin a little inflamed where the ring pierced the lower edge of her navel.

'Hi, Crystal,' he said, picking up a plate and following her down the line of salads.

'You're staring at my ring,' she said.

'Yes, I'm afraid I was,' he said, transferring his gaze to the sliced cucumbers.

'Don't be afraid, at least not of that,' she laughed. 'When they put this ring in, I had an orgasm right there in the shop, it was wild. The guy said, "This is definitely your energy centre."'

Peter was silenced by this information, but recovered in time to say, 'Does it still have that effect on you?'

'Sure, that's why it's there.'

Gosh, thought Peter, these California girls are amazing. He felt his own Englishness and stiffness and inability to decipher Crystal's candour. If an Englishwoman told you about an orgasm the second time you chatted together, you knew that she either wanted sex straight away, or that she'd been educated at a convent. Over here, one had no idea what it meant.

Peter wanted to ask Crystal to sit with him, but in the communal dining room he felt the usual sense of personal and social meltdown known locally as 'lodge psychosis'. Instead of the sense of community it was designed to promote, the lodge shipwrecked its occupants by presenting them with a series of treacherous whirlpools and rocky dilemmas. Acquaintances imagined they were friends, friends turned into strangers, seminarians were looked down on by residents, and residents exploited by staff, teachers appeared to be available to students but were suddenly ringed by jealous lovers and competitive sidekicks. Anyone at any time could come and 'process an issue' with you, however turgid or trivial, whether you could remember meeting them before or not. The person to whom you told the secret of your mother's mental illness the night before might not remember your name by lunchtime the next day. The permissiveness that made sex seem pleasingly inevitable made you realize more sharply the internal constraints that prevented you from approaching the object of desire, but the same permissiveness could not stop the bore you most dreaded from bearing down on you with greedy tactlessness when you were deeply engaged with someone else. Like the place as a whole, the lodge made a partial transcendence of the formalities and hypocrisies of ordinary social life, but at the same time generated a longing for the good manners and the privacy which those formalities, until they became corrupted, were designed to protect.

Psychologically bleeding and half drowned, but still hoping to preserve an air of purpose and self-possession, Peter had often wandered back and forth in the last three days, plate in hand, meeting or avoiding glances he was no longer calm enough to interpret accurately, or being dragged with a fixed smile on his face to a table of people he had no reason to spend time with.

'Shall we sit together?' he murmured almost inaudibly.

'Sure.'

What a miracle. She hadn't promised to spend the whole of dinner 'processing' with some deluded monster. He knew that she was doing a meditation workshop and wanted to ask her about what had happened to him on the massage table. Was there such a thing as spontaneous meditation, like spontaneous combustion but less messy?

'You're doing this meditation thing, so you might know: do you think one can start meditating by accident?'

'How do you mean?'

'Well, do you think that someone who wasn't trained could start doing it spontaneously?'

'Oh, ya, I think people bliss out spontaneously without meditating. Meditation is just a bunch of techniques for getting you into that reality.'

'Is that reality with a capital R?' asked Peter. 'I mean, do you think this "blissing out" is an insight into some fundamental truth, or is it just another state of mind to add to a menu which already includes guilt, boredom, anguish, despair, hatred, longing, nostalgia, and so forth?'

'Great menu,' laughed Crystal. 'You should join our

workshop. Those are the kind of things we discuss when we're not observing "noble silence".'

'How many kinds of silence are there?'

'You're the expert on lists. I guess there must be guilty silence, nostalgic silence, despairing silence . . . but the only kind you have to worry about this week is the noble type.'

'Can I really switch workshops?'

'I think you've got till tomorrow evening to switch.'

'This place is so strange,' said Peter. 'You're in an ego-dissolving workshop and I'm in an ego-building one, and here in the lodge there's a convergence of the cool and warm currents.'

'I guess you've got to have an ego before you can dissolve it.'

'So, do you think that some people set about trying to eliminate a sense of self they don't have in the first place?'

'That can happen but it's really more like trying to awaken a sense of self that you don't recognize in the first place. It's just there . . . you just have to turn the mind back to that source.'

'Hi.'

Peter looked up and saw a square-jawed woman he could vaguely remember talking to for a few minutes on the day he arrived.

'Oh, hello. Crystal, this is . . . um.'

'You've forgotten my name. It's Flavia,' she snapped.

'Flavia, of course, I'm frightfully sorry.'

'Don't you hate the British?' Flavia asked Crystal, sitting down with a plate of vegetarian chilli. 'They apologize for everything and then when they really have something to be sorry about, they sound like they just bumped into you by mistake in the street, "Oh, I'm so awfully sorry to have destroyed your life",' she sneered in a dreadful English accent.

'Well, I'm sorry you don't like the English,' said Peter, crashing down the nearest manhole.

'Oh, I'm so awfully sorry you're awfully sorry,' said Flavia.

'I'm just going to get a drink,' said Peter. 'Excuse me a minute.'

'Off to get a cup of tea,' chimed Flavia in her grating accent.

Peter retreated to the tea counter. Behind him he could hear Flavia saying, 'Black tea is dreadful. It's just tannic acid and caffeine. That's why the British are so fucked up: they drink too much tea.'

After helping himself defiantly to a bag of Earl Grey, Peter returned to the table. He listened distractedly while Flavia told them about her mother's schizophrenia. He was bored and annoyed by this second intrusion, but at the same time felt elated just being near Crystal.

9

'Now listen up!' said Martha Goldenstein, resting on her crutches.

'The way you language it up really matters, so part of our letting go and moving on process is to let go of some of the labels we put on things. The way of the warrior is a path of the heart, and this week we're hopefully going to be trying to open up that chakra,' she leant heavily on her left crutch, and spread her right hand over her chest, 'and live from this part of ourselves.'

A frenzied smile broke out on her glazed face as if a cord had been tweaked behind the swagged draperies of her cheeks.

She was really pleased that they had five days together in what would hopefully be a very dynamic situation. She did weekends too, which could be very transformational, but a week gave them that much longer to get into the group process.

In the dimness of the large white room, thirty seminarians formed a rough circle. Sleepy after dinner and relaxed by the introductory nature of the meeting, they slouched, stretched or leant on huge cushions; some sat in a half-lotus position; others rested their chins on their clutched knees. Occupying the noonday point on this human clock, Martha and her assistant were languaging up the aims of their workshop. Outside, the sea let go and moved on with a fluency which even Martha must have regarded as an unobtainable ideal.

'My name is Carlos,' said Martha's assistant in a Brazilian accent. 'You may not be familiar with this name. Perhaps it will help you to think of C. G. Jung. The C stands for Carl, which is the same name.'

'And Carlos Castaneda,' said Karen helpfully.

'Yes,' beamed Carlos, pleased to find another famous person who had the same first name as himself.

'He thinks he's bloody Carl Jung,' Jason whispered to Haley.

She narrowed her eyes at him to express contempt for his facetious tone.

'My name's Jason,' Jason whispered. 'It might help you to think of Jason and the Argonauts pursuing the Golden Fleece across the ancient world.'

Haley glared at him with renewed hostility, and Jason conjured up a chastened expression which competed unsuccessfully with his enormous grin.

Karen just could not get over the fact that Martha, like herself, had broken her ankle. It was another one of those unique little signs confirming that she was in the right place, and was meant to be doing this workshop. Stan had fallen asleep on the cushion next to her, but Karen was serene about that because she had heard somewhere that we absorb information even better subliminally than we do consciously. It was an amazing thought but Stan might be benefiting more than anyone else.

Peter was too happy to mind, but he couldn't help feeling that the comparison with Jung was a bit pretentious. On the way over to the Big House, where this workshop was taking place, he had noticed Carlos struggling to get Martha's new car off a rock on which he had driven it by mistake. Martha stood beside the stuck car on her crutches, and Peter wondered if these were the best-qualified instructors in the art of letting go and moving on.

When he was about to make this mildly irreverent observation to his neighbour, he saw Flavia on her other side and fell silent.

'Doesn't he look pleased?' said Martha, indicating Carlos with her chin. 'He loves it that you compared him to Carlos Castaneda,' she said, nodding at Karen. 'You know, one time I was here at Esalen, and I was out running along Route One, and there was a thick fog rolling in off of the sea, and suddenly, I don't know why, I shouted out, "What are men?" And this voice came out of the fog, and it said, "They're little boys. They're little boys."'

There was a murmur of appreciation for this anecdote. Many of the women nodded their heads resignedly, while many of the men shook theirs guiltily. Stan slept. Peter, absorbed in the excitement of meeting Crystal, withdrew from the room by concentrating on the sound of the sea.

'And that voice,' confessed Carlos, 'I have to tell you, it was me!'

Mild laughter broke out among the seminarians, and

Martha's face convulsed with pleasure. Her eyes, astonished by surgery, looked as if they'd just seen a tiger leap through the window.

'They're little boys,' she whispered.

Blue-Eyes looked towards Martha with an earnest desire to confess his part in the crime of his gender's immaturity, but frowned from an equally genuine feeling that he was a whole and wonderful human being.

The African Queen wondered if she had been a man in a previous lifetime, and if this might explain the sticky patches in her own personality. Perhaps she had to grow up as a man in order to grow up as a woman. How was she going to integrate that awesome task with being a white African? God, life was complicated when you started to think about it.

'OK,' said Martha. 'Do you wanna hear the good news or the bad news first?'

'The bad news,' groaned some stoical voices.

'OK, this is the bad news: nobody is going to save you. And what's the good news?' She looked tantalizingly at the group.

'We can save ourselves.'

'That's right,' beamed Martha. 'What's life? It's relationships,' she answered, before anyone could advance a rival theory. 'And what's the most important relationship of all? Your relationship with yourself.'

She paused so that the full horror of this truth could blossom before the group.

'The way you behave here is the way you behave in life . . .'

'No it isn't,' whispered Jason.

'You're right,' said Haley. 'You're even more of a git here than you are normally.'

'Do you two have an issue you wanna share with us?' asked Martha.

'Oh, no,' said Haley, embarrassed.

'Like I say, the way you behave here is the way you behave in life. Perhaps the two of you can't stop arguing at home and so you can't stop arguing here,' said Martha shrewdly. 'You don't listen to me, and so maybe the problem is that you don't listen to each other. We're all so busy talking, we forget that half the art of communicating is listening. When you're a child, you're full of "shoulds". I should do this and I should do that,' explained Martha, holding up one hand and then the other. 'Being an adult is this,' she said, leaning precariously forward on her crutches and mingling the frantically outstretched fingers of both hands.

'In the office they said to me, "Martha, when are you going to give another workshop? You're always doing this moving on and letting go," and I said, "Moving on and letting go, what else is there in life?"'

'Keeping still,' someone suggested.

'That's part of the process,' said Martha possessively.

'Making out and running away,' said a wag in the audience. Ostentatiously virile, his black T-shirt and tight jeans seemed unlikely to contain his rippling musculature for much longer.

Martha's mouth shot open in a silent scream of laughter.

'What's your name?'

'John.'

'Well, we've all found out something about John,' she cooed. 'We're going to have to move that kundalini life force past your diaphragm, which is a very big muscle, and into the heart space, which is the middle way, and then upward to your throat, so you can express it. I mean, someone like Hitler, he had a lot of fire down here,' she pointed to her belly, 'and he expressed it,' she clasped her throat. 'But he didn't have anything here,' she said, patting her heart.

Karen was very struck by the idea that Hitler hadn't developed his heart space. What a world of suffering might have been avoided if only he'd had the privilege of attending one of Martha's workshops.

'Now listen up,' Martha went on, 'we're going to play a game. You all like to play games, right?'

Compulsory games, thought Peter, please don't make me play compulsory games. He didn't want to be interrupted, he was thinking about Crystal and thinking about his perfect moment by the sea. If he concentrated, he could still feel the breeze sharpening his blood. The beauty and the terror of that self-annihilation had cooled with reflection and he imagined walking away calmly from his discarded personality like a woman stepping out of the crumpled circle of the skirt which has slipped to her feet. This vision merged with the thought of Crystal performing the same action, the ruby on her navel ring shining in the phosphorescent light of the churning ocean.

Get a grip, he urged himself.

'Do you wanna pair up?' asked the man to his left.

'I'm sorry?'

'We're meant to get into pairs.'

'Oh, right, yes.'

'I'm Frank, by the way.'

'Peter . . .'

'Now, listen up,' said Martha. 'You're four years old and you've just found some treasure on the beach, and you wanna take it home and hide it in your treasure box – you remember what it's like to be four?' she gushed.

Peter could remember loading caps into his toy pistol and being told by his father not to point guns; and breaking into a run and being told by his mother not to run; and trying to build a house out of pieces of toast and being told not to play with his food.

'Who wants to be four again?' he said to Frank. 'You can't even get a credit card in your own name.'

'The shorter person in the pair is your best friend,' said Martha. 'They wanna see your treasure, but you don't wanna let them see it,' she lisped, stamping her good foot. 'So, I want the best friend to do everything to try to persuade you to let her see the treasure, but you're not going to give in and you won't let her see it. OK? Has everybody got that? When I say "change" you swap roles and the taller person plays the best friend.'

Frank, who was slightly smaller than Peter, played the best friend.

'Can I see your treasure?'

'No.'

'Please.'

'No.'

'I'll pay you.'

'How much?'

'A million dollars.'

'No,' said Peter reluctantly.

'But I love you and I'm your best friend.'

It was really absurd, thought Peter, if this chap was his best friend, not to show him the treasure. Why had Martha told them to say no? He was going to defy the rules, he was going to run if he felt like running.

'You're absolutely right,' he said, 'since you're my best friend, I think you should see the treasure.'

'Great.'

The two of them smiled vaguely at each other and relaxed. All around them two-stroke engines of pleading and refusal whirred on tirelessly.

'It was love that brought you round.'

'Love and boredom,' admitted Peter.

'I didn't know what unconditional love was until I met my wife,' said Frank.

'Is she here?'

'No, I came here for me and, also, she needed her own space this week. When we found each other, we just sat around at home for a long time and cried about our unmet needs.'

'Are you still . . .'

'No, we're over that phase.'

'Oh, good, it's nice to get out occasionally.'

'Change!' shouted Martha.

'Can I see your treasure?' asked Peter.

'No,' said Frank.

'But I showed you mine.'

'Sucker.'

'Well, I don't think that's very fair.'

'You're four years old and you don't know the world's unfair yet? Wise up,' said Frank.

'You little bastard, I thought we were supposed to be best friends.'

'We are, but this is my treasure.'

'I love you,' said Peter disgustedly.

'You do?' said Frank, suddenly wide-eyed and vulnerable.

'Yes.'

'OK,' said Frank, opening his cupped hands with histrionic tenderness.

The two men subsided into idleness. Peter was annoyed at having deployed the word 'love' like a password in a computer game. Frank was looking round to see if they were the only ones to have found this exit from the loop Martha had condemned them to. Only one other couple seemed to be in repose.

'I have to admit, I've done this workshop before,' said Frank. 'I knew we were really meant to show our treasure.'

'You've moved on and let go before?'

'Yes, but Martha says that you can always come back because you can always go deeper,' said Frank.

'Ah-ha.'

'OK,' shouted Martha. 'Time's up! Which one of you showed the treasure?'

Peter and Frank, Karen and Blue-Eyes put up their hands.

'Only four of you,' said Martha.

'But you told us not to,' said some protesters.

'And who told you to obey the rules?' said Martha. 'Your parents? Your teachers?'

'I wanted to,' a number of people cried out in self-defence.

'No,' said a woman's voice over the hubbub of excuses. 'I'm pleased I didn't show my treasure.'

Peter looked at her carefully: she was in her sixties with a kind, maternal face.

'And what's your name?' asked Martha.

'Carol.'

'Why are you pleased you didn't show your treasure, Carol?'

'It was my gift to myself; I've had to learn a lot about my boundaries,' said Carol. 'I was giving it away until two years ago,' she groaned.

Everyone laughed, not least Martha and Carlos.

'I read *Women Who Love Too Much* and it really changed my life,' said Carol.

'Well, we've certainly learned something about Carol, haven't we?' said Martha with relish. 'She's been "giving it away" until two years ago. But don't you feel you may be overcompensating, dear, by not showing your treasure to your best friend? You "give it away" to a stranger, but you share with a best friend. The Middle Way is the path of the heart. We don't want to be a spendthrift or a miser.'

'No,' said Carol firmly. 'I feel really good about not showing it. I wasn't just giving it away to strangers, I was giving it away to my children and my husband. I don't blame him, we were just playing the roles we'd been taught, but when he passed away two years ago I was completely lost because I had no way of living except through serving others.'

'But maybe now,' said Carlos, 'you look at the situation with the eyes of someone who realizes that she has given away too much. Abraham Maslow used to say that if you only have a hammer, every problem in the world looks like a nail. One reason why we asked you to imagine you were four years old is so that you could come to the problem freshly.'

'Ya,' said Carol, 'I see what you're saying, but we're all individuals, right?'

'Yes,' said Carlos, without sparing a thought for what the other Carl might have said on the subject.

'And maybe what I did wasn't what you and Martha wanted to show, but maybe it was right for me.'

'We'll see how you feel about it at the end of the week, dear,' said Martha, cutting short this rebellion. 'Now, the ones that showed your treasure, why did you do that? What's your name?' she asked Blue-Eyes.

'Paul.'

'And why did you show your treasure, Paul?'

'Well, you know,' said Paul, rubbing Karen's back, 'Karen reminds me of my mom, and she was such a great lady I couldn't refuse her anything.'

'Oh-oh-oh,' wailed Karen, 'I think I'm going to cry.'

'Plus,' said Paul, 'I'm pretty active in my local Zen centre in LA and I've taken vows of generosity . . .'

'Well, it's great when we can act from principles,' said

Martha, 'but when we can do what's right spontaneously, that's even better.'

Her fingers meshed again, but this time on a vertical axis, the right hand swooping down to meet the rising spread of her left hand.

'How about you?' she asked Jason. 'The great communicator.' She turned to the group and wrinkled her nose humorously.

'You're the great communicator,' said Jason. 'Forget women who love too much. What about women who talk too much?'

A simmering disapproval passed through the group.

'What about arrogant British men who shoot their mouths off?' shouted Flavia.

'This is typical Jason,' said Haley, sensing the opportunity to graft her grievances onto the group's burgeoning hostility. 'I give up, I really do.'

'You know,' said Martha to Jason, 'there's a lot of aggression in what you're saying.'

'God, they didn't give you that psychology degree for nothing,' said Jason. 'You do have a psychology degree, don't you?'

'My background is in Gestalt and EST,' said Martha proudly. 'I also trained as a chiropractor.'

'Oh, well, we're going to be all right from the neck down,' said Jason. 'It's just from the neck up that I'm worried.'

'What are you worried about in particular?'

'Well, for a start, we were meant to end at ten o'clock and it's already ten-thirty . . .'

'Big deal,' said Flavia. 'Jesus, you should be grateful that Martha and Carlos are giving us so much of their time.'

'No, no,' said Martha, 'I want to thank Jason for pointing that out. I'm not very good with time and anybody who wants to leave at the advertised time can do so. If I get excited and I see that things are cooking, I just like to stay with it as long as anybody needs me.

'But tell me, Jason,' Martha went on, 'what are ya really mad at? Remember, the way you behave here is the way you behave in life, so what are ya getting in touch with here? Is it your relationship?' she said, pointing to Haley. 'Is it your parents? Is it your work?'

'No,' said Jason breezily. 'As Haley'll tell you, I'm a very superficial person, and I'm angry with what's happening right *now*.'

'Well, that's great. You know, a lot of people have a problem with living in the present. But as I like to say, it's a real gift, and that's why it's called "the present".'

Several people expressed their wonder at the insight afforded by this pun. The African Queen strained to catch Paul's eye, hoping for acknowledgement that she had already quoted Martha's self-quotation to him in the hot tub, but Paul was still pondering whether Martha had been rebuking him for lack of spontaneity. He felt that he was a pretty go-with-the-flow, spontaneous type of guy, and he didn't want the group to think that he was some kind of Zen robot.

Failing to connect with Paul, the African Queen sank back into the exasperation of realizing that if she hadn't been a man in a previous lifetime, the flow of sacred feminine energy would have been strong enough to free her from the patriarchal cringe which had made her obey Martha's deceptive authority instead of following her own perfect instincts.

'Yeah,' said Jason, 'but sometimes "the present" is the spiritual equivalent of the archetypal pair of socks your granny gives you for Christmas.'

'Have you got an issue with your grandmother?' said Martha.

'No,' said Jason, temporarily thrown.

'Ya see,' said Martha, 'I don't believe it when you say that your anger isn't rooted in the past.'

'You sort of win the argument in advance by using the word "rooted", don't you?' said Jason. 'Where else can anything be rooted?'

'According to Terence McKenna,' said Flavia, 'who happens to be a genius, instead of an arrogant British jerk, history is rooted in the future.'

'What's your fucking problem?' said Jason. 'Your English boyfriend walk out on you? He must be a happy man.'

'You bastard,' said Flavia.

'Children!' said Martha.

'All I'm saying—' shouted Jason.

'Go, go, go, Jason,' said Martha, 'get in touch with that anger.'

'All I was saying,' Jason resumed, 'is that I was in a perfectly good mood until I had to listen to you and Carlos Jung here blathering on past my bedtime.'

'You have a bedtime at your age?' asked Martha. 'Or

is it Little Jason who has a bedtime, and Little Jason who's mad at us?'

'I was interested that you use the word "archetypal" about your grandmother's socks,' said Carlos.

'I wasn't talking about my grandmother's socks,' protested Jason.

'Sometimes we are correct to resist the idea of a personal crisis,' explained Carlos, 'because what we are in fact experiencing is a *transpersonal* crisis.'

'Listen, Yungos,' said Jason, 'I'm not experiencing any sort of crisis, except that I'm about to gag from listening to the two of you.'

'Why is Little Jason being such a bad boy?' said Martha. 'Does he wanna be spanked?'

'Not by you, darling,' said Jason with a curt laugh.

'This is real dynamic,' said Martha excitedly. 'We don't normally get the energy moving this much on the first session. I wanna thank Jason for getting us all stirred up.'

'Any time,' mumbled Jason.

'Now is it past everybody's bedtime,' asked Martha ironically, 'or do we wanna play one more game?'

'Let's play,' replied a number of voices, now united against Jason.

'You know,' said Martha, 'when we're children we know how to play but we need to learn how to work. Now we know how to work but we need to learn how to play.'

'But this play,' said Carlos, '*is* work.'

'Don't tell them that,' said Martha in mock consternation.

In the next game they paired up again and the shorter

person had to start as many sentences as possible with the phrase 'One thing I don't want you to know about me is . . .' Then they would swap again.

People milled about the room looking for new combinations. Carol, seeing Jason shunned, went over to his side and offered to play with him.

Haley, furious with Jason, attached herself to Paul, who she thought was attractive in a sincere sort of American way.

Peter couldn't help agreeing with Jason that the session should end at ten o'clock, but he also found himself embarrassed by Jason's manners and more conscious, because he had been mercifully free of this consideration for some time, of how much he was conditioned to react to other English accents. If he couldn't throw off this habit, the most superficial layer of opacity, how could he hope to see clearly? Perhaps all he could hope to do was to see clearly why he couldn't see clearly – was that the limit to freedom? He refused to believe it, but then why had his wild mind-annihilating passage on the massage table left this sociological tic untouched?

He was suddenly revolted by the idea of England, like an impacted tooth collapsed on itself and rotting. The prospect of returning there filled him with depression and impatience. Leaving Martha's workshop was an incentive, but he could do that by stepping outside and standing on the edge of that mysterious ocean whose other shore was China, under the named and the unnamed stars, the pulse of Crystal's presence as unmistakable as spring in the branches of a cherry tree.

There was only a sleepy old man in a tracksuit left to play with, and so Peter went over to Stan's side and smiled at him weakly.

'One thing I don't want you to know about me,' said Peter, who was slightly smaller than Stan, 'is that I think I must be a very superficial person because I keep falling in love with different women. One thing I don't want you to know about me is that I had the most amazing experience this afternoon and I'm already murdering it with sceptical analysis, but at the same time I want to give the irrational an intelligible place in the scheme of things. One thing I don't want you to know about me is that although my childhood wasn't bad it was dull, dull, dull, and sometimes I worry that I must be fundamentally dull as well. There wasn't any cruelty but there wasn't any magic either; perhaps that's why the sort of thing that happened this afternoon feels like an alien invasion. One thing . . .'

'Swap!' shouted Martha.

'One thing I don't want you to know about me,' said Stan eagerly, 'is that I'm impotent. One thing I don't want you to know about me is that I sometimes wish my wife would take it easy with some of this New Age stuff. One thing I don't want you to know about me is that, that, well, that I don't wanna die. I'm not allowed to say that at home 'cause I just get an audio book about being over-attached to my earth suit, but I wanna say it now: I'm real scared of dying.'

Stan swayed a little on his feet, as if he'd been punched in the face by his own honesty. Peter was pierced for a moment by compassion.

'Time's up,' shouted Martha. 'Now listen up! We haven't got time to process this work tonight, so I want ya all ta remember what you said and how it felt to trust another person. Trust is a real big issue for most of us and we'll be looking at that tomorrow morning. At eleven o'clock we've got an appointment with some of the body work staff down in the baths. For those of you who haven't been to Esalen before, nudity might be an issue for you, so if you wanna raise it in the group tomorrow I'd encourage you to do that.'

'And also,' said Carlos, 'try to write down any dreams you have tonight. Remember your unconscious is your best friend.'

'Speak for yourself,' muttered Jason.

'That's right,' said Martha. 'And we've got a storm system coming in right now, so there's gonna be a lot of negative ions in the atmosphere which means real exciting dreams.'

'Finally,' said Carlos, taking out his half-moon glasses and unfolding a piece of paper, 'I would like to read you a very short poem I wrote about old age:

"Old age is when your back goes out more often than
    you do.
Old age is when the little old lady you are helping
    across the road is your wife."

'Or the little old man is your husband, um, if you're a woman, of course,' said Carlos.

'Isn't that great?' said Martha, carrying most of the group with her in bleating acquiescence.

Peter glanced at Stan. Stan smiled fixedly.

Christ, thought Peter, old age is when you smile in terror because the idea of death gets in everywhere, like sand in the desert, whispering under the door, and snaking its way into the saddlebags.

As the group filed out of the Big House, Frank stopped several men, including Peter, with the words 'Do you have a problem with your back?' and, if they answered no, press-ganged them into helping shift Martha's new white Range Rover from the rock onto which Carlos had driven it. When he heard why he had been asked about his back, Jason cried, 'I think I've just slipped a disc,' and staggered groaning into the night.

Frank, Carlos, Peter and Paul stood outside in the thick drizzling darkness.

Paul crouched down and peered at the chassis with an air of calm expertise.

'Can't see a damn thing,' he said, still staring.

'I can't believe she bought this car,' said Frank, the perplexed disciple.

'Why not?' asked Carlos.

'It's so big and ostentatious. In LA it's a target car.'

'Well, eh, don't tell her that,' said Carlos.

'Oh, no, God, this is just between you and me.'

'Maybe she's influenced by the fact that I have the same car,' said Carlos.

Each man felt he had to have a suggestion which would establish his mastery of mechanics, physics or engineering. The car remained immobile.

Peter couldn't think what to say. Paul had already

asked if the transmission was in neutral, the one thing Peter knew somebody always said on these occasions.

'Perhaps we should wait until tomorrow to move Martha's car,' he finally blurted out, and then without the slightest effort added, 'We could show that we were all prepared to collaborate *as a group* to overcome our individual problems.'

'Sounds good,' said Frank.

'Way to go,' said Paul, finally getting up from his crouching position.

'Yes,' said Carlos, 'tonight we learned that play can be work, tomorrow we will show that work can be play.'

Peter was amazed by the ease and success with which he had learned to manipulate the new language at his command.

He was learning, he was definitely learning.

10

Crystal changed course abruptly and headed down the steps and onto the lawn. She was determined to keep up the noble silence of her Dzogchen workshop for at least one day.

If she overheard one more person say that light was both a wave and a particle, or talk about left-brain and right-brain activity, she was going to throw up. Who did they think she was? She had been turning physics clichés into spiritual metaphors before most of them had given up jogging for t'ai chi.

She had been a child of the alternative scene, amazing the questing hippies of her mother's endlessly shifting and yet monotonous circles with the precocity of her questions. When she was nine, during her mother's Zen phase, they had gone to Tassajara, a remote monastery in the hills behind Carmel.

'When will impermanence end?' Crystal had asked a balding student from the Bay area.

He smiled comically as if to say, Who will rid me of this turbulent child?

'Are you attached to non-attachment?' she persevered.

'Quit bugging the man, he's trying to be mindful,' her mother said, bowing apologetically to the student and dragging her away.

It was at Tassajara, visiting the shrine of the monastery's revered founder, Shunryu Suzuki, that she'd had her first taste of that magical reality she had been pursuing ever since.

Standing in the clearing where Suzuki was buried, she bowed to the shrine and asked him with childish earnestness to teach her something about Buddhism. Mosquitoes clouded the air around her, landing on her face and whining in her ears. Too frightened of being bitten to stay in the clearing, she immediately ran down the path, flailing her arms and slapping her face to get the bugs off. Halfway down, she was overcome with guilt at having shown so little equanimity and given Suzuki no time to offer her an answer.

She doubled back, determined to withstand the distraction of the mosquitoes for at least a minute or two in case he had something to tell her. The air was still smudged with bugs and they still danced around her, but this time they remained a foot away from her face, like a ring of debris around a planet, as if she were radiating a force that held them in place. She stood in the clearing, amazed. Unable to understand what was going on, and unable to mistake it, she burst out laughing, like a spring that gushes out of the ground when the right rock is kicked aside.

By the time she was twelve, and her mother entered her Spanish phase, Crystal had already meditated in four different countries and six different traditions.

In Spain they attended an 'English-speaking' meditation class.

'Relax de ties, relax de boathooks,' said the teacher solemnly. 'De mint is your enemy, de mint is fool of false contraceptions. Let go of de mint! Let go of de contraceptions!'

They'd had to leave because they were laughing too much. After that, one of them only had to say, 'It's all in the mint', or 'mint over matter', and they would both giggle helplessly for several minutes.

Then adolescence hit. She suddenly stood critically removed from her mother's enterprise, and at the same time inescapably immersed in its fascination and self-importance.

How vulgar to think that every guru was corrupt, how naive not to realize that most of them were.

Why did her mother pursue her spiritual longings so indiscriminately? Again and again Crystal saw her set out with fawn-like credulity, only to end up stalking disappointment like a tigress, bringing it down expertly and living off it for days; ferocious, possessive, alone, while it putrefied beside her. Her mother's aspirations to communal life always collapsed into a territorial craving for her 'own space'. At the same time Crystal's family life kept shifting from tribal kinship to semi-nuclear isolation. One month she would be circle-dancing in a yurt with a community of seekers; the next she would arrive back to an empty apartment, some tofu leftovers and a note from her absent mother, who was out at a part-time job, or being empowered by some dubious class on the other side of town, or doing 'service' by nursing an acquaintance through a repetitious crisis.

Crystal's diagnosis that her mother lacked psychological stability because her analysis had been interrupted carried with it a measure of anxiety. The interruption had after all been caused by the pregnancy of which she was the result. She undertook an analysis of her own to complete the one she had interrupted for her mother. She also hoped to snuggle up to her unknown father, if only in the cool laboratory of his profession. The elegant formulas yielded by this tight familial matrix proved less liberating than she had hoped, and this search for a distinct identity curved back into the capitalized Universe in which she had been brought up, where Self and Reality came in those giant sizes which are only stocked in the hypermarkets of the Divine.

Liberation seemed to lie beyond a self-knowledge that described her, however precisely, as a product of her past. And yet without it she would end up like her mother, too unstable to live with any other kind of knowledge. She interrupted her own analysis on the grounds of youth and expense. Her analyst said she was leaving because she had been trying to reconcile her parents by finishing her mother's analysis, and that next time she should come back for herself. Slick bastard. She didn't pay his last bill. They were moving again anyhow.

A second attempted rebellion, with daily acid trips and hits of Hawaiian grass from water-cooled bongs, foundered even faster as the analogies between the unreal and the Absolutely Real multiplied mockingly before her eyes.

The brilliantined palm trees and the humming air, the way in which space collapsed into two dimensions and became perfectly pictorial, only to give birth by Caesarean section to a mental reality of potentially unlimited dimensions: all these flashy effects seemed to mimic the ecstatic promises of Realization. She felt the guilt and exhilaration of artifice, as if she were eating tropical fruit in a snow-bound city.

She only really broke away from her mother when the trips started to go wrong and the surface excavations of her analysis opened into the deeply grooved fissures of an earthquake zone.

This time it was Crystal who left a note for her mother in the empty apartment. She was only seventeen at the time but seventeen years later the embarrassment of that note still sometimes ambushed her.

Dear Lynda,

I've gone to live with Krater and Stash. We've decided to *grab* and *grasp* at the debris of the American Dream you've always so despised, before the Nuclear Winter gives birth to the ultimate Cockroach Civilization.

Stash says that Roaches are going to be the only survivors and that they're going to evolve into a superintelligent Roach race with weird myths about the Beautiful Bipeds who once ruled the planet, knew the secrets of flight, fission and long-distance communication but *abused their power* and destroyed themselves.

Skeptical young Roaches are going to say that those are just myths, but we know that it's true, because we're living in the backward-stretching shadow of the Age of the Roach.

Krater says that in view of the gravity (and the entropy) of the situation, we should get as many kicks as possible before we get the ultimate cosmic kick of Extinction. The only thing we have to do, of a religious nature, is to *bow down* every time we see a roach and say, 'I salute the future.' After that you can step on them while you've still got the chance to show that two feet are better than two dozen.

'When I got this note I felt middle-aged for the first time,' Lynda told Carla, an acquaintance of hers who was a therapist.

'The note is about standing on her own two feet,' said Carla. 'She feels you've been involved with too many religions. Two feet are better than two dozen because when you're looking for independence, your own despair is better than someone else's hopes.'

'Oh, my God,' wailed Lynda, 'my daughter sees me as a roach.'

'Ya, but she's a "sceptical young roach", so she's still your daughter.'

'Anyhows, it's not her own despair,' said Lynda, 'it's Stash and Krater's.'

'Those are her two feet for the moment. They may not really be hers but at least she chose them.'

'Here I am trying to be a good midwife to the New

Paradigm and all the thanks I get is that my own daughter wants to squash me like a bug.'

'It's tough being a parent,' said Carla, 'but you gotta let go of her, she's in her own process now.'

'You've helped me a lot,' said Lynda, but somehow she lost touch with Carla after that.

Crystal entered a period of overwrought nihilism, cruising around LA on amphetamines. Fidelity was for the faint-hearted and everyone fucked everyone else.

'It's no coincidence,' Krater used to say, 'that "committed" is the word they use when they lock you in a mental institution.'

Before abandoning formal education for TV, Krater had discovered that Goya was supposed to have said 'Nada' on his deathbed. Instead of 'Yo' or any other traditional gang salute, Krater, Stash and Crystal said 'Nada' to each other at breakfast (a meal they usually ate in the evening) and 'Nada' to each other when it was time to crash at lunch the next day.

Televisions blared in every room, artfully tuned by Stash to 'self-surf', switching channels haphazardly so you couldn't lose a sense of the triviality of the medium. If visitors were uncool enough to want to watch a programme, the gang would shout 'Nada'. Sometimes, if Krater was up, he would launch into the fuller rap.

'TV is the sewer pipe of this society. We stand underneath it, we *shower* in it, because that's where the biggest roaches are.'

They would clasp their hands together and bow reverently, 'We salute the future.'

One day, the gang was so bored by their own boredom, so underwhelmed by their own negativity, that they decided to stay awake until they died, in an amphetamine equivalent of *La Grande Bouffe*. Krater couldn't do anything without a sound theoretical context. Although he regretted this lingering positivity, at least his need for meaning was dedicated to Nada, and so he said that there would be an exemplary sarcasm in dying of starvation in an obese society. They would represent an imploding population amidst the population explosion, homing in on Nada by diminution, consciously conspiring with the real nature of the world rather than struggling against it pathetically.

He was worried by the respect for harmony inherent in this last part of the theory, but Stash and Crystal, who wanted to get going, told him it was perfect.

Everything was fine for the first three days. They bounced around LA telling everyone that this was It, Adios, The End. Their friends were too cool to dissuade them; they were too proud to dissuade themselves. During the next three days the insomnia started to take its toll. Krater worked on refinements of the Theory. Should they stretch out their terminally weakened bodies in a roach-infested room, or did this show an unreconstructed desire to be part of the future? He argued each side of the case with increasing violence.

Stash's teeth started to fall out of his bleeding gums like ripe fruit. This blow to his vanity seemed to undermine his desire to die. Only Krater's incandescent personality held the operation together. Stash was burning through a layer of cultural conditioning, he claimed. Romanticism had taught them that death was beautiful. Naturally they would have to break through the barrier of this myth as they descended into Nada. There would be a layer of horror also, he warned them. That too was superficial. Nada was flavourless, odourless, without affect: when they hit Nada there would be no pain and no peace, just an indifference he called White Time which would cancel the presence of either possibility. As usual, Krater was thrown into crisis by his own claims. Was he giving a transcendent value to White Time?

Crystal tormented him with questions about the relation of White Time to the Buddhist Void and other rumours that had floated through the questing skies of her childhood. 'Avoid the void,' she wrote hundreds of times on the walls of her bedroom. This simple phrase shattered her addled mind again and again, sometimes itself disintegrating into 'A void, the void.'

'The definite article is definitely out,' screamed Krater on the seventh day. 'We can't turn it into a place.'

Later that day he crashed his car but failed to kill himself. Stash, unplugged from Krater's rhetoric, fell into bed and slept for three days.

Crystal, demented and sleepless, went out in search of the vitamins and honey she desperately needed, her exhausted mind reduced to a metronome, a void, the void, a void, the void. Clasping a pot of honey and scooping the golden liquid into her mouth, she staggered down Santa Monica Boulevard weeping with gratitude.

Krater had a near-death experience and said there was nothing to worry about. Stash went to the dentist, who said there was plenty to worry about. Krater resumed formal education and went on to teach in the comparative religion department of UCLA. Stash started a computer company which gave ten per cent of its profits to the environment, without even building an advertising campaign around its generosity.

After her Nada days, Crystal sat firmly on the fence, worrying that she was neurotic when she worried and worrying that she was becoming stupid if she ever briefly and haphazardly stopped.

One day when she was twenty-nine, she almost crossed the street to avoid walking past the Be Here Now Metaphysical Bookshop. Glancing distastefully into the window, expecting the usual hotch-potch of Crystal Rainbow Quantum Self-Help Healing Miracle books, their authors' photographs bearing witness to the twin miracles of hairspray and marginal publishing, she saw instead a photograph of Shunryu Suzuki's austere and imperturbable face. There seemed to be a certain tenderness in the one raised eyebrow. 'I'm still here. Where have you been?' it said to her guilty soul. She remembered the mosquitoes, and she remembered that she had a story of her own to pursue, distinct from the maternal see-saw of credulity and disappointment to which she had been strapped until her Nada days.

The often-repeated claim that meditation was more like coming home than going anywhere was in her case literally true.

*

But what was going on now, in the famous present moment which, like a naughty child, couldn't be left unattended for one second?

'You know the way your parents used to say, "Don't just sit there, do something,"' Surya had said that morning. 'Well, what I like to say is, "Don't just do something, sit there."'

She folded her legs and sat on the lawn. Why was she so uptight? Why was she fleeing from the other people on the deck? Why were they bothering her?

Why was she bothering to ask? She knew she mocked these fumbling seekers, whose left brains didn't know what their right brains were doing, because she was shocked by her own clumsiness. During meditation that morning she had been daydreaming about sex. She hadn't even watched the thought of sex arising and announcing its ephemerality, like the landscape from a train window. She'd been right in there, craving, projecting, tuning her fantasy so as to make it more gratifying, worrying about how many affairs to have at once. It was so uncool.

Yesterday in the tubs, she had felt the adhesive longing of Peter's glances, and she knew she hadn't managed to let go of them. The reason was obvious: the desire was also in her. She had been touched by his desire to understand what had happened on the massage table. He hadn't said anything to her at the time that it happened, but she had felt that sudden moment of involuntary concentration, she had seen him stagger back to the tub and she knew that he'd been mingling with the stars. It had happened to him spontaneously, just as it had not happened to Jean-Paul, either spontaneously or under the wild duress of psychedelics.

She was shocked by her lascivious daydreams because she had come to rely on meditation at least delivering that first level of detachment, from which to observe, unmoved, the movement of her desires and dilemmas. Neither fear nor hope, neither optimism nor pessimism, could distract her from looking into the real nature of things, which meant, at this level, looking into the unreal nature of things.

A cold demolition of the self lay at the core of her practice, but instead of making her feel cold it released her into a more passionate life, not focused on the volatile and exhausting play of her impressions, but on the clarity that enabled her to cut through them.

From this foundation rose a hierarchy of states which she had classified in a private lexicon.

There was that silvery dilation of consciousness in which awareness was itself the object of awareness, as if two mirrors were resting face to face with nothing to reflect except the power of reflection.

Sometimes, as if it were tired of hurrying everywhere, time stopped and instead of one thing after another there was one thing, a moment rising out of the plain, like a mesa from the desert floor. The witness and what she witnessed arose at once, without a word of explanation, and stood in the silence of that single image. The whole mental landscape stretched skywards, as if it had agreed to El Greco's gaze.

If these long moments were reimmersed into the stream of time, it took on an erotic pulse, as if Tantalus's torment had been reversed and she could eternally take the first bite of a white peach, over and over, perfect each time and each time freshly perfect.

The key was to throw herself beyond the parapets of language, where a linguistic junkie like Jean-Paul could only imagine vertigo or nonsense. He had never tired of quoting to her the ominous and taciturn last sentence of Wittgenstein's *Tractatus*, 'Of which we cannot speak we must pass over in silence', but he took 'pass over' to mean dismiss, as you might pass over a candidate, whereas she took it to mean contemplate, as a hawk might pass over a landscape, missing nothing.

Beyond the parapets of language, meaning could take flight into a realm of purer metaphor. But if images were further up the metaphoric stream than words, what was the object that revealed itself through these metaphors? What was the source?

There was a silence that lay under the noise of life, and then there was what George Eliot had called 'that roar that lies on the other side of silence', the roar of the growing grass and the squirrel's heartbeat. For Crystal the descent didn't stop there. Under the roar she had found another layer of silence, and, concentrating carefully, under that silence she had heard a hum.

How many strata could an archaeologist of silence discover, and what secret communications were packed in their hushed embrace? Was that hum the sound of some fundamental life? Or was it the sound made by the chanting of discarnate Tibetan monks who occupied a fairly shallow band of secret articulation among innumerable sub-basements, each sealed off by layers of apparently final silence, and including, in their descent towards the final object of contemplation, the chattering of extraterrestrial elves, as yet inaudible to her unrefined ear?

She could only guess.

What she knew was that beyond any fabrication there were those moments in which all sense of self was replaced by the sense of limitlessness. Who was having the sense of limitlessness if the sense of self had disappeared? That would be the logical question, but it could only be asked from the point of view which the experience had abolished. If these terms could be preserved at all, they had to be reorganized: if there was limitlessness, how could you exclude yourself from it?

She could of course take a dose of psilocybin or LSD or DMT and bring on the melting boundaries, but then the limitlessness was paradoxically limited to the substance that induced it. Psychedelics could point the way to being free but in the end she wanted to be free of them as well. The experience of limitlessness in any case created its own natural resistance in the form of crippling impracticality and the terror of madness which shadowed the disappearance of the self. She didn't want to add to it the toils of dosage and availability.

Besides, the flamboyance of the psychedelic realm, its seductive way of suggesting that everything invisible could be visualised, kept her in thrall to imagery, when what really fascinated her was the persistence of consciousness beyond both words and images. Sometimes she struggled to provide a structure for this persistence, imagining the total absorption of the personal mind into an impersonal mind whose metaphorical play, if it had any, her mind was not designed to register, but whose presence she could detect by this vivid and palpable breakdown, by the sense that there was something she couldn't grasp because it had grasped her.

The joke was that she was sitting on the lawn at Esalen, picking the sultanas out of her grated carrots and musing about these high meditative states, when today she had failed to achieve even the most rudimentary concentration.

Apart from the stew of sexual fantasy in which she'd spent the morning simmering, she had continued to speculate about whether she should fraternize with Adam Frazer.

What did she care if she saw him here or not? The twists and turns of his career were really none of her business, she decided in a burst of simplification. Either Adam would arise or he wouldn't. Such a useful word, 'arise' . . .

'Hello.'

Crystal looked up.

'Adam!' she exclaimed. 'I was just thinking about you.'

'That's what happens when you think about people hard enough,' said Adam. 'They manifest.'

'Well, I wasn't even thinking that hard,' said Crystal. 'I must have special powers.'

'I don't like someone not thinking hard about me,' said Adam. 'By the way, have you heard about Brooke and Kenneth?'

'No.'

'Well, apparently, they've had a Wagnerian squabble.

It turns out that Kenneth hasn't written a word of the book which Brooke has been subsidizing for the last two years. He's a complete mountebank, a snake-oil salesman.'

'Is Brooke furious?' asked Crystal.

'Furious,' said Adam, 'but mature. They're coming here for a weekend ritual workshop, for a weekend ritual reconciliation. Actually, they're coming tomorrow to spend a few days on the coast, baring their souls. You know that they had an affair, don't you? Or tried to have an affair. Poor old Kenneth couldn't manage it, even when he closed his eyes and thought of the Morgan Guaranty Bank.'

'I guess some people just don't find banks sexy,' said Crystal. 'How do you know that's what he thought about? Were you there?'

'I can read his mind, and it has Morgan Guaranty written on every page,' said Adam firmly. 'Brooke's threatening to sit in on some of my talks and to bring Kenneth with her. Typical of the extremely rich to want something for nothing, don't you think?'

'Humm.'

'Remind me, you're here for . . .'

'Dzogchen.'

'Oh, my God, isn't that supposed to be silent? I've dragged you from the crystalline air of Himalayan contemplation into the dusty and toilsome plains of gossip.'

'I was in them already,' said Crystal, 'but on my own.'

'That *is* contemplation,' said Adam; 'gossiping alone.'

He pressed his fingers exaggeratedly to his lips and tiptoed away.

Crystal looked out to sea and emptied her mind.

11

'What a divine evening,' said Brooke. 'It's probably global warming, which isn't so divine, but let's try to enjoy it anyway.'

Kenneth smiled in agreement. His wise superior smile had given way to a grin of genuine relief. He was enormously grateful for Brooke's magnanimity. She could have taken a harsh line about the entirely unwritten book which she had subsidized for the last two years but, after admitting to her sense of betrayal, she had headed for higher ground and looked for a way to handle the situation constructively.

'It's what Ralph Abrahams calls the "sunset effect",' said Kenneth. 'While there's a beautiful sunset, even if the optical effects are produced by pollution, people won't understand the magnitude of the crisis.'

'You see, you know so many interesting things,' said Brooke, 'even if you haven't gone to the trouble of writing them down.'

There was an appreciative silence.

'Kenneth, do you think the seals know?' asked Brooke, as their car flashed past the glittering sands of Andrew Molera beach.

'Know what?' asked Kenneth.
'That it's the end of the world.'
'Oh, they know,' said Kenneth. 'They know.'

Karen lay on the bed in her pink tracksuit listening to her *Waves at Sunset* tape which always filled her with a unique sense of peace and wonder. Stan, with that literal-mindedness which sometimes challenged his wife's patience, walked along the cliff's edge looking at the sunset and listening to the waves.

'Do the seals know the world is coming to an end?' Stan found himself thinking.

A seal barked from the kelp in what seemed to Stan an affirmative fashion. But affirmative of what? That they knew the world was ending or that, on the contrary, there was nothing to worry about? He wanted to plunge into the water with the seals and have a transpersonal experience. Now that would make a radical workshop.

Stan felt the richness of his own imagination. Even Karen didn't have crazy ideas like that. In a strange way, Karen was utterly sane; that was why he'd married her. It was just that she believed everything she was told, everything. That had been fine in New Jersey when the rumours had been the neighbourhood gossip, the milkfloats of the daily news, and the suburban consolation of horrifying crime statistics from New York City. Santa Fe rumours were a different matter.

Carlos, sitting on his balcony watching the reddening sky, dreamt of the unnecessary income that would come his way if his ear massage mufflers (patent pending) went into production and became one of those stress-appeasers that several million people find in their stockings one Christmas.

The sea still looked pretty, but how many flecks of heavy metal and radioactive isotopes crowded its cubic kilometres? The waves beat themselves against the rocks like washing, and then collapsed back into their own suds. While money still had some meaning, he would buy himself a stretch of primary rainforest back home in Brazil, far from the mutant viruses ravaging the great cities. There he could relax a little longer than the rest of his guilty species, behind a veil of rabies, yellow fever and malaria which would by then have taken on the character of old friends.

Peter was resting after a revolutionary afternoon. He had moved on and let go of his workshop. That morning in the baths Martha had lectured them on the importance of nudity while she wore an unusually long T-shirt. In the afternoon she had picked on a particularly lost and unhappy woman and told her to choose her 'mother' among the group.

'Tell her you hate her,' she commanded.

'I hate you.'

'Tell her to stop trying to control your life.'

'Stop controlling my life,' echoed the hapless seminarian, stamping her foot.

Martha then told the group to pile cushions on top of the woman and sit on her while she screamed, with increasing desperation and difficulty, 'I want to live, I want to live.'

'I can't hear you,' Martha kept saying.

'*I want to live! Let me out of here. Please!*'

'I can't hear you.'

'*I want to live!*'

Peter, on the other hand, wanted to leave. He took the opportunity to switch to Crystal's Tibetan workshop. It was technically too late, but the Tibetan chap, who turned out to be an American, and happened to come into the office at that very moment, was so relaxed about it that they let him do it anyway.

They also told him that a message had just come through to call his mother. Slightly irritated, and slightly worried, Peter phoned England.

'I've joined a group,' said Mrs Thorpe.

'You've done what?' said Peter.

'I've joined a group. It's called Cult Busters. We're all worried friends and parents. It's been such a help, and I've stopped worrying because there's no point and it doesn't do the earthliest bit of good.'

'I'm glad you've seen that, especially as I haven't joined a cult.'

'But what I find absolutely fascinating is my group. They've all had such extraordinary lives, if you put them in a novel nobody would believe it. And there's a sort of thing that happens . . .'

'A group dynamic.'

'I suppose you could call it that. I prefer to think of it as wartime spirit. It's not a bit like charity committees and the other groupie things I've done; because everybody is so *revealing*. I couldn't talk at first, but then I thought I really must buck up and I told them my son had been kidnapped by the Moonies and I got tons of sympathy and at least twenty telephone numbers. I haven't put them in my proper address book – I'm waiting to see which ones I like *in that way*.'

Peter smiled.

'That's great,' he said. 'It sounds like they're being really helpful.'

'Well, watch out, or we'll come and bust your cult,' said Mrs Thorpe excitedly. 'I went with Fiona, and I warn you that she's met a man she's rather taken with.'

'Good,' said Peter.

'His girlfriend joined one of those dreadful suicide cults, and naturally he's been down in the dumps for ages, but then Fiona said a great friend of hers had committed suicide and they became as thick as thieves.'

'Gavin?' said Peter. 'She hardly knew him.'

'It's no use being jealous of our group,' said Mrs Thorpe serenely. 'We were told about that. You get very jealous because you've been feeding off our anxiety for years.'

Peter didn't bother to point out the flaws in this theory but congratulated his mother on her group.

'It may not be my *only* group,' said Mrs Thorpe. 'I'm thinking of becoming frightfully green. What we've done to this planet is disgraceful. If you make a mess, you have to clean it up. I met a fascinating man in our group – he might well get into my proper address book – who said that all the animals are starting to behave differently. They can sense it, like fire on the wind, he said.'

Jason was amazed to find that he was obeying Martha and Carlos and writing down the dream he'd had the night before. He reassured himself that this collapse into conformity was only a feint in his dedicated subversion of the workshop. What had got him going was the woman they'd buried under the cushions that afternoon. It was just like his dream.

'I dreamt I was buried alive by mistake. There was this really loud noise, like rain on a roof, and I thought, "Hang on, that's too loud for rain," and it turned out to be a shovelful of earth landing on the cheap pine box I was buried in. I punched my way out, and instead of a crowd of cheering friends, there was just this horrible old git with a roll-up in the corner of his mouth, earning a bit on the side by burying me alive. The sight of me standing there finished him off. He rolled in and I rolled out. I brushed the earth off my favourite leather jacket – the one I lost in Berlin – and swore I'd never play dead again. It felt good to be alive, but I knew it was only the contrast, and it was bound to wear off.'

Was he going to tell them that he constantly fantasized about faking his own death in order to see who would turn up at the funeral? No need to ring Vienna to know that there was a bit of a question mark hanging over his sense of popularity. Should he admit to this? These bastards didn't really teach you anything, they just activated the superstition that if you didn't confess everything, you wouldn't see the light of whatever they were peddling. Then if you didn't get it, it was your own fault. Cunning. After you got caught in the mangle of your conscience, you couldn't afford to do anything but come out the other side praising the system that had just wrung you dry.

Bastards, with their essential oils and their pillow-bashing, and their colonic irrigations. What was all that about anyway? Even if you didn't believe that we were made in God's image, it seemed a bit iffy to think that the human body was so badly designed that it could only function properly with a pressure hose up its arse.

Well, he certainly wasn't going to tell them about the second half of his dream, the wet half. He hadn't had sex for so long that he wasn't surprised, but the trigger for his unsolicited discharge was a girl he'd only met at Monday lunch. God, was it only yesterday? He had thought about her so much that he felt he had known Angela for weeks. He even felt a song coming on. The only lyrics Haley could inspire were vicious and sterile. What rhymed with aroma-therapist anyway? Twist, fist, pissed, cut your wrist . . .

Angela was a workscholar, that's what they called the people who paid to work here. Yes, paid to work here. He must get some workscholars in his band. He was going to meet Angela now in the baths. What a great place. You got to see someone naked straight away. What a crazy place where they got to see you naked straight away.

The door of the room opened and Jason stooped studi-ously over the page.

'Are you coming to dinner?' asked Haley.

'No, I've got to write my dream down for Jungos.'

'Isn't that rather goody-goody of you?'

'Look, if I don't write it down you criticize me, and if I do you criticize me.'

'See you later,' mumbled Haley, leaving the room.

Gotcha, thought Jason.

A blue jay (Angela had told him that's what they were called) landed on a tree she hadn't yet named for him outside his room. It was beautiful here. He wasn't really the urban thug he pretended to be. Can the birds tell it's apocalypse time? That might make a good first line. As they beat their way through the rich brown air of Hollywood, they might start to wonder, but on this untamed coast, while the sun played its classic solo in the storm-washed sky . . .

Isn't that what we're all looking for? thought Jason, practising for Angela. Our own untamed nature. He felt another song coming on. What would we do if there was no untamed nature to guide us?

She'd love that, she'd definitely love that.

Angela had prayed to the Goddess to bring a beautiful man into her life, she had handed it over and trusted, and now she'd met Jason, a rock star from England. Life was beautiful. And the timing was perfect too. Without having a boyfriend, she had told all her friends that she was going to the Tantric workshop that weekend. You had to be a couple to attend. She'd just handed it over and trusted. Jason had a girlfriend, but she had a beautiful feeling about that too. The Goddess had sent her a dream last night showing her that they weren't really suited, and that Jason was meant for her.

Crystal didn't quite know what to make of the long, disturbing letter Jean-Paul had sent her from Paris. At its core there seemed to be genuine confrontation with the horror he had felt in Canyonlands but been unable to embrace. A lot of his time on the Lakoda reservation had been spent acting out the fantasies he had stored up from his passion for Western films, ululating and waving his power shield at the once indifferent but now paternal sky. In addition to this lonely pursuit, and with a bravery she couldn't help admiring, he had done several tepee ceremonies, swallowing nauseating doses of peyote and discovering in the fire at the centre of the tent the chaotic video of his own fears, as well as the healing messages that Great Spirit transmitted through the earnest and practical prayers of his new brothers.

He described, in a surprisingly lyrical passage, how he had seen again the knotted balls of newborn vipers that rolled and writhed along the gravel paths of his aunt's house in the Loire. As a child he used to watch them obsessively during the Easter holidays. His uncle put out poison and soon most of the vipers died, limp and scattered, like a burst bag of liquorice, around the fatal bowls. The flickering leaves of the poplar trees, the silvery ringing of his bicycle bell, all became vivid to Crystal as she sat beside the Esalen waterfall at sunset.

The others forgot about the vipers but Jean-Paul could

not forget. The mockery and the disapproval of his aunt silenced the 'viper-mad' boy, but also shaped the solitary confinement into which all his terrors were later thrust, and out of which his cleverness, for what it was worth, was born. And now, out of the burning coals of the tepee fire a new ball of vipers writhed and rolled, and Jean-Paul, with the unbearable poignancy of a scalded child, writhed and rolled around the tent as well.

Snake medicine was powerful medicine, his new brothers told him. Whatever belief he was able to muster in the emblematic language of Great Spirit, he could not lose the sense that these were *his* vipers. This clinging to the uncollective unconscious drove him back to Paris, where they spoke his own dialect, but he returned irrevocably changed. Where was the subversive analysis of American culture he would have done better to write in the greenhouse of the Bibliothèque Nationale? His best friend said that it had been a grave mistake for him to leave France. 'Nothing is more fatal to one's judgement than evidence,' he told Jean-Paul. Instead of being ludic he had become ludicrous, he told everyone else, who hastened to report back to Jean-Paul. His publishers told him that the French public's love–hate relationship with American culture was crying out for his penetrating deconstruction. An old girlfriend found a pair of beaded moccasins in his cupboard when she quickly scanned his room for signs of a woman. His neighbours became grumpy about the monotonous drumming that issued from his apartment every evening.

Here, Jean-Paul started to describe how he had struggled

to come to his senses, and the tone of the letter changed. The vulnerability which Crystal had rather admired gave way to a more familiar voice, but one which was giving birth to a somewhat obscure insight.

I remember attending a lecture by Jacques Derrida in which he described the ideal text as being 'like a vagina, infolding and outfolding at the same time'.

I admired his audacity and his eroticism, but I imagined they were at the service of plurality and indeterminacy, the gods of my intellectual pantheon. I never suspected that this infolding–outfolding was the only structural expression that could be given to the rhythms which I would see and feel as I hurtled through the infinite depths of my peyote purgatory. It charms me that this copulative and generative image should be at the heart of true structure. We must have known something when we were born. The truth was, as it were, staring us in the face but, never formulated, it was easily forgotten as we learned to live in a world ruled by that sick tyrant and his part-time nurse, absurdity and stoicism.

How proud I was of my self-doubt, that bed of nails on which the existential yogi ostentatiously takes his rest. But if we do not doubt our doubt, if we are not sceptical about our own scepticism, it becomes the opposite of itself and is merely complacency wearing the mask of science. I doubted everything and then stood strangely pleased on the ground of my own doubt. What happened in Canyonlands is that the ground gave way, and I found, under the crust of my inadequate scepticism, a visionary realm where I stood in terror before the birth pangs of thought itself, the infolding and outfolding pulse of *la pensée*.

When we look at the detailed physiology of the brain processes which 'cause' consciousness (even though qualia may be 'emergent properties' which are categorically different, etc. – sometimes the instrument panel of language tells us we are on the ground when the windows are stained with a stratospheric blue), we see that the boutons at the tips of the axions that fire into the cleft of the dendrites are making love *before* they make thought . . . *Je fais l'amour donc je suis!*

Crystal had no precise idea of what Jean-Paul was saying. She must look into the riddle of consciousness one day. What the hell were axions? She realized that the synapses must look as if they were fucking – at least something in her was getting laid. Jean-Paul's own style of lovemaking had a surprising amount of what he would have called 'eroticism'. He appreciated a holiday from the cerebral even more than a belligerent sensualist. In the end, though, she wanted sex as well as everything else to be a form of meditation.

She watched the waterfall turning back into a stream and rushing to meet the waves of the sea. The ceaseless chatter of the stream was silenced by the booming chant of the sea. A wave disclosed a seam of cloudy emerald before it came in a white rush among the rocks. God, she was at it too. Maybe everything *was* making love.

Looking at this scene, it was hard to believe an earlier passage in Jean-Paul's letter.

I announce the death of Nature. The ancient dialogue between Nature and Culture, and its reconciliations in the pastoral, the Arcadian and the romantic, are over. Culture stands alone on stage and, like a bereaved husband who has 'let himself go', no longer seeing any reason for restraint without his old partner and his old opponent, gorged on sleeping pills and junk food, bloated and self-regarding, shouts out his repetitious soliloquy to an audience of widows like himself.

A seal popped up inquisitively. Those eyes that looked as if they had been swimming through their own tears.

'Is it over?' said Crystal out loud.

The seal made no reply.

12

Some people said, 'Be here now,' but what Brooke said was, 'You're always missing something.'

Here she was in an absolutely fascinating Rumi class, but she could be doing something else absolutely fascinating instead. She knew that Crystal Bukowski was at Esalen doing an exciting-sounding meditation workshop. Brooke was no stranger to meditation, she had built *the* most beautiful, completely authentic zendo in the garden of her summer place in Rhode Island. She even sent the architect to Kyoto to study the whole thing and get every detail right.

What finally convinced her that she was in the right place, that most elusive category of all, that spot you could never find at a party, was the secret thought that she was in a room with two men who, God forbid they should think she thought so, were on her staff.

Adam was a star, an absolute star, on her staff. And Kenneth was a complete failure, on her staff. The sinister thing (where was Dr Bukowski when you really needed him?) was that she had grown much fonder of Kenneth since his compromising admission of failure. Pathetic, downtrodden, powerless, he was only a step away from being completely perfect.

The wonderful thing about Adam was that he made Rumi so *relevant*. She had thought to begin with that he might be a little too homocentric, if that was a word, but she had soon substituted the permissive thrill of imagining she liked his introductory refrain, 'Through the grace of the Divine Mother and the love of my husband . . .'

Her initial recoil from the suggestion that she see sperm as holy water was swept away by the thought that the comparison would have annoyed her own far from Divine mother. It also would have failed to make her mother think of sperm as any more sacred – for that, Adam would have had to compare it to a mint julep.

Both Adam and Rumi were fond of culinary comparisons. Rumi had said, 'My poetry is like Egyptian bread.' Brooke, who had been to Egypt, couldn't help regretting this news. Apparently what Rumi had meant was that you had to eat it straight away, whereas Brooke felt that you shouldn't touch it at all. Luckily the Johnsons, who were the most thoughtful hosts you could possibly imagine, had croissants flown in from Paris every day. They appeared miraculously at breakfast as their boat throbbed down the Nile, past the fundamentalist children gesticulating on the ragged banks. Poor Rumi probably never tasted a croissant. Anyhow, the point about the Egyptian bread was the same as what Blake meant when he said you had to kiss joy 'as it flies' in order to live in 'Eternity's sunrise'. She was learning so much.

Then Adam had said you had to seal the vessel of love

with fidelity, that it was like making a good soup. Although there were no dogmas, you had to be faithful to one person for the rest of your life, and stay on your knees adoring God through that person. Once you were doing that, there was no *room* for any more dogmas.

Kenneth took notes discreetly in the back of Adam's class. 'Stop complaining and start contemplating; stop rebelling and start co-creating,' he wrote.

Life was complicated; sometimes hypocrites and even idiots said things that were true. He was a hypocrite himself, so he ought to know. His conscience, like a sunburnt scorpion, was stinging itself to death. Adam's case brought out all his new agonies of self-reproach. If only Brooke had been nasty to him, he could have hidden his failure in retaliation and escape.

Instead, here he was, Kenneth Shine – even his name was false – the former 'ambience director' of the Blind Parrots, a group whose ambience was more celebrated than anything else about them, sitting beside his patroness to whom he had sold himself as a New Age Prometheus, proposing to steal the forbidden fire of every spiritual fad anybody had ever thought of and stoke it into a single inferno of wisdom, but failing in fact to produce a single word. And here was Adam Frazer, whom he had always billed as a total fraud, turning out to be an unreliable soprano, occasionally hitting an unmistakably high note amid the shuddering props, gushing orchestration and weird melodrama of his performance.

What made the horn of Kenneth's paranoia overflow completely were the attacks on fake gurus and New Age thinking which sometimes erupted from Adam's tutorials on the incomprehensible splendour of Divine love.

'It's time for all of us to *grow up*,' Adam was saying, pausing like a nanny who wishes to show that her own tantrums are more terrifying than anything her little charges could manage. Kenneth prickled with unease.

'You don't need complicated mantras, all *that's* bullshit too. The Divine is always listening to the soft whisper of your heart . . .'

Or, in my case, thought Kenneth, the loud scream.

'I used to go and visit an old Sufi,' said Adam, 'who lived in a small room with lots of books, and always had a bowl of fresh roses in the corner, and one day he said to me, "You know of course that Rumi and Shams were lovers?" And I said, "Of course they were lovers, they met at the highest point of the soul where hearts fuse, and their souls became one . . ." And he said, "Yes, but you know that they were lovers." And I said, "Yes, at that level there's no body any more . . ." And he said, "My dear Adam, go over to that bowl and take the rose out of the bowl" – I was completely confused by this point – and so I took the rose, this great big open red rose, and he said, "Smell the rose and tell me if it's physical or spiritual." I just took the rose and something very strong happened which I can't put into words, and the full impact of that rose exploded all over my body and my soul and I realized the shattering stupidity of separating soul and body.

'This is the secret that is being given to the whole human race now, which we're at last adult enough to receive. Not the pasteurized, patriarchal version which splits off the spirit and the body, but the full secret of the full human Divine experience.

'If you want to see the light that is streaming from everything,' Adam incanted, 'if you want to see the light streaming from your lover's body, then you must be in a naked state of adoration and gratitude. If you want a rose to speak its secret name when you gaze at it; and if you want to be fed in dreams and visions; and if you want to feel with every second you spend on this earth that you are a Divine being; if you want that experience and it's the only experience you want, because all the rest is pointless bullshit and vanity and stupidity and ego; if you want that experience, the Beloved asks only one thing – it doesn't ask that you be brilliant, it doesn't ask that you write three hundred and fifty books . . .'

Just as well, thought Kenneth.

'. . . it doesn't ask that you live on a glass of orange juice,' said Adam, 'and stand on one leg and mortify and torture yourself in the Himalayas. All those things are too easy. Anybody can adopt a few forms, anybody can have a discipline that makes them feel good about themselves. *All that is bullshit!*' he screamed. 'The Beloved, who created all of this, is asking only one thing of us: that we become one love.

'Don't think it's easy, because it's not easy. It's simple but it's not easy. It demands one very important thing of us, it demands humility, always being on your knees . . .'

Funny how 'our' turned into 'your' with the mention of knees, thought Kenneth. Standing on one leg is bullshit but being on your knees is crucial. Posture remains an important issue.

Kenneth was pleased with the sharpness of his observation, and with the joke of hearing Adam promote humility, and yet at the same time he was uneasily impressed by Adam's passion. How could he split himself off so consummately from what he was saying? In the end there was no substitute for self-deception, Kenneth reflected enviously; it left insincerity standing, or kneeling, on the starting line.

'The Sufis say that there's a gate for each one of us,' Adam continued, 'through which each one of us can enter into the garden of Eden, but the shape of that gate is the shape you make when you're on your knees. You can't get through it standing up and you can't get through it jogging; no guru can take you through it, you have to go through it yourself, *on your knees*.

'All these philosophies which have been patriarchal and destructive have said that the point is to get out of here. What an absurd idea to be told that you're just a pathetic little worm trapped in a million lives of bad karma, brought to this appalling Earth which is nothing but illusion, darkness, suffering and disaster, and the only thing you can do is scourge yourself and batter yourself and purify – never forget that word purify!

'This is not an illusion,' wailed Adam, pointing to the pretty view out of the window. 'This is a masterpiece of the Divine. The Beloved is looking at the Beloved through your eyes. Ramakrishna says that knowledge will get you into the courtyard, but only adoration will get you into the bedroom. Poetry is the sign saying "This way to the bedroom".'

The bedroom, thought Brooke, that was another place where she might be having a wonderful time.

'Adoration is the opposite of capitalism,' said Adam. 'In capitalism, the more money you spend, the more money you lose. In adoration, the more love you give, the more you feel. The soul's extravagance is endlessly returned . . .'

Now that was the kind of investment adviser she really needed! God was great, there was nothing he didn't do better than everyone else. And yet it was Kenneth, sweating with guilt and probably plagiarizing Adam's pronouncements, who was in danger of securing her adoration.

'The Divine wants you to have the whole thing,' said Adam. 'Not just a banana . . .'

A banana? thought Brooke. That certainly wouldn't be a good return on your adoration investment.

A banana? thought Kenneth. Why not at least say 'the Presidency'? What catastrophic prompting of the unconscious had led Adam to say 'banana'? The guy was losing it, thought Kenneth gleefully.

Kenneth and Brooke looked at each other and frowned.

'The elite, the hierarchies, have not worked,' said Adam. 'We're twenty years away from extinguishing life on this planet. There are people who know all the facts about the forests, there are corporations that know exactly what they're doing, and still sit swilling Château Lafite, on their electrical chairs, in their Armani suits, discussing how to kill the peasants so they can get their land . . .'

They didn't sound *that* elite, thought Brooke, in their

Armani suits. And Adam sounded as if he'd be happy to see them in another sort of electrical chair, being turned into little wisps of smoke.

Kenneth yawned. The trouble with the end of the world was that it was taking so long, it was difficult to hold anyone's attention. He definitely wasn't going to mention it in his book.

'Clearly what is needed at this time is a massive infusion of love into the heart of the world, a vast awakening in everybody of a deep, deep ecstatic connection with the body, and with Nature and with each other, because if we don't have that connection with bodies and nature and each other, we won't do everything we can to save the planet. We'll be sitting on our futons when the last tree is burnt down, saying all this is an illusion, and actually choking to death. It'll be that stupid.'

'Adam,' said a woman with a French accent.

'Yes.'

'I don't feel comfortable with you saying . . . well, you can say what you want . . .'

'Yes.'

'But I don't quite agree with "Everything else is bullshit". Because you've been through it and so now you can see that it's bullshit, but for those who want to go through it, that's OK.'

'Oh, I agree, I'm just trying to point out that it may be a waste of time,' laughed Adam. 'I'm just trying to transmit something.' He paused.

Thinks that 'transmit' makes him sound too much like a guru, thought Kenneth. He's cornering himself.

'I think you have to be very aware,' Adam resumed, 'of how the ego can entrap you in another game. I think you have to be very aware of how the ego can appropriate the image of the seeker as one of its theatrical roles. I think you have to be extremely aware that you can fabricate experiences for yourself, experiences that you think of as Divine visions. I think you have to be very aware that there's something hilarious in the whole enterprise of seeking something which you already are.'

Kenneth watched Adam leap from his guru corner on the spring of rhetoric, saw him stiffen with confidence as he regained his audience of seekers by recalling them to these sensible precautions.

'Unless your seeking has that continual subversive humour, unless it has that continual self-awareness, unless it has that humility about its potential vanity, arrogance and *silliness*,' roared Adam, 'then you're going to be trapped by seeking and you're going to be trapped by every other activity.'

'And being a lover too,' said the Frenchwoman.

What an annoying woman, thought Brooke. Why doesn't she just let Adam fly? He's such a star, and he's on my staff.

'Exactly,' said Adam. 'I wrote a book claiming that this woman who is half crazy is the Divine Mother, simply because I was having real experiences which I was projecting on to her. It's very hard to grow up, and most of us avoid it as long as possible, because then you have total responsibility, and you have to look at all the things in yourself which don't want the real truth but want magical solutions.'

'What made you realize that your guru was half mad?' asked the Frenchwoman.

'Well, simply when she sat down and said you've got to get rid of Yves, and become a heterosexual, and write a book about how the force of the Divine Mother has transformed you into a heterosexual, because homosexuals play no part in the future of the Divine Mother. It doesn't reek of the holiest of wisdom, and I realized that she was mad and that she was vicious and controlling and very frightened of Yves because he's very truthful and could see everything.'

'Why do you think it took you so long to see that?'

'Because I'm a fool, darling, and you are, and we all are,' snapped Adam. 'I think a lot of the relationship with the Master is a rewriting of the family romance,' he continued more sweetly. 'I had a disastrous relationship with my own mother which took me years to uncover. I thought I was choosing the exact opposite to her, but in fact I was choosing the same person.'

He's so compellingly honest, thought Kenneth, so impressively passionate, but honest and passionate about what? It might just be the latest confusion, the latest defence against the delusion before last.

'I think that what I went through is what the whole of the New Age is going through,' said Adam. 'I now believe that the guru system is over. The dribble of scandals about gurus is going to turn into a monsoon. We wanted transformation on the cheap – naughty us. I had a partial awakening through the power of adoration, but I was very lucky because at a moment when I was about to go round the world announcing my guru, the Divine Mother revealed to me that she was not real. If I'd gone forward I would have been locked into a system of my own creation. So the whole thing was broken by the real Mother at a very important point, to help me to get free and also to help me discover the direct path.

'The New Age has been in some ways a good thing,' Adam went on. 'It's opened people up to this whole new area, but it's usually been done in the context of the old Western ego that wants to appropriate and wants to possess. Now that God is fashionable, everybody is talking about God, but as soon as God stops being fashionable in five or ten years, and Stalin becomes fashionable, everybody will be wearing Stalin jackets.'

Not everybody, thought Brooke proudly.

Not a bad idea, thought Kenneth. It just might work.

'This is not a fashion,' said Adam; 'this is the final call to *wake up*. We have to travel through the narcissistic phase of the New Age, the absorption with beautiful bodies and living a long time, and having your perfect aura, and seeing visions and all the rest of it, very fast, because all that's child's stuff, and we have to get to being spiritual adults, real Divine children, who are seeing quite clearly, without any consolation, the desperation of a world hurtling towards catastrophe, the horror that we could be about to enter, the horror of injustice and the holocaust of nature, and seeing it without panic and without fear, because you're rooting yourself, as Rumi suggests, in Divine Love.

'I think it's very important to look at how some people have acted in final situations, in Auschwitz for example. Unless we're all armed with vitality and courage and heaven-may-care heartfulness, we're going to be reduced to *screaming animals*.'

Adam shuddered to a pause and began to cry.

'The whales have got AIDS, *the whales*.' Tears flowed down his cheeks.

He was rehearsing this at my dinner party, thought Brooke. You get so much more than just Rumi in an Adam Rumi class.

'If you've ever seen a whale up close, you know that you're in the presence of God, you know that it is the representation on earth of the Divine Mother. They're so incredibly beautiful and intelligent. To think that the whales are dying because we're *so* selfish and *so* cruel and *so* stupid is so unbearable. And it should be unbearable, it's properly unbearable.'

Adam paused, and resumed in a steadier voice. 'We must let it become unbearable. Not because we're pain queens, and hysterical, but because we're slowly learning to become responsible.

'We could say, like some of these fashionable gurus, that it's all an illusion and so don't let it get to you, but the whole point of the mystical path is *to let it get to you*,' he roared angrily.

'This is what it means,' he said, his voice changing to pleading, 'to arrive here, to let your heart break. There is no otherwhere that we're going to; this is the Divine world, and we are the children of the Divine, and it's because we haven't recognized that, and because we've invented else-wheres and otherwheres, that we haven't had the supreme beautiful experience that Rumi is talking about.

'Rumi says there comes a point in the search when you're not seeking, you're *being hunted*. That's the most wonderful moment of all, when you wake up to the fact that you think you've been seeking, but in fact the Divine has been appearing in your coma, shaking you, dancing around you, making funny noises, giving you the odd illness and heartbreak, hoping that you'll wake up to its presence.'

What funny noises? thought Brooke.

Funny noises? thought Kenneth.

'There's a lovely story about a priest who went to see Ramakrishna,' said Adam. 'And he found a very peculiar-looking man leaping up in a field like a rabbit, surrounded by rabbits. And he thought, this is probably the village idiot, but he might be able to direct me, and he asked, "Where is the great swami, the illumined one, the child of the Divine Mother, Ramakrishna?"

'And of course it was Ramakrishna, and he was actually lying in the grass, and he was talking in rabbit language to the baby rabbits, and what he was saying was, "You're very silly baby rabbits," ' Adam lisped, ' "because over there are baby snakes and you think they're rabbits, but they're not rabbits they're snakes. Don't go and play with the snakes because they're going to kill you. Do you under-stand?" And the rabbits said, "Yes."

'And then he lay down with the baby snakes and said, "I love you and you're right to be snakes, Mother made you snakes, but you're not to kill those baby rabbits. You're cleverer than they are and you know they think you're rabbits and it's very naughty and you must stop it."'

This guy's got more voices than a jukebox, thought Kenneth.

'There he was,' Adam resumed in a voice which had discarded its copy of Peter Rabbit: 'he wasn't in the lotus position, he wasn't emanating peace, he wasn't collecting cheques for being enlightened. He was in the space of total love, and he was protecting the baby rabbits from the snakes, so he was honouring both of them.'

What were the snakes supposed to do, thought Kenneth, in a fit of compassion, become vegetarians? Or were the mice they ate not made by Mother?

'When you hear stories like that you realize you're having such a limited experience. Here we are trapped in our identities, in our clothes, in our vanities, in our plans, in our projects, in our disciplines, in our dogmas. But the Divine itself is extremely humble, that's the point we always miss – the Divine is so humble that it appears in a ladybird. We're so busy thinking about the sixteen types of emptiness that we don't notice that this thing we're brushing off our sleeve is God.'

In that case the sleeve it's being brushed off is God's, thought Brooke with relief, a bigger God's.

'Here is a poem that really speaks to this condition. Rumi is really giving us the neat vodka in this poem.

' "In that moment you are drunk on yourself, you are prey to a mosquito . . ."

'Everything is too much,' Adam explained. 'Oh, I'm feeling too neurotic to go into town today; oh, I'm feeling too desperate to go and feed the poor. "In that moment you leap free of yourself, you go elephant hunting . . ."

'I love that line. Anything is possible.

'I remember seeing a programme about Mother Teresa in Lebanon. LE-BA-NON. Everybody killing everybody else, because they're all in such a drunken rage. Mother Teresa arrived and said, "Well, actually, across the valley there is an orphanage of spastic children, and tomorrow I'm going to get all those children out."

'And all the military authorities said, "You're nuts! Do you realize that if you even walk out of that door you will probably be shot? Leave those children be, and if they're all going to die, that's fine. You're going to walk through ten miles of enemy territory, and how do you even know that they're alive?"

'And she answered, "I'm going to ask God for those children, and I'm going to get what I want." And the next day there was a ceasefire and she and a few old Lebanese ladies walked those ten miles and they took those spastic children out, and every one of them was saved, because she was mad enough to say, "*I don't buy your logic.*" ' Adam shook with contempt.

' "I don't buy it," ' he went on, calmed by his discharge. 'There is another rule, there is another law, and there is another power than your pathetic little games. And that power is the Divine power, and love can call upon it, and she could, because she was humble enough and awake enough.

'If you are on the side of love you can change the world – one person.'

The room became silent.

Brooke was crying. She didn't quite know why, but all her other thoughts had disappeared and she was suddenly overwhelmed by pity and relief. Someone had gone in and saved the children. It was so moving.

Kenneth looked at the effect Adam had created. Life was complicated. Sometimes Adam could shift the whole room by invoking the perspective of an absolute truth, but he was such an unreliable witness to that truth. His slash-and-burn, rave-and-squabble progress filled the air with the smoky perfume of burning bridges. But then, Kenneth pushed his logic forward, he, Kenneth, was such an unreliable witness of Adam's unreliability. And who was the reliable witness of his judgement of Adam? What was the value of these judgements we all spent our time formulating so carefully? It was like one raindrop trying to estimate the position of another raindrop as they fell together through space.

'Last year I came to a moment when everything was falling completely apart,' Adam resumed. 'We were being persecuted and divided and had no sex for nine months. It was a horrible, horrific story. I had told the truth about my guru and I had the demonic force of all the disciples against me. I thought we'd be murdered, and then a voice said, "Even if you die, the fact that you are trying to bear witness to the truth of life will mean that in invisible occult ways anybody who stands for truth will be fed by you, even if you're killed, even if people believe the worst of you, it doesn't matter, stand for life anyway. Get annihilated . . ." '

Get annihilated? Is this still 'the voice'? Kenneth wondered.

' ". . . that standing, even if you're defeated, puts you in the eternal order, not in the order of the world." '

Oh, so standing is good, thought Kenneth, who was getting hungry. It's just standing on one leg which is bullshit. Standing and kneeling are good. He'll be walking next; a proud moment. And what about that 'eternal order', sounds like an 'elsewhere', an 'otherwhere'? Is this a man looking at life 'without consolation'? Kenneth's blood sugar plummeted.

'Christ was, after all, in wordly terms, defeated . . .'

'Christ, now he thinks he's Christ,' muttered Kenneth.

Brooke smiled at him enquiringly. Kenneth smiled back obediently.

'. . . defeated in this dimension, but the act of standing for what he believed really transformed our vision of life.

'There's an astonishing new discovery,' Adam continued excitedly, 'that, in Aramaic, Christ is punning with the last words he spoke on the Cross. They could mean, as they're traditionally translated, "My Lord, my Lord, why hast thou forsaken me?" But the very word which means "forsaken" in Aramaic could mean, wait for it, "My Lord, my Lord, why hast thou glorified me?" The pun gives us the clue to the whole inner nature of the Crucifixion. The ultimate dignity comes from the total embrace of that abandonment, that's the paradox.

'Real mystic alchemy is not a game, because you're dealing with the fundamental powers of the universe. It's very, very difficult, because what's trying to be born between two people on that path isn't Shams and Rumi, but Shrumi or Rams. That's why Rumi often signs the poetry Shams, because he genuinely didn't know, he'd crossed over, they'd done it, Rumi was transformed by Shams and Shams was transformed by Rumi, and Shrams wrote the poetry.'

'Adam?' asked a middle-aged woman in a grey tracksuit and thick white socks. 'Is Yves your Shams?'

'Yes,' said Adam calmly.

Shall we call him Adamy or Yvam? Kenneth pondered. Or perhaps Jesus Shramdric? Or Mother Jesus Yvansham? Or The Gloriously Forsaken Mother Jesus Ramashramydam? Weak with hunger, Kenneth started to laugh silently but uncontrollably.

'This is a new model,' Adam resumed. 'The tragedy of the guru disciple thing is that the guru isn't implicated, whereas in this relationship both go to another stage of love and discover the non-duality which occurs when both beings are fused. And that's what Shrumi is communicating.'

Kenneth had a coughing fit and had to leave the room.

'The only comparable relationship is a young child,' Adam confessed. 'I mean, when you're a mother and that child is in pain, all the therapists in the world can tell you to be detached but you can't sleep: the suffering comes from this immense identification with the other person. You're not in any kind of theatre in that love, you're not on any kind of stage, you're not posing, you're deprived of all the normal games by which people control each other and control themselves.

'Really, what goes on is that Shams says, "You fool, don't you understand what's at stake? Stop it." And Rumi has a nervous breakdown which is exactly what he needs, because he has to have that breakdown to get to the next stage. And Shams then leaves because Rumi has to be broken by that leaving. This would look to a normal San Francisco therapist like madness. They have all sorts of fancy names like co-dependency and sado-masochism. They wouldn't be anywhere near what was going on in the relationship, because what's actually going on is atomic fusion, nuclear fusion.'

'Do we have to have a nervous breakdown too?' asked the woman in the grey tracksuit.

'No, no, no. Bless you. You may be lucky enough to have a harmonious relationship, and that may be a karmic gift.'

'Add children to this dynamic, Adam, and it's totally different. You can't afford to do this stuff if you have children. These two guys didn't have to deal with children.'

'Of course they didn't, but they had to deal with homophobia. Try homophobia, darling.'

'Why do you think the disciples were so vicious?' asked the Frenchwoman.

'I think they were freaked out that Rumi, who they were projecting on as a Master, suddenly appears as a person shattered by love, crying and unable to organize his experience. And then he was with Shams, this utter nutcase who is obviously going through something immense. They don't want a Divine experience, they want security, and so they do absolutely everything to stop it, out of a mixture of fear, panic, anxiety, rage at other people's happiness, incredible self-accusation at not feeling as much as other people, and hatred of beauty – don't underestimate that: I think we all have it. And so on, and so on, we're all in this game of comparison.'

Kenneth tiptoed back into the room, looking studiously solemn.

'But let's not dwell on all of that,' sighed Adam. 'After all, is there anything more sublime in the world than sitting with a group of friends thinking about these things, in a place as incredibly sacred and radiant as this place has been for centuries and centuries. Being here with you I feel gratitude for the Earth, immense gratitude for the Sun. I feel affection for everyone that I'm looking at, because I know that everyone is sincere and searching and Rumi is the great wine-pourer, and something wonderful is going to happen whether we like it or not. We're in the hands of powers greater than ourselves.'

There was a murmur of appreciation from the room.

'Let's end with a poem. I might try to sing it for you . . .'

'Uhmm,' said several people encouragingly.

' "Those tender words we spoke to one another,
     They will be stored in the secret heart of Love,
     And one day,
     And one day," '

Adam repeated the line, belting it out at top volume.

' "They will fall like rain,
     And the whole earth will be made green
     With our love." '

Cheers and applause rose from the audience.

'Isn't that beautiful?' purred Adam. 'The springtime is coming, the real springtime, and this is the agony of child-birth.

'I love you all,' said Adam, hurrying towards the door like a man expecting to be mobbed. 'And I'll see you at four o'clock.'

Brooke dashed after him. She had arranged a special lunch for herself and Adam, Kenneth and Yves.

'Let's not dawdle,' said Adam, 'or they'll all come and ask me to read their poems. How was I?'

'Brilliant,' panted Brooke, trying to keep up.

13

The windows surrounded Peter with faint reflections of meditating figures, upright on their cushions. Slumped on his own zafu, he discreetly lifted his ankle from a pressed artery. His lower leg had been tingling its way to death on the carpet and he couldn't bear it any longer. He was resigned to the ache in his knees which had taken up residence immediately, but he was surprised by the skewer of pain running from his neck to his right shoulder. He discreetly – discreetly again, although in this room full of statues every blink felt like an Olympic event – arched his back in the hope of bringing some relief. What was he supposed to do, meditatively speaking? Pretend it wasn't happening? How was all this sitting around related to the strange experience he'd had in the hot tubs?

In one respect he didn't really care. He was in love with Crystal and he was in love with the possibility of a renewed ecstasy. Physical ruin was a small price to pay for these promises of self-transcendence which seemed to merge in the mysterious light of next weekend's Tantric workshop. Although it was for 'committed couples', he still had twenty-four hours to persuade Crystal to come along with him. If she agreed, he would be completely broke and miss his last chance to go back to the bank on Monday morning. Peter felt the thrill of finally detonating the edifice of his old self.

Everybody knew that being 'in love' was a state of temporary insanity, that's why it was so important to make it last as long as possible. It was the bubbling up of the absurd conviction that he had just met a human being unlike any other: not wounded or demanding or confused; not deceitful or egotistical or cruel; not lost or weak or stupid; someone generous, splendid, inexhaustibly intriguing, and reciprocally deluded.

Love was such a small word, how could its single syllable attend to so many catastrophes at once? Like a doctor in an emergency ward, it was always on call, covering for a fondness compounded of pity and duty, rushing to the scene of a violent sexual obsession, falling to its knees in a mountain monastery, throwing stale bread to clockwork pigeons, meeting somebody else's wife in a hotel room, changing a nappy at four in the morning. What time could it possibly spare to certify his romances?

Perhaps this time it was true love: not the insomniac registrar but the brain surgeon with steady hands. And yet, how had Crystal so convincingly replaced Sabine, and how had Sabine so convincingly replaced Fiona, all in a few months? Fiona, it was true, cried out for replacement. Her opinions were doomed expeditions, her voice a futile gesture, her kisses kamikaze pilots. Now, she seemed not to have been born into the complexity of the world at all, but to have slipped thinly and diffidently to the ground, like a page from a fax machine, the announcement of some fading appetites and sociological facts that stuttered, almost noiselessly, from the roller of her genetic fabric.

He hated Fiona for the use she had made of Gavin's death in the Cult Busters meeting she had been to with his mother. Hatred was famously close to love, people wrote books about that sort of thing, but it also had a justified reputation for not being close to it at all. As this thought passed through him, Peter could feel his hatred break up into guilt, and see pity rushing in to soothe the guilt. These Buddhists were certainly on to something. The exhausting business of turning his colliding and scattered emotions into a story about who he was was matched by the exhausting business of editing it into a story he liked. The first thing he asked about a situation was whether he liked it or not, and the next question was how it would 'turn out', which meant whether he would like it or not later on.

During the last forty-eight hours he had been forced to see the extent of this tyranny. Even 'meditating' he kept asking, 'Do I like this?' 'Is this for me?' 'Will I get enlightened?' 'Will I like that?' 'Are the others bored too?' And that was when he was concentrating. The rest of the time he just drifted through the ghostly landscapes of the future and the past, arranging and rearranging them until he liked them more, or decided that he didn't like them at all. It was pathetic. There he was again, having an aversion to his own mental life. It went on and on.

Once or twice he had stopped asking, 'Do I like this?' and had felt the encroachment of a subtle and alien calm. Needless to say, in the face of this opportunity for a new experience, he had painstakingly reconstructed the story which had just dematerialized. 'Am I the sort of person who kisses a woman he hardly knows as he leans on a wooden fence above the foaming Pacific?' Yes! 'Am I the sort of person who then invites her to a Tantric workshop which will cost him his job?' As soon as possible!

He was in a radical frame of mind, partly thanks to Lama Surya Das, who was leading the meditation. Peter had expected a wizened ethnic type in a saffron toga, smiling tirelessly and bowing to the insects. The Lama in fact turned out to be a burly American who walked to his zafu as if it were the striking plate on a baseball field. Peter dimly sensed that somewhere in the depths of his meditating mind the Lama was perpetually hitting a home run, but instead of dashing around the field he stood there, watching the ball arc into the open space which was the true object of his attention.

'Now that the mind is extremely spacious,' said Surya Das, as if to confirm Peter's speculation, 'turn it back abruptly on itself with the laser-like question, "Who or what is experiencing right now?" Sense that directly, no need to analyse it too much, just pop the question and let go. Who or what is experiencing, controlling, thinking? See through the seer and remain free. Plumb that gap, that bottomless abyss, that luminous openness, pure presence. It's too close, so we overlook it. It seems too good to be true, so it's hard to believe. It's too simple, we can't get our minds round it. It's too transparent, we can't even see it. It's not outside us, so we can't reach it. That's the innate great perfection. Don't overlook it.'

He fell silent again.

Yeah, thought Peter, just pop the question and let go. He pictured himself falling through space, like a Magritte businessman. He let go of his umbrella, and fell faster. He heard the wind rushing in his ears. That rushing sound, that was pure presence.

Who or what was experiencing right now? Perhaps he was a 'what' after all. Perhaps under the sociological 'what' was a psychological 'who', and under that another impersonal 'what'. Poor old 'who' was sandwiched between a 'what' hardly worth knowing, and another 'what', hardly knowable. 'Buddha nature' made it sound like a big who, that was the lure, but actually it was a big what. It never belonged to you, you belonged to it.

There he was pondering again. Pondering wasn't meditating, or was it?

Just pop the question and let go. Rushing sound in the ears, pure presence, free fall. Wasn't this fabrication, wasn't this fantasy? God, meditation was a nightmare, one got in such a muddle. Still, he'd better look as if he knew what he was doing, or Crystal might never kiss him again.

Begin again. Shed his armour, and shed the bandages under the armour, throw away his masks and the sincere countenance under his masks. Say goodbye to his body, his cherished body. Watch it fall away, like the discarded section of a rocket. And his mind, his cherished mind, watch it fall away. Who watches it fall away? Sense that directly.

For a moment, sharp as a paper cut, Peter sensed it directly.

What was that?

It disappeared.

Shit.

'Let's chant the Prajna Paramita mantra,' said Surya Das, 'number three on your sheet. It's said that wherever this sutra is chanted the dharma will flourish. Beings will be awakened and benefited and blessed. The land and the denizens of the forest will have the seed of enlightenment sown in their fertile heart-minds. So I think it's a good thing to do,' he added casually.

People laughed.

'It can't hurt, right?' He chuckled. 'I should say, "thus have I heard" to show that I didn't make it up,' said Surya. 'Somebody else made it up.'

Crystal smiled. She enjoyed watching Surya walking the line between mischief and respect, between being an American man and being a Tibetan monk. After playing with these conditions, he would cut through to the 'heart of the matter', the fact that Dzogchen teachings claimed to deal with 'things as they are'.

The subtlety of his positions was not always shared by his audience. Yesterday a woman had said that when she was growing up, 'It was real important to be American. I have a problem with all this foreign chanting,' she complained. 'Do I have to accept this stuff to be enlightened?'

'You have to accept everything to be enlightened, that's the trouble,' said Surya.

Crystal heard Surya chant the end of the Heart sutra and prepared herself.

'. . . and therefore set forth this mantra and say, "Gate Gate Paragate Parasamgate Bodhi Sva."'

The chant swelled through the room:

'Gate Gate Paragate . . .'

'Break up your mind,' urged Surya.

Peter imagined a clay pigeon shattering in the air.

Crystal imagined a machete slicing into a watermelon, its two halves rolling quietly apart.

Peter played the image again and again, wondering if he was doing the right thing or just having a fantasy.

Crystal watched the image dissolve as she had watched it arise, by itself arising and dissolving by itself. 'We don't need to get rid of our thoughts, they're empty enough already,' as Surya liked to say. The mind had a capacity to be enchanted by its own display, but that enchantment was also part of its display. By not interrupting this flow of appearance and disappearance, and not wanting anything from it, Crystal made room for everything, let everything be just as it was. She did not call this allowance stillness or spaciousness, because stillness could be ruined by agitation and spaciousness by confinement. If there was room for everything, there was room for agitation and confinement as well.

This accommodating state of mind had started two days before, when she took the afternoon off and went for a walk. The clouds were strangely symmetrical that day. Each tower of white vapour rose from a dark, cleanly cut base. Widely spaced enough not to obscure the sky, they receded all the way to the horizon, like the intersecting points on a grid that described the curve of space.

Crystal started to notice that her thoughts and perceptions gained admittance without the obstruction of a reaction. The noise of the cars that passed her on the highway was no more intrusive than the beauty of the clouds. Everything was being itself, there was no need to interfere. She tested the Dzogchen soft-focused gaze, looking, without looking at anything in particular. Flies and birds passed through her field of vision as effortlessly as her field of vision passed through her. A jogger drifted by in a melting passage.

She stopped trying to meditate because she was living immersed in the unobstructed sympathy that meditation tried to procure. She knew that there was an absolute continuity between herself and the other forms which shimmered on the surface of emptiness. There was no need to be less fundamental than that. She knew that the grammar of consciousness was reversible. Instead of saying, 'I had the experience,' it was no less true to say, 'The experience had me,' but then again it was no more true either, and the flashy pleasure of playing with the transitives did not tempt her. It was not a question of boundaries dissolving, as they did so ostentatiously in the psychedelic realm, but of the boundaries not being there. Dissolving, transcending and cutting through gave substance to the illusions over which they claimed to triumph. If there was no wall, there was no need for a pole vault. When there was a wall, it was pretentious to call it an illusion.

Further down the highway she came across a dead fox. Flattened by a car, it was alive with flies. The stench of its putrid entrails was overlaid by a much sharper smell, like the stab of ammonia. She drew the air unemphatically into her lungs and walked on. There was room for that too.

She saw the beckoning finger of a 'symbolic' interpretation, and saw how the provocation of a corpse could form a whirlpool in the stream of her perception. Opposite this whirlpool, another one was formed by the vanity of think-ing, as so many seekers seemed to do, that the world had organized itself into a lesson for her benefit. The excitement of those times when everything seemed symbolic (*'Tout devient metaphor,'* as Jean-Paul had moaned all night in their tent in Utah, quoting some French author) now seemed a lower-order vision compared with this unimpeded clarity. There was no need to reject the fact that the fox was a *memento mori*, or that its death tested the resolve of her inclusiveness, nor was there any reason to become fasci-nated by it. The meanings of the fox's death could not be exhausted: the appearance of the corpse, its chemical com-position, its absent inhabitant, its affinity with all other corpses, its difference from all other corpses, the velocity of the impact, the mood of the driver, the hunger of the flies.

Back at Esalen, there was a party. To see if she would be distracted, she took on the music and the crowd and the darts of distrust and the grappling irons of desire. There was no essential change, just more perceptions to work with. She was seeing the Buddha nature in each person while at the same time seeing the personality that enclosed it. She was filled with extraordinary tenderness. She saw that every unhappiness was caused by the desire for happiness, and it prised open her heart. She had no trouble in operating on two levels at once, as she had always wanted to do. It was completely natural, but quite inexplicable, like being able to circle above an airport and meet someone in the lobby at the same time.

She danced in the crowd and when Peter came up to her she danced with him. When they kissed, they kissed.

Nothing else could have happpened at that moment. She knew that Peter would become her lover, she knew that he would ask her to the Tantric workshop that weekend. She could see over the horizon of ordinary knowledge, rising on the natural thermals of her awareness. She saw no reason to imagine any limits to its widening perspective.

Nothing interrupts Nothing, she thought, and she was still thinking it now.

'Gate Gate Paragate Parasamgate Bhodi Sva
Gate Gate Paragate Parasamgate Bhodi Sva'

Surya accelerated the chant.

'Let go of the brakes,' he urged.

The mantra became a syllabic blur, slowed down again to individual sounds, and then died to a whisper. Surya sounded the meditation bell and silence resumed.

Crystal remained in the same state of subtle and effortless generosity. The mantra couldn't take her there or take her away from there. Chanting had been happening; now silence, charged by the chanting, was happening instead.

Peter felt himself fall into that electrifying silence, like a child jumping into the sea from a high rock and suddenly plunging into a cooler, denser medium, in a thrill of bubbles and slow limbs. The silence was his held breath, was everyone's held breath. Kapow! he couldn't help thinking. That was as good a mantra as any other, as long as it kept him feeling this lightness, this vitality.

The next time the bell sounded, it was the end of the session and time for lunch. Peter unlocked his legs and staggered out of the meditation room. He waited for

Crystal in the hall, and passed the time by reading various quotations pinned to the notice-board.

Follow your breath right out of your nose
Follow it out as far as it goes.
You can't think straight
And you don't know who to call
It's never too late to do nothing at all.
    – Allen Ginsberg

You do not need to leave your room. Remain sitting at your table and listen. Do not even listen, simply wait. Do not even wait, be quite still and solitary. The world will freely offer itself to you to be unmasked, it has no choice, it will roll in ecstasy at your feet.
    – Franz Kafka

Within that birthless wide open space, phenomena appear like rainbows, utterly transparent . . .

As Peter began to read this third quotation, the woman he had last seen buried under a pile of cushions in Martha's workshop swayed towards him, as if to challenge the claims of transparency with her soft bulk.

'Hi, how are you doing?' she said.

'Fine.'

'You left our workshop, right?'

'Yes.'

'That's too bad. Martha and Carlos have completely changed my life. I feel like a great weight has been lifted off my mind.'

'Oh good.'

'But maybe you've found what you need. I hope so.' She smiled and swished her way through the door.

A great weight *has* been lifted off her, thought Peter, remembering Carlos, Martha and Paul sitting stoutly on the cushions from which her stifled screams of protest could be heard. *I wanna live. Let me outta here.* And now she's grateful. Why had he wasted his indignation on this useful therapy? How could he know what benefits it might not hold for someone whose life was already worse than being sat on in public?

He looked into the meditation room and saw Crystal stretching out. She sat on a cushion, her back arched forward and her head touching the floor.

'That's not necessary,' smiled Surya.

'Ah, Guruji,' said Crystal, entering into the joke and bowing reverently.

Peter glanced back at the notice-board, and wondered vaguely whether you could get rainbow gridlock, with the phenomenal world arching iridescently in one direction or another. The rainbow marquetry of a place like Manhattan might represent a substantial insubstantiality. He decided not to carry on reading but to wait for Crystal outside. After retrieving his shoes, he went out onto the lawn and stood with his hands in his pockets looking at the flowers, and thinking he must look like lovers are supposed to.

When Crystal came out, they walked together to the lodge. Peter wanted to keep the silence they were meant to observe, but he was desperate to ask if she would join him that weekend. As they crossed the bridge over the waterfall, he pondered various hopeless ways of formulating the question.

'Yes,' said Crystal, as they started the ascent beyond the bridge.

'What?' said Peter.

'You wanted to know whether I'd spend the weekend with you. The answer is yes.'

'How did you know I was going to ask that?'

'I don't know *how*,' said Crystal. 'I just knew it was troubling you.'

'I don't know why I asked you how you knew,' said Peter, after a pause. 'I suppose,' he went on, unused to talking after two days of relative silence, 'I suppose it sounded like the next question, if you know what I mean. It's not that it might not be interesting to look into, but I asked it then because it was the obvious thing to say.

'It's like earlier,' he went on, 'when I was waiting for you, I leant over and sniffed a flower, and it smelt of nothing, and I thought of the word "odourless", and then I thought of the phrase "odourless, colourless liquid". It was completely meaningless, except that the phrase was lying there like invisible ink, waiting for the heat of an experience to tell me what to think. I can't bear it, it's completely unfree, during that moment my mind was just a chain of words.' Peter was surprised by the thoughts that were tumbling out of him. He felt himself becoming more real as he spoke.

'Even when I was beating myself up about being distracted during meditation, I thought "I'm living in the past" – another chain of words – but I wasn't living in the past, I was thinking about the past. Thinking about the past was my present experience. What stopped me from having it was that chain of words, that misguided self-reproach. Do you see what I mean? I'm rather new to all this, I've probably got it all wrong.'

She smiled at him and he knew that she understood. Her silence invited him to be silent. Did he need words at all? And when he did, why arrange them in a chain? They were not his enemies. He understood, and smiled back.

At lunch, Crystal and Peter found themselves next to a man from their group. With aquiline nostrils and an emphatic vertical crease between his eyebrows, he sat on the redwood bench, both hands planted on his thighs, looking at his salad bowl with the implacable concentration of a duelling samurai. He breathed heavily through his nose, a pearl diver about to plunge, and then with a sudden burst of speed impaled a lettuce leaf on his fork, thrust it in his mouth, replaced the fork, planted his hands back on his thighs and resumed his wakeful snoring. Chomping the leaf with reptilian equanimity, his half-closed eyes remained focused on the same spot. A minute later he repeated his raid on the salad bowl, bringing a piece of celery back to his ruthless mouth.

Peter looked on, lost between amazement and laughter. Glancing at Crystal to see if she was leaning in either of these directions, he saw a complex but relaxed expression on her face. She seemed to sympathize with his desire to laugh, without losing sympathy for the person who had caused it. She held his gaze and he felt himself slipping into the atmosphere she was inhabiting, where the mind's dragging plumage could slowly spread to reveal the full glamour of its design.

14

'I'm not angry with Jason,' said Haley. 'I'm sorry for him, I really am.'

'I hate to say this,' said Panita, 'but what I saw in the car had all the classic signs of a sick relationship. I've been *really* worried about you, stuck somewhere with no meetings. I could just imagine Jason throwing your tapes out of the window when you were trying to get some sanity.'

'He's been humiliating me in our workshop,' Haley confessed. 'And now he's started up with this woman who lives here. My self-esteem is at about minus ten thousand at the moment.'

'You need a meeting,' said Panita, once again relieved by her exclusion from the dangerous world of romantic love. 'I'll pick you up at the airport if you like and we can go straight to the Thursday evening Earls Court Women's Group.'

'Thanks,' said Haley, suddenly breaking into sobs.

'Let it all out, love,' said Panita.

'He's such a bastard,' sobbed Haley. 'Why do I still want him to love me?'

'That's the disease,' said Panita.

'It's not a disease,' howled Haley, 'it's me, me and Jason. Can't you understand, it's the end of three years? Oh God, how can you hate someone and still feel closer to him than anyone else? It's so horrible.'

Haley abandoned herself to grief.

Panita, shocked by Haley's rejection of her generic diagnosis, was tipped into a free fall of unconfidence and hostility which made her ache to call her CoCo sponsor. Refraining from quoting her favourite slogan, 'If you stick together, you're sick together', she hastily wrote down Haley's arrival time, said goodbye and dialled the proleptically healing digits of her sponsor's number.

After hanging up, Haley went on sitting in the wooden phone booth, glazed over and strangely peaceful. The solvent of her tears seemed to have disengaged her from the confusion of her recent life. In an hour she would be leaving Esalen and leaving Jason too. What was she wailing about? She should be celebrating. What was she doing in California anyhow? She was longing to get back to Clapham. She wanted to build up her business, and get proper offices, and advertise, and marry someone who had a really positive attitude to life. She was finished with her old life, completely finished. She didn't even like Panita, and she wasn't going to go to CoCo meetings either.

It was so Aries, she loved it. Just make a new start. No problem. Except that it would be no problem for Jason either. Little bastard.

There was a tap on the window. Christ, it was him.

'Listen, doll,' said Jason chirpily. 'I was wondering if you could lend us a few hundred dollars. I'll pay you back – I've been writing some great new material.'

Haley gave him her contemptuous look.

'I'm not going to lend it to you,' she said coolly. 'I'm going to give it to you.'

'Great!' said Jason.

'On one condition. You never call me, never write to me, and if you see me in the street, you keep on walking.'

She threw down two hundred dollars on the ledge under the phone.

'I don't keep walking for less than four hundred,' said Jason in his John Wayne voice.

'Oh,' said Haley, picking up the money, 'in that case, I'll keep walking.'

'No, you've convinced me,' said Jason, lurching forward as Haley started to leave. 'I'll walk away.'

'Too late.'

'Don't be such a mean bitch,' said Jason indignantly.

'You wanker,' said Haley, striding towards her car with all the dignity that the word 'wanker' left in its wake.

'You won't be able to get away from me,' said Jason. 'Every time you turn on the radio, I'll be there.'

'I think someone's done that song already,' said Haley sarcastically.

'Listen,' said Jason, switching tactics as they got closer to the car, 'Angela has been on these conflict-mediation workshops. Maybe we should try to end on a more, sort of . . . generous note.'

'You mean four generous notes, don't you?' said Haley. 'I don't know how you can ... I mean ... you're un-believable.'

'Thanks,' said Jason with a grin. 'That's what Angela thinks too.'

Haley got in the car and slammed the door.

Jason watched her cerise Fiesta ascend the hill to Route One, unable to forgive himself for not taking the two hundred dollars. He really could have done with that money. He had used Haley's unrefundable deposits and some of Angela's cash to get them into the Tantric work-shop. Now he was totally broke. He had not mentioned to the office that Haley would not be attending, nor had he warned Angela that she might have to pretend to be Haley if a list of participants was read out. Not a perfect start to a workshop for committed couples.

'Jason?'

He turned aound and saw Flavia.

'Was that Haley?' she asked.

'Yeah,' said Jason. 'She left with all my money. I was standing here talking about conflict resolution, and return-ing to love, and honourable closure, and she just pissed off with all my dosh.'

'You need a ritual,' said Flavia.

'I need a credit card,' said Jason.

'Listen,' said Flavia, 'I feel *we* need an honourable closure as well. I want to apologize. I arrived at Esalen with a lot of anger, and I feel I projected it on to you.'

'People are always doing that,' said Jason.

'I had a lot of realizations about my patterns during

Martha's workshop, and I want to say that my behaviour was immature.'

'Don't worry,' grinned Jason, 'I'm at home with immaturity.'

Flavia smiled back. She opened her arms to indicate that the moment had come for a hug. Jason, who had nothing better to do, hugged her. He could feel that she was standing on tiptoe so that her chin could clear his shoulder; it was quite sweet really.

They disengaged, and Flavia let loose a loud sigh, still holding on to Jason's forearms with her long fingers.

'Oh, that felt good,' she said. 'My personal rock bottom was living with this English guy in LA and I was projecting all that stuff on you. I can't believe I did that, it's so primitive.'

She seemed as elated at the end of the week as she had been angry at the beginning.

'Listen, I don't know how appropriate this is,' she blurted out, 'but if Haley left with all your money, I could lend you some until you get it back.'

'It's *totally* appropriate,' said Jason.

'I could give you my address in LA and you could send me the money next week.'

'Definitely.'

'This feels good,' said Flavia.

'It's beautiful, beautiful,' said Jason, giving her another hug.

Kenneth prodded and squeezed his crushed feet. Over the last two days, Brooke had cajoled him along several hiking trails, his wheezing progress only inspiring her to more ambitious combinations of hill and stream and wood. These country walks, or Vision Quests as Brooke preferred to call more or less anything that took place outside a department store or a restaurant, were a medical hazard from which he scarcely expected to recover. Radiated by the carcinogenic sun, they had scrambled over blond hillsides, exhuming muscles from the graveyard of Kenneth's thighs and shocking them brutally into life. He could remember seeing, through his sweat-blurred vision, the purple splashes of wine-coloured rocks in the soft and intricate gloom of a redwood grove. He had swayed giddily as wild mineral water frothed under a fallen tree. Brooke ballerinaed across with outstretched arms and girlish cries; he lumbered behind like Frankenstein's monster, while she extolled the beauties of the scene.

If only he had finished his book, he could have turned down these bucolic humiliations. As it was, he could refuse nothing to Brooke. He had always exhausted his imagination wondering what to wear for the television interviews accompanying the publication of his finished book. Now he tiptoed apprehensively to the other end of the process and wondered what to put in the book itself. At first a hideous sense of blankness and panic washed over him, but as another ravine edged into view, he started to compose spontaneous fragments of Streamist philosophy.

'You see, you're being inspired by Nature,' said Brooke, when he took out his notebook.

'You better believe it,' he muttered.

'Oh, God,' said Brooke, 'it's so beautiful here, I think I'm going to buy a ranch.'

'You should be teaching the Tantric workshop,' said Yves, leafing through the Esalen catalogue.

'We should be teaching it together,' said Adam.

'Everyone could sit in silence and just watch us,' said Yves.

'Don't get me excited, I'm trying to pack.'

'But Ad-um,' said Yves, imitating the annoying French-woman Adam had been telling him about. 'Did Rumi and Shams have Tantric sex?'

He caught hold of Adam and pulled him backwards onto the bed.

'Scholars are divided on this point,' said Adam, in his silly don's voice, 'but I think that the best approach is the experiential one adopted by Fraser and Lamartine in their seminal work, "Having It Off".'

He rolled over to Yves's side and they stared adoringly into each other's eyes.

Karen spotted Martha tossing her crutches into the back of her liberated Range Rover, and felt compelled to tell her that unique was not a unique enough word to express her appreciation and gratitude for the inner journey Martha and Carlos had taken them on during the course of the week. Clad in a pink tracksuit of the softest fabric and with one hand pressed to her heart, she walked over to Martha and congratulated her.

'Well, you know, I thought it was real dynamic,' said

Martha, her fists racing about aimlessly in the air. 'The energy was really moving around the room,' she boasted. 'And when Stan shared with the group about his impotence – that was one of the high points, for me personally.'

'It was really an important moment for me also,' said Karen. 'I was sort of embarrassed at first, and then I broke through to another level.'

'You should be proud of him.'

'He should be proud of himself.'

'I'm sure he is, dear,' said Martha, closing the back door and hoisting herself into the passenger seat.

Carlos came striding up the hill, his suitcase swinging lightly by his side. 'The patent has been processed,' he declared. 'The Auricular Acupunture Massage Muffler is now official.'

'Oh, I . . . that is so . . . we were . . .' Karen didn't know where to begin. 'When you get the Nobel Prize don't forget that we were praying for you,' she finally said.

'I'll be sure to mention that,' said Carlos suavely.

Peter wondered if it could all be true. Not just the miracle – how easily that word now slipped from his lips – of meeting Crystal, but the paradoxes – how indispensable *that* word had become – which emerged from his brief experience of meditating and listening to the question-and-answer sessions in the evening. Meditation appeared to be a mad game of hide-and-seek in which the seeker stubbornly overlooked the hidden and the hidden longed to be found, while an audience of giggling lamas shouted, 'Look behind you!' 'Look within you!' 'Look beyond you!'

'Look around you!' like children at a Christmas panto-mime. If you took any of these propositions seriously, there was always someone ready to bash language, and say that teachings were just a 'finger pointing at the moon'.

The time had come to change rooms. He was going to share a room with Crystal for the weekend. It was strange, they hadn't made love yet and that evening they would be starting the Tantric workshop together.

Peter came to an abrupt halt. Here was something really unbelievable. A few yards away from him stood Jerome, the appalling man he had met in LA, stretching out his arms and arching his back after taking some suitcases out of the boot of a car. Jerome looked round at him and nodded vaguely.

'Hello, Jerome,' said Peter icily.

'Hi,' said Jerome. 'Do I know you?'

'You seem to have a lot of trouble working out who you know,' said Peter. 'The last time we met you thought you knew Sabine but she, or he, turned to be Shalene.'

'Peter!' said Jerome. 'Peter, my friend. I'm sorry I didn't recognize you.' Jerome stood back and looked at Peter discerningly. 'You've been going through some changes.'

'Not as many as Shalene, I'm pleased to say,' said Peter. 'Has she had the full operation yet?'

'I *know* I don't know Shalene,' said Jerome.

'She was the little charmer you introduced me to in 222.'

'Oh, Shalene, sure I know her,' Jerome corrected him-self. 'I guess maybe you're mad at me about that evening, huh? That's what we call crazy wisdom, Peter, kinda shocks you into a realization. That's me, the Jester, the Trickster. When the crazy wisdom gets going, even I don't know how crazy it's going to get.' Jerome pranced around in front of Peter, shifting convulsively from leg to leg. 'You know, Sabine is going to be very happy to see you again.'

'You're still claiming to know her?' said Peter wearily.

'Claiming? We're here for a Tantric workshop.'

'You're not serious?'

'Couldn't be more serious,' said Jerome seriously.

'I don't believe you,' said Peter.

'We just arrived. Sabine had to go to the bathroom. She'll be back.'

'So likely.'

'Here she is right now!' Jerome exclaimed, spreading his hands copiously in the direction of the sea.

Walking across the lozenge of lawn that separated the office from Jools's car, a hippie harlequin in baggy trousers of emerald and beetroot velvet, Sabine billowed into view.

Peter was startled into a moment of detachment. He saw the walk of a model who has been told to look preoccupied, the vigorously insipid expression of a woman who is doomed to be stared at, and the devouring sexual confidence, as easy as a panther's stride. As she came closer, though, he was engulfed by his old longing, and its vast entourage of panic and frustration and unreality.

'Hey, Peter!' said Sabine in her husky German voice, throwing her long arms around him and kissing him on the mouth.

Peter stood there as if a bucket of water had just been emptied over his head.

'It's great to see you guys get together,' said Jerome, placing an avuncular hand on each of their shoulders.

'You realize that I tried to get hold of you in LA and this man stopped us from meeting?' asked Peter.

'Yeah,' said Sabine, laughing. 'He's so naughty, huh?' She looked at Jerome with mock reproach, at the same time draping an arm around his neck and biting his ear. 'You shouldn't have dumped Peter at that stupid club.'

'I knew why you wanted to see Sabine,' said Jerome, 'but she's my Tantric consort.'

'She could have told me that herself.'

'What we had in Germany was very sweet,' Sabine explained, 'but then the universe gave me Jerome.'

'Clever old universe,' said Peter, suddenly sounding to himself like Gavin.

'He's a crazy and stupid man,' said Sabine, playfully slapping Jerome and then biting his ear again. 'But the energy between us is something incredible,' she gasped.

'It certainly is,' said Peter. 'He's lucky to have any ears left.'

'She can have my ears,' said Jerome, crucifying himself against the side of his car. 'She can have all of me.'

'Yummy, yummy,' growled Sabine.

I want to throw up, thought Peter.

'So did you just quit a workshop, or are you going into one?' asked Sabine.

'Both. I'm doing the same one as you.'

'Hey, cool,' said Sabine, moving over to Peter's side. 'Maybe I go with him instead,' she taunted Jerome.

'And maybe I'll go with him too,' Jerome threatened.

'Sorry, I'm already booked,' said Peter. 'I'm sure you could get Shalene biked up for the weekend. Listen, I've got to move rooms. We're bound to see each other very soon.'

'*Hasta luego*,' said Jerome.

'*Ciao*, Peter,' said Sabine, kissing him on the mouth again.

What an appalling woman, thought Peter, wishing he could fuck her one more time. How could he have turned her into an emblem of depth and mystery? He wandered towards his new room in a state of turmoil which centred, if anywhere, on the facile consolation of thinking that if he hadn't pursued Sabine he never would have met Crystal. If he started thinking like that, he might as well get a set of beads and start circle dancing.

15

'I can't get over Sabine turning up here,' said Peter, 'with that unbelievable jerk I met in LA – the one I told you about who dumped me at the transsexual club. She seems so ghastly, I'm embarrassed to have given up so much time looking for her. I suppose I was really looking for you, or enlightenment, or a long holiday, or something. How do *you* feel about it? It must be strange for you too.'

'It's perfect,' said Crystal. 'It's better that she should be here disappointing you, or delighting you, than not here, haunting you.'

'You're so grown-up,' said Peter.

'I'm grown-up when I'm grown-up, the rest of the time . . .'

Peter leant over and kissed her. They sat beside the waterfall in the late afternoon sun.

'The trouble with that theory is that she wasn't haunting me until she turned up, and now she's just puzzling me for a minute or two. You're the one who's been haunting me. But you're right, seeing her again is liberating. It makes me realize that what happened between us – which *was* extraordinary – wasn't something contained in her, or in me for that matter. We were just the landing site for a strange ecstasy. It was a sexual ecstasy which didn't connect with anything else. We were just in bed for three days, hardly even talking, and when we did talk I was rescheduling flights to London and she was saying something unfathomable about the universe.'

'It's a hard thing to say anything fathomable about,' said Crystal.

'Quite,' said Peter. And then, changing the subject, 'I wanted to clarify something that John said about ejaculatory control. This PC muscle, should you clench it without clenching your buttocks, or as well as?'

'It's a free country,' said Crystal. 'You can clench anything you like. I guess if you're trying not to ejaculate you'd better use every muscle you've got.'

'It's hard to imagine that it would do the trick on its own,' admitted Peter, experimenting. John had said that the PC muscle was the one you would use if you wanted to stop peeing halfway through. It seemed a feeble instrument to pit against the sense of manifest destiny which was the birthright of every ejaculation.

'Maybe we should concentrate on the sacred spot massage,' said Peter, 'rather than the ejaculatory control.'

'Let's concentrate on everything,' said Crystal.

'Definitely,' said Peter, getting up. 'I just wanted to "process" Sabine with you.'

'She's in the can,' said Crystal, accepting Peter's hand and letting him pull her gently to her feet.

*

'One of the sisters in our circle was raped at gunpoint,' said Karen. 'It was just so upsetting to hear her . . .'

'Gee,' said Stan solemnly.

'One of the other sisters said that we should take a moment to grieve for all the women who had been raped in the history of the world. I thought it would be nice if we could take a moment to grieve for the woman who was right there in front of us, crying.'

Karen rarely allowed herself to question another's path, but she had to admit that she had taken a dislike to the hawk-eyed sister, or stepsister, who had stolen and generalized the suffering of the rape victim. Her face was lean and angry and her jaw muscles spoke of an Olympic dedication to clenched teeth.

Now, nobody was more planet-minded than Karen, but sometimes you had to be practical, and so she had gone to fetch a Kleenex box, only to find that it had been emptied during John's demonstration of the loosening and opening effects of the sacred spot massage. The empty Kleenex box now symbolized the perfectly liberated *yoni*, and the pile of tissues, which Karen soon located, stood for the discarded layers of shame, guilt and fear. She hesitated to offer this pile of toxic emotions to her weeping sister. Everybody else in the room seemed to be channelling the female predicament since the eclipse of the Goddess had cast the shadow of war, industrialization and rape over the Earth. Sensing the insult of this transpersonal sorrow Karen, heartbroken and precise, picked up a handful of pale-orange tissues and sat next to the crying woman.

'I want to honour your courage in sharing that,' said

the muscle-jawed woman, noticing the counter-attack of personal sympathy. 'It gives me hope for all the other women who've suffered a similar experience.'

'There was a man in our men's group,' said Stan, interrupting Karen's memory of this incident, 'who was caught masturbating by his parents, and got sent to a psychiatrist.'

Karen came to a halt and let loose a deep sigh.

'That poor man. Can you imagine the effect that had on him?'

'I didn't have to imagine it, I could see it.'

'We are so privileged to be in this workshop,' said Karen, shaking her head. 'Just talking about sexuality in an open way is a healing process. Our generation was given such double messages. What was it that John said? "Sex is dirty: save it for the one you love."'

'Right!' said Stan. 'Can you believe that?'

Stan and Karen drifted back to their room, hand in hand. Stan felt the calm depths of a forty-year marriage being stirred by the influx of new perspectives. He loved Karen and had always been faithful to her (except that one time at the insurance conference in Oklahoma City) but the idea of sexual passion with his aged wife was a challenge he had barely considered. Now he felt ashamed of the rift between devotion and excitement which scarred his sexual nature. Could the tranquillizing familiarities of their marriage be transformed into the conscious intimacy which, according to John, was the fuel of sexual ecstasy? John had even deprived Stan of the painful refuge of his impotence, when he had talked about sex with no goals, and non-ejaculatory orgasms, and the pleasure a man could give his beloved with a soft-on.

Stan was confused and apprehensive, but also excited, as he opened the door of their room.

'This isn't our bedroom any more,' said Karen.

'It isn't?' said Stan, thinking his wife had planned a surprise.

'It's our love temple,' said Karen.

'Oh, right,' said Stan bashfully, descending deeper into his mixed emotions.

Jerome was standing on his head in lime-green boxer shorts, his legs slowly scissoring the air. Standing on her feet in the bathroom, Sabine looked quizzically at her red and gold sari. That *shakti* red was guaranteed to make her feel like the ultimate temple dancer. On the other hand, Jerome had seen it before. The alternative, which Jerome had not seen, was a kind of tattered suede wrap, hardly big enough to polish a windowpane. Very cavewoman at the dawn of history, it was devastatingly sexy, with its rough edges effortlessly failing to hide her freshly groomed *yoni*. The trouble was that it lacked any obvious spiritual quality, and Sabine wanted Jerome's soul, not just his *lingam*.

She finally made her decision and went through into the bedroom.

'Shall we chant?' she asked, walking past Jerome with a little spin.

'Woah!' said Jerome, leaping back onto his feet. The only mantra that goes with that rag is "Yabadabadoo".'

As if inspired by the laws of cartoonland, he threw

himself on to the bed in one smooth gesture, his head already resting in his palm as he hit the mattress. He raised one knee and lay there in the posture of a feasting Roman.

I knew I should have worn the sari, thought Sabine.

'Do you like it?' she asked, pretending to pull a few strands of suede over her pubic mound.

'You bought your own nakedness at a clothes store,' said Jerome. 'That's what I call capitalism.'

Sabine joined her hands together in prayer and bowed to Jerome.

'Yabadabadoo,' said Jerome.

'You are a silly man,' said Sabine, beginning to be irritated. 'This is supposed to be a meditation.'

'Meditate on this,' said Jerome, clasping the silken bulge in his boxer shorts.

'Be serious,' shouted Sabine, stamping her foot.

'You come in dressed in a couple of moose sinews, and you want me to behave like I'm in church.'

'My God,' said Sabine, 'what are you doing in a Tantra seminar if you are making a separation between sexuality and spirituality?'

'Lighten up, will you?' said Jerome.

'I think you're the one who needs to relax,' said Sabine, getting up and stepping into a pair of jeans. 'I'm going for a walk, maybe when I get back we can start again.'

'Start what again?' said Jerome. 'Your process?'

'*My* process? You know, John warned us about this: one person starts an argument because they're afraid.'

'So what are you afraid of?' asked Jerome.

'Don't try that cheap trick on me,' said Sabine, buttoning

up her trousers. 'You know, with you I've always had this feeling that Tantra was just a way of learning some fancy moves so that Mr Irresistible could go on getting cool young chicks into bed. For me, it's part of my spiritual journey. Like John says, "Don't be afraid of inviting God into the bedroom."'

'John's the one you're inviting into the bedroom,' said Jerome. 'Are you going to quote him all night?'

'You're jealous of John and you're afraid of inviting God into the bedroom,' Sabine taunted him. 'What if somebody else was in charge of the energy? What if Jerome wasn't running the show? You wouldn't like that so much, huh?'

'Cut the psychology,' said Jerome contemptuously.

'When you've worked out your little problem, why don't you come and fetch me in the hot tubs? I need to be with my own body right now.'

'I'm not afraid of inviting God into the bedroom,' Jerome called out as Sabine swept towards the door. 'I just don't want Her to come dressed as Wilma Flintstone.'

'How do you expect God to dress? In fluorescent green shorts, like some low-class gigolo?'

'They're Italian silk,' shouted Jerome. 'These shorts cost me a fortune.'

Sabine walked out, leaving the door open. Jerome collapsed onto the bed with a loud groan.

Both Brooke and Kenneth felt tense as they headed north on Route One. They had switched workshops. The drumming in their ritual workshop had been so powerful and transformational they had decided to leave and try sex again. Three years earlier there had been a fumbling encounter between them, initiated by Kenneth when he was first establishing the subsidy for his book. It had almost lost him Brooke's support. She knew that he wanted to blame her unattractiveness for what she had described to Adam as a 'catastrophe', but if he found her unattractive, what had he been doing in bed with her in the first place? He had never really been honest about the confusion, his motives for taking her to bed, and the backlash of his revulsion. Perhaps it was too horrible to go into. Their friendship had survived with its sails torn, and now they were risking another storm. This time Kenneth had not taken the initiative. He had agreed, though, and agreed at a time when the subsidy he had first courted was in danger of extinction.

Brooke had taken a room in the Post Ranch Inn, a small house in fact, overlooking the ocean from a thousand-foot cliff. The rooms in Esalen, with their Ivory soap and their bewildering lack of maids, were just a little too alien for her to quest in.

'So, what d'ya think of this non-ejaculatory orgasm?' said Brooke, taking a hairpin bend.

'I guess I'm pleased my father wasn't a practitioner,' growled Kenneth. 'Why would Nature make it feel so good if we weren't supposed to ejaculate? It sounds counter-evolutionary to me.'

'According to John you'll feel even better if you don't ejaculate. Maybe Nature wants us to know that right now. Even evolution's got to evolve.'

'I've got nothing against *delaying* orgasm,' said Kenneth.

'For how many weeks?' asked Brooke.

'Oh,' Kenneth pondered for a while, 'just over half a per cent of one week.'

'How long is that?'

'Almost an hour.'

'That's not bad.'

Brooke paused and wondered whether to say what was on her mind.

'You know, this is hard for me after what happened.'

'I know,' said Kenneth, with the alacrity of someone who has been dreading talking about a subject. 'But it's not the same,' he went on. 'We've been through a lot, and this is a way for us to explore a new level of intimacy.'

Feeling that he was drifting, he switched abruptly to declamation.

'The point is not to try to sanctify the genitals by giving them foreign names like *yoni* and *lingam*, but to be able to say "cunt" with such a radical sense of wonder that the word is restored to its ancient . . . I want to say "virginity".'

'Well, try to resist,' said Brooke, laughing.

'But seriously,' said Kenneth, removing himself further from the awkwardness of the personal. 'For me this is connected with something that came out of Adam's class: the point is not that sperm is like holy water, but that it's *sperm*, which is quite wonderful enough. Lightning isn't the emanation of some Divine mood, it's *lightning*, which is quite wonderful enough.'

The road became more precipitous, a ribbon of perpetual vertigo carved in a cliff.

'Well, Professor,' said Brooke, with uncharacteristic boldness, 'I guess the question I ought to ask, the one with the radical sense of wonder, is, "Do you want my cunt?"'

Kenneth coughed sharply.

'Yes,' he said, sympathizing with the view, 'yes, I do.'

'I don't like the word *lingam*,' said Jason. 'It doesn't rhyme with anything. Unlike "prick", which rhymes with – well, "dick" for a start. Or "cock", which rhymes with "wok" and, eh . . . "sock".'

' "My cock is in my wok", is that the kind of lyric you want to write?' asked Angela.

'Well, it's better than "My *lingam*'s in my wok", isn't it?' said Jason with a lively sense of justice.

'It's hard to judge,' said Angela. 'It might be better to keep the wok and the cock entirely separate.'

'In an ideal world,' admitted Jason. 'But sometimes the chemistry is just overwhelming,' he said, grinning at Angela.

'Like John says,' said Angela seriously, 'Tantra is about replacing chemistry with alchemy.'

'Yeah,' said Jason. 'It's certainly having an alchemical effect on my writing. Tantra, yantra, mantra.'

Jason had often written lyrics about himself in the third person. Now that he was with Angela songs were pouring out of him in the third person plural. That was love for you. 'They', the token of crowded anonymity, of paranoid

conviction, of midnight grudges, the parasite of a belea-
guered ego, had become the pronoun of confessed love.

'You know, I've done a lot of personal growth work,'
said Angela with unquiet pride. 'I've lived in communal
situations, I've worn crystals and I've prayed to Navajo
gods, but I don't need to prove that I'm cool any more.'

'Right,' said Jason.

'I trust my intuition now and go with what comes up,
if it feels right.'

'Sounds good to me,' said Jason, daydreaming about
his career.

'When I heard about this Tantric workshop, I started
getting this tingling all over my body and these little
mystical events in my life. I hadn't even met you, but I
knew that I would be doing the workshop with someone
totally appropriate.'

'That's me,' said Jason, 'Mr Totally Appropriate.'

'It was like the first time I heard about the Goddess,'
said Angela.

Jason tended to glaze over at the mention of the Goddess. If there was one thing that worried him about
Angela, it was this Wiccan trip she was on. He really had
no idea what it was about but his imagination was seized
by disturbing images of neo-pagan harvest festivals, of
chicken's blood irrigating blazing straw effigies on a rainy
night, of body-painted mudwomen moon-dancing around
windblown coals, empowered by the music of dry beans in
a pig's bladder.

'What's so great about the Goddess is that she has so

many faces,' said Angela. 'I was into this Gaian model which identifies the Feminine with the Earth. I'm still totally into that, but now, thanks to Tantra, I've met her as a sky dancer. So she's in the Sky too, which is *really* cool.'

'She's everywhere,' said Jason uneasily.

'Definitely,' said Angela. 'I really appreciate being with a man who understands that.'

She skipped around him laughing and waving the edges of her skirt.

Jerome had been darting through the garden with a pair of nail scissors and a torch, collecting flowers to garland himself for his beloved. He wore a bedraggled crown of Mexican daisies, a mayoral sash of Californian poppies, a couple of lupin bracelets and a snapdragon behind his ear. Like a heavily medicated King Lear, too serene to notice his own madness, he wandered naked through the baths, holding in each hand a fistful of petals to strew on the sulphurous waters in which he expected to find Sabine.

Instead, to his surprise, he found her lying naked on a padded white massage table next to a strange man. They were whispering conspiratorially.

Jerome was cool. He had lived through the sixties; he had an open relationship with Sabine; he knew that she had an issue with him that evening, and he owned his part in it.

'What the fuck are you doing?' he asked.

Sabine turned round slowly and looked at Jerome.

'Oh, my God,' she said, bursting into uncontrollable giggles, 'you look so funny.'

'I asked you what you were doing,' said Jerome, letting the petals fall from his hands.

'Having a great time,' said Sabine. 'This is Paul. Paul, meet Jerome. He's not in a very good mood,' she whispered to Paul.

'I can't believe you're doing this,' wailed Jerome.

'Doing what?' asked Sabine.

'Lying here naked with another man on the night of our Tantric seminar.'

'I sense I oughta leave at this point,' said Paul.

'Oh, don't go,' moaned Sabine. 'We were having such fun.'

'I take back my love,' screeched Jerome, suddenly losing his temper and tearing off his lupin bracelets. 'I take back my devotion.' He threw his sash of yellow poppies to the ground. 'I take back my passion,' he concluded.

'And why don't you take that stupid crown off as well?' said Sabine, flicking the Mexican daisies off his head. 'You make a lousy King.'

'You're acting out your abuse issues,' said Jerome coldly.

'Don't try that, you fucking man,' said Sabine, pushing him on to the neighbouring massage table.

'I sense that you have some personal issues to clarify at this point,' said Paul. 'I'm really going to leave now.'

'Great,' said Jerome. 'Take a hike.'

'For your information she told me she was alone,' said Paul, pointing a finger at Jerome's nose.

'You said that?' said Jerome.

'I thought maybe the three of us could have some fun together,' lisped Sabine, looking down coyly.

'Oh, I get it,' said Jerome, with a relief verging on glee. 'Poly's here tonight, isn't she?'

'Yes,' said Sabine girlishly. 'Poly wants more than one.'

'Jerome knows what Poly wants.'

'Yes,' said Sabine, picking up the daisy crown and placing it back carefully on Jerome's head. 'Jerome is Poly's hero. Jerome is King.'

Paul hesitated. Sabine was the most attractive woman he had met in years. On the other hand, there was a question mark over her mental health.

'You're a very lucky man,' said Jerome, putting an arm around Paul's shoulder. 'This beautiful woman, this quintessence of erotic . . . I tell you, man, she's hot.' Jerome punched him in the shoulder a little too hard. 'This vision of loveliness has chosen to share her *shakti* with you this evening.'

He looked deep into Paul's blue eyes, his face paralysed with friendliness.

Crystal sat on the bed, cross-legged and naked, her brown hair falling in spirals down to her breasts. The darker curls of her pubic hair were half hidden by her heels.

Nervous in his underpants, Peter stood at the end of the bed, at once seduced and reproached by her physical ease. The atmosphere of giddy spaciousness that had surrounded her in the Dzogchen workshop radiated even more strongly from her nakedness. She wasn't going to tell him to relax because she was so relaxed herself that she was immune to his nervousness.

How could he offer her his pale body with its tufts of wiry black hair? Was it bad manners not to be naked as well? Would it be better to have an erection, or should he be content with what he had learned to call a soft-on? His waist was not narrow enough, his cock was not big enough, his throat was too dry, his . . .

'Hi,' said Crystal.

'Hi,' said Peter.

Peter crawled across the bed and sat opposite Crystal.

'You look as nervous as a virgin,' said Crystal.

'I'm trying to relax,' Peter defended himself.

'Why? It might be fun to be a virgin.'

'The only time I tried I was confused and incompetent.'

'Let's get it right this time,' said Crystal, placing a hand on Peter's chest.

He felt his shoulders sink a couple of inches. She reached out with her other hand and cupped it under his balls. John had spoken about these funny hand positions which 'ran the energy' from one chakra to the other.

'Is this a mudra?' gulped Peter.

'Yes,' said Crystal. 'Do you like it?'

'Oh, yeah,' said Peter. 'Only I feel like crying.'

Crystal smiled at him.

He felt a warm current flowing upwards between Crystal's hands. She was definitely running the energy and now the energy was running him.

He smiled back at her.

'You're so lovely,' he said.

Whereas Jason was well capable of getting depressed about his career, he had absolutely no worries about his body. His compliments to women were adjuncts to his self-congratulation as a lover. 'You're not bad yourself,' he would say, or 'It's nice to be appreciated.' He knew his wizzer was above average, and he offered women his genital confidence with the breezy conviction that it might blow their circuits if he were to offer them anything more. He certainly felt no need to give a woman his attention while he was making love to her. If she was lucky enough to be getting his pelvic thrust, his mind was free to stalk through the masturbatory routines which had drained him since adolescence. His sexual formation, like that of almost all his friends, had taken place among inaccurate rumours, dirty mags, clumsy gropings and hopeless hopes. Nothing had made him question the mental habits which grew from this thin soil.

Of course it was easier to pay attention when you got some new flesh, especially a dishy, turned-on, tuned-in girl like Angela. For a while his experience could map over his desire for conquest, novelty and accident. There was still a subtle gap. The contours of longing might be perfectly traced by his lived experience, but the tracing paper still intervened. Jason wouldn't even have noticed this gap if it hadn't been for something Angela had said the night before. It had really got on his wick at the time.

'You don't have to leave to experience pleasure, the

pleasure is right here,' she had said, and she had given him a little squeeze with her vaginal muscles.

Normally he would have found it dead sexy, but he was too pissed off. The truth was that he had been fantasizing. Not about anything gross like another woman, Angela would have to wait a few weeks for that, but about another version of themselves. He was a famous rock star, of course, and she was an adoring groupie. They were in his vast hotel suite, and she was overwhelmed that he had chosen her out of all the groupies and was having the most unforgettable experience of her life. And then she'd said, 'You don't have to leave to experience pleasure . . .'

Crash. That had really brought him down. He'd played all hurt and innocent, and he really was all hurt and innocent because he wouldn't have noticed the fantasy if she hadn't said that.

And now, when they were supposed to be having Tantric wondersex, they were sitting on the bed naked, talking about their feelings.

'So give me a weather report,' said Angela. 'What's happening for you right now?'

'I was just thinking, "Girls aren't for getting on with, they're for getting off with."'

'To begin with I'm not a girl, I'm a woman. And secondly, that's the most—'

'Joke!' said Jason. 'What I was really thinking was that I used to enjoy sex, but now I'm worried that if I spice it up a bit the fantasy pigs'll nab me.'

'What fantasy pigs?' asked Angela, thinking that Jason's problems might be more serious than she had imagined.

'It's an English thing,' Jason explained. 'It means police.'

'I'm not the police,' said Angela. 'I was just saying that you don't have to fantasize to experience pleasure. And I also want to say that there's an element of disrespect – you're inside me, and you're thinking about something else.'

'That's what sex is,' protested Jason. 'Doctors have proved that it's all in the head. This is where the orgasm is,' said Jason, tapping his skull.

'God, I can't believe what I'm hearing. Consciousness is everywhere in your body, Jason. This is the wound of men, this is the Beast of Society that Barry Long talks about. It's—'

'Barry Long Dong,' chuckled Jason.

'Can't you ever be serious?' said Angela. 'You know, I want what John was talking about, I want the *amrita*, the female ejaculate, but I'm not going to surrender to someone who's jerking off inside me, thinking about another woman.'

'I wasn't thinking about another woman, I was just being a rock star, that's all,' said Jason. 'It's practically not even a fantasy.'

'The point is I could feel your absence,' said Angela. 'Yesterday you had to be a rock star, tomorrow I'm going to have to be a movie star. Pretty soon, we'll be a couple of fantasy pigs making out in a fantasy pigsty.'

They looked at each other, and luckily they burst out laughing.

Jason grabbed Angela by the waist and started snuffling

around her body making porcine noises. He was secretly impressed by how much more focused Angela became when she was angry.

'Can we just try it the way John suggested?' asked Angela. 'Plenty of eye contact, communication and conscious breathing. I want the *amrita*, Jason, I want to realize my sexual potential, that's why I'm in this workshop.'

'No problem, doll,' said Jason. 'There'll be *amrita* dripping from the ceiling.'

'LAM ... VAM ... RAM ... YAM ... HAM ... OM ...' Karen intoned.

Stan got the RAM and the YAM the wrong way round and was lagging behind on the rest.

John had said you could tune your chakra system like a guitar.

'LAM,' Karen began again, tuning her base chakra and imagining the colour red.

'VAM,' she said, tuning her genital chakra. This time she could remember the yantra – the sacred shape – that went with the mantra – the sacred sound – because it was like a smile, a horizontal crescent. Yes, she was smiling from hip to hip. She could feel it!

'VAM,' said Stan, thinking how hard it was not to think of van.

'RAM,' chanted Karen, moving up to her navel. Wasn't that the name of God? She had read somewhere that Gandhi had said 'RAM' when he was shot. Or had she seen that in the movie? What a wonderful person Gandhi was. It was a privilege to be a human being when there were people like Gandhi to show what human potential really was.

RAM, thought Stan. A male goat, that at least was more appropriate than van. They really oughta take van out, in his opinion.

'YAM,' said Karen and she felt her heart opening out and just pouring love into the room. The colour was green, like spring.

YAM, thought Stan. Was that a fruit or a vegetable? HAM, the next one up, was definitely a meat, like LAM. Stan started to imagine the LAM and the HAM and the YAM being driven round in the van, sort of like a grocery service. Gee, he really wasn't entering into the spirit of the thing. These were sacred syllables imbued with thousands of years of practice. Maybe you *could* tune your chakras. Maybe he could tune the old second chakra and get a hard-on.

'HAM,' said Karen, imagining blue light radiating from her throat. She hoped she would find beautiful words to speak to Stan during their lovemaking, words to reassure and inspire him, and words to express her own needs as a woman.

'HAM,' said Stan. Where were they now? The throat? Nothing wrong with his throat. Mind you, John had said a lot about 'allowing sound', which evidently meant keeping your neighbours up all night, since John had described being thrown out of a couple of hotels for allowing a little too much sound. 'Tell them you're on honeymoon and they'll cut you a lot of slack,' was his advice. Maybe Stan could make the folks next door bang on the wall and beg for sleep!

'OM,' chanted Karen, visualizing a purple circle spreading from her third eye and then, as it rose over her forehead and hovered over her crown, turning into a thousand-petalled white flower.

Stan figured that OM was the most famous mantra. You knew where you were with OM. He'd even heard about it way back in the sixties when he was about as square as you can get. It also didn't mean anything in English, which was a help. Now, he really must concentrate next time round. Tune the old second chakra. 'LAM,' they began again.

Brooke told Kenneth to go for a 'quick vision quest' while she prepared the room. She was relieved to find the fifty honey-coloured beeswax candles, twelve dozen red roses, and the punnets of tissue-wrapped *fraises des bois* she had asked Moses to send down from San Francisco. She already had some Guérlain L'Heure Bleu to put in the deep grey-tiled double bath.

Kenneth set off on the hotel's little circular trail with the sad knowledge that he was going to be exposed to more ticks, midges, poison oak and sock-soaking streams, as well as the lethal rays of the setting sun winking at him through the branches of another gloomy redwood grove. He toyed with the idea of walking down to the highway and hitching a ride to LA. He could become an ambience manager again, pimping and scoring for rock bands; half-eaten sandwiches on top of his TV in the Château Marmont, a telephone like an injury permanently crooked in his neck. Those were the days.

Kenneth stood halfway down the path, conflicted and uncertain. The dark wood lay ahead. Maybe he should go back to the bar and have a drink. Maybe he should think about what he was doing, maybe he shouldn't. Yesterday he had felt inspired, not by charlatanism, his usual source of seriousness, but by that gratuitous vitality which had filled his body during the drumming. The trouble with this inspiration was that it made it impossible for him to cheat Brooke. She so longed to be treated with enthusiasm, rather than the cheap deference commanded by a plutocrat. Some gallant part of him, buried under the ambience manager and the sterile guru, wanted to give her exactly what she needed. Tonight he must delight not in what she was but in how she was.

He pressed on into the wood, alarmed by the task he had set himself. With her thin hair and her tired face and her expensive clothes, and that unstable combination of imperiousness and diffidence, it was easy to overlook the passionate woman asleep inside Brooke's body. When he thought of the awful simplicity of the question she had asked in the car, 'Do you want my cunt?' he couldn't deny that the obvious answer was 'No'. But when he considered her courage in asking the question at all, the opposite answer shimmered into view. There was no way to resolve this conflict, he thought, inadvertently stepping into a puddle, except to revive the vitality he had felt the day before and share it with Brooke.

Back in the room, Brooke had found that twenty candles

were already a fire hazard and she put the last thirty into a drawer, unlit. Taking Kenneth's vision quest into account, she had run the bath scaldingly hot, until thick wisps of steam curled on its surface. With an oil spillage of L'Heure Bleu in the tub, the seething and wobbling refulgence of the golden candles on all the walls and ceilings, the bedroom floor ankle-deep in red rose petals, and logs burning silently behind fireproof glass, the cottage had taken on an exotic appearance. Heaped on a plate beside the bed were the wild strawberries she would feed Kenneth as they lay in post-coital calm among the moistened sheets.

It was pre-coital calm which eluded her grasp. Her secret aphrodisiac, and her most brilliant act of long-distance shopping, was the CD of Mtumbe's *Drums of Africa*, the very sound which had transported Kenneth the day before. She had found the perfect volume, tested the remote control from every point in the room she could reach without climbing the walls, and finally put the disc on 'pause'. Now, there was really nothing left to do, except to stand in front of the mirror and adjust her bathrobe for the twentieth time.

Kenneth approached the cottage along a manicured forest path. If he was going to do this thing he must do it right. He stopped to watch the bloodstained fingers of the sun drag the slaughtered day below the horizon. He breathed deeply a few times, walked the last few yards, and knocked on the artistically rusted door.

Jason leant forward, caught one of Angela's breasts in his mouth and gave her nipple a little bite. Women loved that, didn't they? He was already shagging her and rubbing her clit, so she ought to be well happy. Get them every way at once, that was his policy. It blew their circuits. And she couldn't complain that he was fantasizing either, because he was totally in the present, thinking about what a great time she must be having thanks to him. What really turned him on was the thought of how much he was turning on the women he was with. The truth was that unless he hadn't come for ages, he really didn't feel that much *physically*. His record for not coming was ten days. It was a sort of experiment to see if it made him more intelligent.

Until a couple of days ago, Angela had been dead keen on his performance in the sack. Then she had been exposed to a bit of Tantric propaganda and suddenly she was the Teacher, with a capital T, going to show him how to have a totally spiritual shag. Of course he wanted better sex (who didn't?) but he hated being patronized. The horrible thing was that Angela could tell if his mind was wandering. Luckily, he wasn't making up a fantasy at the moment. Unless he was fantasizing that she was having a good time. Fuck, this whole thing was a nightmare. She was ruining his life.

Jason pumped away indignantly.

Angela could feel that Jason's energy was blocked. She prayed to the Goddess to release the block and let the *shakti* flow between them. She really wanted Jason to feel that connection, that beautiful connection, to the Goddess.

'Let go,' she whispered.

Jason released her breast and fell back onto the pillow.

'I didn't mean let go of my breast,' said Angela. 'I meant let go *inside*, inside yourself.'

'Just stop ordering me about, will you?' snapped Jason. 'If you wanna let go, let go. And you can let go of telling me to let go while you're at it, because half the time I have no fucking idea what you're on about.'

'You have a lot of anger around this issue,' said Angela, abruptly disconnecting her genitals from his and kneeling some distance away.

'Oh, so you're letting go of sex as well, are you?' said Jason. 'Great.'

'No, I just thought we should try yab yum.'

'What's that, then?' said Jason wearily. 'Sanskrit for "processing"?'

'No, it's a position where all the chakras are aligned opposite each other and we can really balance the energy, and become a channel for the Goddess.'

Jason hovered on the edge of rage, but something restrained him and tilted him towards honesty.

'I'd like that. I mean, I can see the problem now, but I can't even imagine the solution. For me, during orgasm, that's when the body takes over from the mind and there's zero fantasy, or whatever you want to call it.' Jason struggled to make progress without the crutches of facetiousness and aggression which usually swung him forwards. 'The ideal would obviously be some permanant state of orgasmic freak-out,' he suggested, 'but that's not possible, is it?'

'I believe it is,' said Angela, 'although that's not exactly how I'd put it.'

'Well, let's go for it, then,' said Jason, all charm. 'What exactly is this position?'

'Just sit up cross-legged like you are meditating.'

Jason followed her instructions.

Angela, noticing that his erection had dwindled during their discussion, made a ring out of her thumb and finger and rubbed his cock up and down. As it stiffened she bent down to meet it, put her lips around the head, and let it slide gradually down her throat. With her middle finger she searched for his perineum, the stretch of skin just beyond his balls. She loved that part of him, the buried root of his cock. It was thick and hard under the softness of the skin. She scratched him lightly there while her head rose up and down on his cock.

Jason groaned appreciatively.

'You like that, huh?' said Angela, looking up.

'Don't stop!' cried Jason.

Angela ignored his command and sat up.

'Oh, no,' said Jason. 'That was great. Your throat was so tight.'

'Wait,' said Angela. Kneeling above him and taking his cock in her hand, she parted the lips of her cunt, and then, guiding it inside her, sank slowly down. She settled comfortably in his lap, wrapped her legs around his back and sat still.

'This is yab yum,' she said. 'You see all our chakras are facing each other.'

'Fan-tastic,' said Jason, feeling something like wonder. 'Yab yum, eh? Make a a great title for a song.'

'Spring has returned to the mountain!' roared Stan. 'I've got a hard-on.'

There was muffled applause from the room next door and a cry of 'Way to go!'

'Oh, my love,' said Karen, 'I'm so happy for you.'

'So is half the building,' chuckled Stan. 'Evidently my throat chakra is in pretty good shape too.'

Stan pressed his palms on the bed and arched above Karen. He looked down into her eyes. For forty-two years he'd been looking into those kind eyes and for forty of them they'd been the eyes of his wife. They were glittering now, with tears, and with a mischievous look which hadn't changed since the day he'd met her.

'You're a good woman,' he said.

She laughed and the tears spilt out of her eyes and ran down the side of her face.

'I guess I won't be needing Walking Eagle's special ceremony now,' said Stan breezily.

'That's right,' whispered Karen.

She had secretly arranged for Walking Eagle to perform the ceremony during their trip to Esalen, but she wouldn't have told Stan that for all the world.

Kenneth and Brooke lay breast-deep in the bathtub, inhaling the fragrant steam, sweat tickling their cheeks and brows.

Kenneth felt himself sliding into some kind of collective male exhaustion. For a thousand years he had been fighting in the salt marshes, hacking with a blunt sword at other angry and exhausted men. His body was covered in cuts, there were purple bruises on his ribs. He was tired from shallow sleep, from a thousand years of sleeping with a sword in his hand. His arms ached from hacking at shields and shielding himself from hacking blows. He wanted to rest, he wanted to surrender; victory lay in surrender. He wanted to stop pretending to be anything except tired, stop pretending to be competent, stop pretending to know what was going on. Brooke was here to accept his surrender, to disarm him and to kiss those buckled muscles, to kiss that grazed skin.

Brooke was beginning to think that *Drums of Africa* might not be the perfect music for the occasion. Thanks to the grey pallor of his complexion, his gaping mouth, his closed eyes, and his appearance of being crucified against the side of the bath, Kenneth looked extremely drunk, perhaps dead. She slid across to the other side of the bath and leant towards Kenneth, not quite daring to touch him. Hearing the water swirl, he opened his eyes and smiled wearily.

'I'm so tired,' he said. 'I mean *really* tired, tired in my marrow. Not just physically, either. I'm tired of all pretences.'

He'll be telling me he's got a headache next, thought Brooke, but she could see that Kenneth was not preparing her for sexual disappointment, he was telling her something essential. His defences were unravelling irresistibly, he was falling apart in the heat of the water. She also sensed that there was more trust in his helplessness than in any sexual act he had ever performed. She suddenly felt touched by the survival of their friendship, despite all the misunderstandings about sex and money. Besides, what else was there to do with sex and money except have misunderstandings about them? They were there to liberate the rest of life for some loftier purpose than bickering, lying and sulking. For the moment she didn't care whether Kenneth desired her, she just wanted to heal him, to touch him where he was helpless, and to enjoy the trust which his helplessness revealed.

She reached out and pressed her fingers into his shoulders and his neck. Kenneth groaned and sank deeper into the water. She knelt in front of him and massaged his shoulders. She could feel his body shuddering involuntarily under her touch. Kenneth reached out blindly and wrapped his arms and legs around her torso. She felt his beard grazing her chest, the panic in his short breaths, the tension in his arms, the contraction in the muscles around his neck. Poor Kenneth, the booming guru, was just a wreck. Running her hands over his back, she could feel emotional collisions piled up in a scrapyard of twisted muscles, and a thousand knots, each telling the story of an unreconciled contradiction.

Everybody was a wreck, but Kenneth was more of a wreck than most. What could you do but heal and be healed? Yes, we're all wrecks, thought Brooke, pushing deeper into Kenneth's troubled flesh, and we must help each other make it through life.

They got out of the bath and Brooke dried Kenneth while he stood swaying with his eyes still closed. She realized that she was in a trance of service. For someone whose napkin was usually caught by a servant before it hit the ground, there was novelty as well as expertise in this role reversal. Stepping through the mirror, Brooke gave away the things she had so often received. The memory of ten thousand massages emerged from her pampered shoulders and rushed solicitously into her hands.

Lying on the bed, Kenneth whimpered pathetically as Brooke pummelled the back of his legs and, finding his exhaustion answered with sympathy, passed through exhaustion into excited gratitude. Brooke, who was by now transformed into the Mother Teresa of Big Sur, was astonished when Kenneth rolled over and presented her with a stubborn erection.

'I love the way you do that,' he said, clasping her by the waist with a manly grip.

She leant forward and they kissed.

'Tight-arse!' said Jerome.

'You're way outta line,' said Paul, putting his clothes back on.

'Poly wants more than one,' said Sabine in a little girl's voice, writhing on the bed.

'And you,' said Paul, turning to Sabine. 'You may be attractive but you're one sick chick. I'm a pretty go-with-the-flow kind of person, but the stuff you guys are into . . .'

Paul shook his head and started to leave.

'Poly thinks Paul is *boring*,' sang Sabine, sticking her tongue out.

'And so does Jerome,' added Jerome.

Jerome and Sabine rolled around on the bed together, sticking their tongues out and laughing. Paul left with quiet dignity.

'Maybe Peter would like to play,' said Sabine.

'Peter?' said Jerome. 'You don't wanna bother with him.'

Sabine rolled onto her back, bringing her knees up to her ears and pulling her legs open.

'Poly wants all the men to come inside her,' she groaned.

'Yeah,' said Jerome encouragingly.

He hoped he hadn't blown it by trying to put her off Peter. Poly was the pure lust in Sabine, a surprisingly separate personality and the hottest lover he had ever known. She couldn't be bridled and if she wanted Peter she must have him.

The Tantric group, because of the sound they might allow, had their rooms in the same area of the property. Sabine used her intuition to home in on Peter's room. She tested the handle and, finding the door open, burst into the room.

'Hello. Who's there?' said Karen, turning on the light. 'Oh, it's you, dear,' she said, recognizing the woman she had comforted in the afternoon. 'I hope we haven't been making too much noise – I mean, allowing too much sound,' she corrected herself.

'What's going on?' said Stan sleepily. 'Are we going to have group sex?'

'Stan!' said Karen. 'I'm sorry, dear, he's a little over-excited, he just had his first erection in eight years.'

'Let's go,' said Jerome, who was standing behind Sabine.

'Poly wants to stay,' whispered Sabine.

'She does?'

'It would be kind of original, no? With these old people.'

'Too original,' said Jerome.

'But Poly wants to,' said Sabine, stamping her foot.

'OK, OK,' said Jerome.

'It's the woman I was telling you about, the one in my group,' Karen whispered to Stan. 'I think she's upset about something.'

'Gee,' said Stan.

'Why don't you come and sit down, dear?' said Karen.

'Thanks,' said Sabine shyly.

'Yeah,' growled Jerome. 'Thanks.'

With gentle bites, Peter traced the tendon that ran from Crystal's knee up to her groin. She spread her knee outwards and made a hollow in the smoothness of her thigh. He bit the tendon harder as he moved upwards, and then he kissed her in that hollow and pressed his lips to that soft crease of skin, rubbing his cheek against the tangle of her pubic hair.

He gazed up at her. She closed her eyes briefly and then

they sprang open again, intensified. All the sadness and all the innocence she had ever known was distilled into a serious delight, and seemed to slide along the thread of her eyebeams and to fall, drop by drop, into his heart.

'I've been waiting for you all my life,' said Peter. 'All my longings and all my fantasies have been about you, but I didn't know you really existed. And now you're lying in front of me in all your beauty.'

Peter, who usually choked on an 'I love you' before falling hastily to sleep, made this speech irresistibly.

He leant down and ran his tongue lightly over her belly until the tip came to rest on her navel ring. As he shook the ring with his tongue, the gold chimed against his teeth. Crystal moaned and rolled her hips.

'You're so open, you're so alive,' he said.

She smiled at him with unguarded eyes, her cheeks glowing in the candlelight.

She opened her legs wider and his chest pressed against the open lips of her cunt. He drew the wetness into his parched heart and, letting out a sigh of amazement, brought his head to rest between her breasts.

She ran her fingers through his hair.

'You're so sweet to me,' she said.

'You're my whole reason for existing,' he said, looking up at her again. His eyes in her eyes and her eyes in his, resting.

He was astonished by the innocence of his feelings. Just for now he was purely defined by making love to Crystal. There was no sense of debt created by the extravagance of his words, no sense that they were being converted into promises. With her, every gesture was made to give life to the moment.

Looking down at her body, he was filled with passion to see her open like a flower. He leant down and kissed her quietly on the lips of her cunt, as if he were kissing her sleeping forehead and didn't want to wake her. And then he parted those lips with his thumbs and ran his tongue along the furrow between them, and when he reached her clitoris he arched his tongue and let it circle and slide over her softly.

Crystal pushed her hips further forward to show him that he could have all of her. Every movement was perfect, there was nothing to add and nothing to take away, nothing to quicken and nothing to slow down. How did he know her already? How did she already trust him? She could feel the clear glass of her meditating mind being stained by the sudden richness of her sensations, but clear or stained it remained translucent.

And now he was slipping his middle finger inside her and at the same time stroking her navel ring with his thumb, as if he were stroking the rim of a glass to make it hum. Their bodies were perfectly intelligent: they knew what to do; they had always known what to do. She breathed in deeply, drawing the excitement upwards, letting it rise through the centre of her torso like mercury in a thermometer. She let out a sigh of delight as Peter's tongue quickened and flickered; she felt the ache in her third eye as the pleasure flooded her skull through the open gate of her throat, and then, fountaining against the inside of her crown, curled round and streamed back down through every nerve in her body.

And now he was slowing down, slowing right down. She relaxed all her muscles and subsided into his palm, which rested at the base of her spine, waiting to receive her. And then he touched her on the clitoris again with the tip of his tongue, as carefully as if he had crossed a wide desert without a drink, and was fetching the last drop of dew from the petal of a rose. And he rested his tongue there, and imagined all the love he was capable of – no, that was not enough – all the love he was not capable of as well, streaming into her.

And then they both lay still. But everything around them was streaming and everything inside them was streaming.

After a brief eternity, he looked up at her and they both laughed in astonishment at the intensity of the lightness they were feeling.

'God,' he said. 'It's amazing . . .'

Crystal's cheeks were flushed. She looked rejuvenated and entirely beautiful. She ran her hands up the centre of her body and said, 'Whoosh.'

'Yeah,' said Peter and, following the same line she had described with her hands, he kissed her belly, and kissed her between the breasts, and kissed the hollow at the base of her throat, and kissed her chin, and kissed her lips and, as he kissed her forehead, he slipped the head of his cock between the lips of her cunt.

'Ahh . . .'

'God.'

He held the head of his cock inside her, his eyes in her eyes, her eyes in his eyes, resting. Slowly, so slowly, because each millimetre was a new plane of intimacy it would be foolish to rush past, he moved further inside her. They gazed into each other's eyes as if they were witnessing a miracle rather than performing an act.

Crystal felt him move from her swollen and sensitive lips up towards her womb, and she felt the same journey taking place from the excited part of her mind towards its silent centre. She felt the reconciliation of everything that was said to be deep and everything that was said to be high; the vertical dimension disappeared and she felt herself disseminated through an infinite horizon.

And then he drew back slowly and she felt herself drawn back into a zone of crowded sensations, of pleasure and the habit of deciding what was pleasurable. But by then she was not herself any more, she was just a woman, and he was a man, and they might as well have been fucking for a thousand years, because she couldn't remember doing anything else.

He got up onto his knees and she hooked one leg over his shoulder and tilted sideways, and he started to fuck her hard, looking down on the spread of her legs and seeing his cock disappear into her wet cunt and reappear glistening and slide back in again. And he became just fucking, not a thought in his head except fucking, and the feeling was so meant to be, first of the tribe lay there, yes, there, yes, there, and he was there, and she was there, and it was there, and there it was, fucking.

He was, he could feel it, he was going to, he could feel

it, he was going to come. Stop everything. Breathe in hard. Clench everything. PC muscle, buttocks, arms, pectorals, abdomen, chin lock. Breathe in further, the last sip of air through taut nostrils. Just in time. He felt the desire reversing and rushing up the centre of his body and flooding his head. He sat back on his heels and closed his eyes.

She felt the walls of her cunt softening and expanding, and then in a series of contractions she gushed *amrita* onto their intermingled pubic hair.

The yab yum had been a big success. Jason still couldn't help thinking that it would make a great title for a song. 'No need to rush/ No need to run/ Just stay where you are/ And yab yum/ ya-ba-di yum.'

He could just imagine himself on MTV with a touch of the Kama Sutra art direction and the whole band in soft-focused yab yum. It could be huge. A little ripple from the sitar, a pelting from the tabla, and his gravelly and laid-back voice singing, 'Yab yum/ ya-ba-di dum.' It would be bigger than 'Be Bop A Lula' and 'Do-Do Run-Run' put together. A world music sound with a neo-sixties message. Perfect.

'I've got to write it down,' he said.

'What?' asked Angela sweetly.

'I've got this song running around in my head,' said Jason.

'You see,' said Angela. 'Sexual and creative energy are really from the same source. Stimulate one and you stimulate the other.'

'Yeah, definitely,' said Jason, getting up to find pen and paper. Under his breath he composed. 'Line up your chakras/ It's time to have fun/ Yab yum, ya-ba-di yum/ Yab yum/ Ya- ba-di dum.'

'Gee,' said Stan, admiring the perfection of Sabine's body, her small voluptuous breasts, her wide tanned belly, and her artfully trimmed pubic hair. Awestruck as he was, he noticed that her wonderful body did not entirely make up for the impression of mental illness which pulsed from her like a lighthouse beam.

'This is your lucky day, old man,' she said, sprawling on the bed and stroking her thighs with her fingertips.

'It was already my lucky day,' said Stan calmly. 'I got to make love to my wife for the first time in eight years.'

'Oh, that's so sweet,' said Karen.

'Well, it's the truth,' said Stan. 'I don't even know this young lady's name.'

'My name is Poly,' said Sabine.

Jerome had stripped down to his lime-green silk boxer shorts. Strangely orange skin hung loosely on his bony frame. From a chaos of serpentine curls, he leered angrily at Karen. He figured that Karen was the price he had to pay for the demented intensity of Sabine's alter ego.

Karen drew strength from the thought that she was not only deflecting the blow of Jerome's sexual attention from poor fragile Poly, but also giving Stan the opportunity to celebrate his rediscovered potency with a beautiful, if mad, young woman. The only thing that could make this blossoming of self-sacrifice utterly perfect would be to avoid any physical contact with Jerome. Perhaps she could find some tactful way to let Stan have his fun while she chatted with Jerome.

'Would you mind if I just watched?' she asked Jerome.

'Watch the three of us?' said Jerome eagerly. 'That's cool.'

'Or the two of them,' said Karen, trying to protect Stan from Jerome's competition, or worse still his contribution.

'I'm not the one who's dropping out,' said Jerome. 'It's up to us to satisfy this sexually devouring woman,' he said to Stan. 'How do you feel about that?'

'Well, gee,' said Stan, 'I don't want Karen to feel left out.'

'She likes to watch,' growled Sabine. 'Everybody can do their own thing.'

She reached inside Stan's white pyjamas and wrapped her fingers around his unconcerned cock.

'I'm not sure what my thing is,' said Stan. 'But, right now, I think I'd like to be with my wife.'

'You could watch us,' said Jerome, leaping astride Sabine's writhing body.

'We'll just go out on the balcony,' said Karen discreetly. 'You make yourselves at home.'

'This is *stupid*,' shouted Sabine, banging the mattress with her fists. 'We might as well be in our own room.'

'That's what I've been saying all along,' said Jerome.

Sabine leapt to her feet, and Jerome hastily gathered up his clothes and turned to say goodbye.

'We'll see you guys tomorrow,' he said cheerfully.

Karen and Stan remained silent while Sabine strode

proudly out of the room, and Jerome shuffled through the door with a presidential wave.

'I guess we'll never have group sex now,' said Stan with a touch of melancholy.

'We could start a group of our own,' said Karen. 'Let's talk to Walking Eagle about it.'

'He's bound to have a ceremony,' said Stan.

'No doubt about it,' said Karen.

Brooke had fallen asleep and was dreaming that the sea was an oriental merchant unrolling bolts of lace at her feet, and with every wave she bought another acre of lace because each pattern was too beautiful to refuse. And then he said he had some silk to show her, and she agreed, and he pointed behind him and the whole ocean was stretched silk. She said she would take the whole thing, but he laughed and said it was not for sale. Couldn't he make her a little dress? she asked. Not even a handkerchief? Nothing? And at that moment all the bolts of lace streamed back into the ocean, and the silk turned into churning sea water and it rushed over her naked body and she was completely free.

Kenneth was standing on the balcony feeling exhilarated and distinguished when Brooke came over to join him.

'I've just had the most beautiful dream and I know I have to give away all of my money,' said Brooke sleepily.

'Make a foundation,' said Kenneth.

'OK, darling,' yawned Brooke. 'But anyhow, I don't need any new dresses.'

'We can make that one of the terms and conditions of the foundation: no new dresses for the director.'

Brooke hooked her hand over his shoulder and rested her head on his chest.

'The ocean looks like silk, but the wonderful thing about it is that it's the ocean.'

'That's right,' said Kenneth.

'And lightning is lightning, and sperm is . . .' She paused.

'Don't say holy water,' said Kenneth. 'Don't give up on me now.'

'I wasn't going to say holy water,' said Brooke. 'I was going to say, yummy.'

'Yummy is OK,' said Kenneth. 'Yummy is allowed.'

Peter lay on the bed, completely still, listening to the whispering sea. An intermittent draught cooled the sweat on his skin. He was immersed in the richness of his own body and yet barely in touch with the bed. He could feel his body coursing with blood and enzymes and glandular excretions and, at the same time, feel nourished by the pulse of the faintest star.

He saw all the causes from the unknowable edges of time which, for all he knew, had no edges, converging on his body in that moment to make it no other than it was. And then he saw that his body was itself a cause dispersing its effects into the future. He saw time rippling in and, caught in the revolution of a moment, rippling out again. History and all possible futures were just the interference pattern of those converging and diverging waves of causality. And then he saw that what rippled in and what rippled out were the same thing, because his body was no more focal than any other point and this moment was no more focal than any other moment. It was as true to call the stillness rippling as to call the rippling stillness, or the stillness stillness, or the rippling rippling . . .

'Far out,' he murmured.

'What?' whispered Crystal.

'I've seen how the whole thing works.'

'What? The *yoni* and the *lingam*?' said Crystal. 'You didn't know that before?'

Peter laughed. 'No. The universe,' he said.

'Oh, the universe,' said Crystal, relieved. 'Sabine's favourite subject.'

'Now you've ruined my mystical experience,' said Peter.

'It was that easy? It just disappeared at the mention of a woman you don't like as much as you used to?'

'Yup,' said Peter. 'I guess we're going to have to painstakingly reconstruct the moments that led up to it.'

'That never works,' said Crystal. 'We'll have to approach it from a new angle.'

Infolding and outfolding at the same time. She smiled as the phrase returned to her from Jean-Paul's letter.

Leaning forward she sucked one of Peter's nipples. The sensation pierced and soothed him like a hummingbird.

Crystal knelt astride him and held his face between her cupped hands.

'A new angle,' she repeated, her knees spreading outwards and backwards as she slid down the sheets to join him.

picador.com

blog
videos
interviews
extracts